PRAISE FOR

THE UNFAILING LIGHT

"Katerina's first-person voice is smart and believable, fitting well into this atmospheric romance." —*Kirkus Reviews*

"The setting is fascinating and quite different from what we have seen in other YA paranormal fiction. Readers will find themselves turning to Wikipedia to find out more about Russian history and the historical characters who appear in the novel." —*SLJ*

"A sequel that is even more exciting, more glamorous and more visually breathtaking than the first book! . . . If you like Russian folklore, culture and history, this is a series you ought to have on your bookshelf!" —*Bookish*

"I love this series so much! I am fascinated by Imperial Russia, and stepping into Katerina's world makes me feel like I'm getting a giant bear hug from a Faberge egg. Bridges makes the architecture, clothing, and customs of Imperial Russia come to life. Add vampires, fairies, witches, werewolves, and a necromancer into the mix and the result is a young adult novel that is a whole lot of fun!" —*The Well-Read Wife*

"Bridges has done it again! The second volume of The Katerina Trilogy surpasses the majesty of the first. I was captivated throughout the entire book, and Bridges made me believe I was with Katerina every step of the way." —*LitPick*

ALSO BY ROBIN BRIDGES

The Katerina Trilogy, Volume I: The Gathering Storm

THE KATERINA TRILOGY

Volume II

THE UNFAILING LIGHT

Robin Bridges

E

EMBER

Text copyright © 2012 by Robin Bridges
Cover photograph copyright © 2012 by Michael Frost

All rights reserved. Published in the United States by Ember, an imprint of Random House Children's Books, a division of Random House, Inc., New York. Originally published in hardcover in the United States by Delacorte Press, an imprint of Random House Children's Books, New York, in 2012.

Ember and the E colophon are registered trademarks of Random House, Inc.

Visit us on the Web! randomhouse.com/teens

Educators and librarians, for a variety of teaching tools, visit us at RHTeachersLibrarians.com

The Library of Congress has cataloged the hardcover edition of this work as follows:
Bridges, Robin.
The unfailing light / Robin Bridges. — 1st ed.
p. cm. — (The Katerina trilogy ; v. 2)
Summary: Katerina Alexandrovna, Duchess of Oldenburg, wants to forget that she ever used her special powers and pursue her dream of attending medical school but is under imperial orders to remain at finishing school where she can be kept safe from Russia's archnemesis, until the protection spell unleashes a vengeful ghost within the school.
ISBN 978-0-385-74024-1 (hardback) — ISBN 978-0-375-89902-7 (ebook) — ISBN 978-0-385-90830-6 (glb)
[1. Ghosts—Fiction. 2. Supernatural—Fiction. 3. Good and evil—Fiction. 4. Courts and courtiers—Fiction. 5. Schools—Fiction. 6. Russia—History—1801–1917—Fiction.] I. Title.
PZ7.B76194Unf 2012
[Fic]—dc23
2012014775

ISBN 978-0-385-74025-8 (trade pbk.)

RL: 5.6

Printed in the United States of America

10 9 8 7 6 5 4 3 2 1

First Ember Edition 2013

Random House Children's Books
supports the First Amendment and celebrates the right to read.

For Tabitha, who dreams giant dreams and weaves stories of her own

A NOTE ABOUT RUSSIAN NAMES AND PATRONYMICS

Russians have two official first names: a given name and a patronymic, or a name that means "the son of" or "the daughter of." Katerina Alexandrovna, for example, is the daughter of a man named Alexander. Her brother is Pyotr Alexandrovich. A female patronymic ends in "–evna" or "–ovna," while a male patronymic ends in "–vich."

It was traditional for the nobility and aristocracy to name their children after Orthodox saints, thus the abundance of Alexanders and Marias and Katerinas. For this reason, nicknames, or diminutives, came in handy to tell the Marias and the Katerinas apart. Katerinas could be called Katiya, Koshka, or Katushka. An Alexander might be known as Sasha or Sandro. A Pyotr might be called Petya or Petrusha. When addressing a person by his or her nickname, one does not add the patronym. The person would be addressed as Katerina Alexandrovna or simply Katiya.

THE UNFAILING LIGHT

The Smolny Institute for Young Noble Maidens
November 1825, St. Petersburg, Russia

Two little girls in identical brown dresses skipped down the long corridor on their way to dinner. It was Thursday, and they knew the cook was making cabbage soup that evening. And cabbage soup meant warm black bread to go with it.

They stopped when they saw the tall, thin woman standing in the shadows at the end of the hall. It was not the headmistress, nor was it one of their instructors. Sophia and Natalia had never seen this woman before.

The woman had dark hair pulled tightly against her head, with loops of raven-black braids twisting prettily from the back. Sophia's eyes grew wide at the woman's elegant red gown, which was trimmed with several rows of lace and embroidered pearls at the sleeves and neckline. She was certain this woman must be the empress. Sophia skidded to a stop and curtsied. She nudged Natalia to do the same.

This did not seem to please the beautiful woman. With a slight frown, she told Natalia to "run along." Suddenly dull-eyed, Natalia abandoned her friend without a single glance back. The cabbage soup would be getting cold, she was thinking, and it tasted best when it was piping hot.

The strange woman stared down at the little girl left alone with her in the hallway. "Walk with me, Sophia Konstantinova."

"Yes, Your Imperial Majesty."

"Foolish girl. I am not your tsarina. I am here on behalf of your father."

Eight-year-old Sophia had never known her father. Orphaned as an infant, she'd been brought to Smolny and raised by the nuns until she was old enough to attend classes. She knew her mother had been a lady-in-waiting to the dowager empress Marie Feodorovna, the wife of the old tsar Pavel, but Sophia did not even know her mother's name. She had, however, overheard the vicious whispers of the nuns regarding her paternity. She knew she was a Romanov bastard, even if she wasn't quite sure what that meant.

The dark-haired woman suddenly clutched Sophia's arm and pulled her into the empty library. "Your father has wanted a child for so long. And I have been unable to give him one. Until now." She smiled a sharp, wicked smile. Sophia gasped as she saw the tiny fangs.

"Why does he want me now?" the little girl asked, turning pale.

"He has watched over you from afar since the day you were born, my dear. But his mother and brother would not allow you to come and live with us."

"His brother?"

4

"And now his brother, the tsar, is dead, and your papa is going to be tsar." There was a gleam in the woman's eyes that frightened the poor girl.

"Who is my father?" she asked. "And who are you?"

"You are going to come and live with us, little Sophia. And we will live happily together forever."

Sophia shrieked, "But you are a monster!"

"Yes, my love," the woman crooned. "And soon you will be one too."

But the poor child panicked and tried to get away from the woman who wanted to make her immortal. She pulled away from her with such force that the woman let go of her arm in surprise. Sophia stumbled backward, not expecting to be freed so easily. She could not catch her balance, but instead hit the back of her head on the doorframe. There was a dreadful thud, and then Sophia Konstantinova slid to the floor, lifeless.

The woman sighed as she picked up her skirts and stepped around the growing puddle of blood. Her nostrils flared slightly, as if she were trying to hold in something terrible. She reached down and picked up the dead girl's hand. It had already turned cold.

The woman smiled. "You cannot run away from a necromancer so easily, my silly child." She ran a sharp fingernail across the girl's palm. Dark, thick blood began to leak out. Closing her eyes, the woman started to chant in an ancient, almost-forgotten language. Using her fingernail again, she cut open her own palm, and her undead blood oozed out. She held her bloodied hand to the dead girl's and resumed her chanting as their blood mingled.

The walls in the cozy library began to shake. Books tumbled from the shelves.

The temperature in the room dropped dramatically. "Do not

fight me, love," the woman said. "Don't you want to come back and meet your papa? He is anxious to see you."

"LET ME GO!" The hysterical voice seemed to vibrate off the walls. A mirror in a golden frame fell from the wall, shattering into several pieces.

The woman looked around her in shock. "Sophia, what have you done?" she whispered with a frown. "This was not supposed to happen."

"LET ME GO!" the voice boomed again.

A small gasp at the doorway caused the woman to turn around. Little Natalia stood there, staring at her friend. She was trembling and pale from shock.

The woman heard voices approaching down the hallway and frowned. Whatever magic was at work here, it was stronger than her own. Konstantin would not be pleased. But she could stay at the school no longer.

The woman vanished before Natalia's eyes. A small black moth flew toward the little girl, lightly touching her cheek before fluttering past.

When the headmistress reached the library, she found Natalia sitting in a puddle of blood, cradling the lifeless Sophia Konstantinova in her arms. There had been some sort of horrible accident.

Natalia had heard her friend's voice shouting at the wicked lady in red. She knew that Sophia was safe from the horrible woman, for now. She promised Sophia she would not let anyone separate them ever again.

CHAPTER ONE

❧

August 1889, The Crimea, Russia

I stood at the edge of the cliff, shouting into the wind and down to the waves crashing on the jagged rocks below us. *"And steep in tears the mournful song, / Notes, which to the dead belong; / Dismal notes, attuned to woe, / By Pluto in the realms below."*

Dariya's laugh was unladylike. "Katiya, must you be so morbid?" my cousin asked as she twirled around in her makeshift toga. We had stolen the snowy white linens from our villa and carried them down to the ruins by the beach. Wrapping the linens around us over our dresses, we looked like ancient Greek goddesses.

"Mais bien sûr," I replied with a curtsy and a melodramatic sweep of my toga. "It's a morbid play." We were reenacting scenes from a Greek drama we had read in literature class last

7

year, *Iphigenia in Tauris*. It was here at Khersones, an ancient Greek temple at the edge of the Black Sea, where the Greek priestesses had sacrificed shipwrecked sailors to the virgin goddess Diana. According to the play, of course.

Our families traveled south to the Crimea every year at summer's end, along with most of the Russian court. This summer marked the end of my childhood. In a few weeks, I would be leaving Russia to attend medical school in Switzerland.

I would never again attend the Smolny Institute for Young Noble Maidens, the school I had attended in St. Petersburg since I was twelve. Dariya had completed her studies at Smolny as well, and had been appointed a lady-in-waiting to Grand Duchess Miechen. Dariya was excited about her new life at the dark faerie's court, and her stepmother, Zenaida Dimetrievna, the countess of Leuchtenberg, was excited for her as well. Aunt Zina, as we called her, was an ambitious woman, always eager to further her own position in the grand duchess's court. She would be keeping a close eye on Dariya.

It was a hot day in late August, cooled only by the salty spray that splashed upward as the gray and green waves churned against the sun-baked rocks.

We poked around in the rubble, searching for ancient coins or pottery shards. "*Mon Dieu!* Katiya!" Dariya picked up something and dusted it off with her sheet.

It was a skull, or part of a skull, at least. Definitely human. But the front teeth had been filed to sharp points.

"What on earth?" Dariya asked with disgust. "Are those . . ."

"Fangs." I couldn't help shuddering. They reminded me of someone I knew. A devilishly handsome but wicked blood-

8

drinking prince in the faraway Black Mountains of Monte-negro.

My cousin laid the skull back on the ground, and I frowned as I pushed the horrid blood drinker's face from my mind.

"Dariya, you girls must come back up here immediately!" My cousin's short, round stepmother shouted over the wind as she stood next to my mother under her parasol. My mother squinted against the bright sunshine, trying to see us from so high up. The countess was Maman's sister-in-law, and she had attached herself to Maman's side for the summer.

It was late afternoon, and time for tea. The servants had brought a picnic basket filled with sandwiches and fruits and pastries along on our expedition.

"I do wish you would be more careful," Maman said when we finally rejoined them on top of the hill. "It's entirely too dangerous among those ruins."

"But it's so beautiful," I said, taking a cup of tea from Maman's maid. "And we saw a few bones down there. Imagine how old they must be!"

"The teeth were pointed, like fangs!" Dariya couldn't help saying. "I think it was an ancient vampire!"

"*Mon Dieu!*" the countess exclaimed, her lace-gloved hand fluttering to her heart. "I'd heard that they lived in this region thousands of years ago." She glanced around nervously. "I do hope there aren't any around now."

"Don't be ridiculous," Maman said. "There are no more vampires in Russia."

Dariya and I both knew better. We'd been roommates with a blood drinker all last year. Dariya had almost died because of the poisonous veshtiza, Elena, who had the most annoying

9

habit of turning into a moth and sipping blood from her sleeping classmates.

But my mother knew nothing about that. She'd heard there were blood drinkers once again in St. Petersburg but had disregarded those rumors as nonsense. Maman had no idea the new head of the St. Petersburg vampires was none other than her niece-in-law, Grand Duchess Militza.

"Katiya, I do not want you girls rummaging around down there anymore," Maman said severely. "If you wish to perform Greek plays, you can do so at our dacha, where it's safe. And more people can watch. We can set up a stage in the garden."

"Perhaps you can find a part for me to play," Aunt Zina said as she piled her plate high with fruit tarts and bits of cheese. "I've always wanted to be Helen of Troy. I know how great a burden it can be too beautiful." She sighed as she bit into a cheese dumpling.

My cousin and I looked at each other and giggled. I saw even Maman stifle a smile. Dariya fell back on the blanket and rolled over onto her stomach. "I think you would be perfect as Helen," she told her stepmother. The countess did not notice the irony in Dariya's voice.

It felt good to laugh and be carefree for a bit longer. We stuffed ourselves on lemon-curd tartlets and closed our eyes to the hot sun shining down on us. The sea breeze kept us from getting too warm.

The countess sipped her tea and gazed out across the breaking waves. "I do believe it's more beautiful here than in St. Petersburg. The landscape is more romantic. Wilder. Don't you agree?"

Maman shook her head. "I'll be much more comfortable

when we reach our dacha in Yalta. The empress and her family are already at Livadia."

My heart sputtered as I thought of the empress's middle son, George Alexandrovich. I wondered what he was doing right now in his family's summer palace. I wondered if he was thinking of me.

I had refused him last month when he proposed, but I still loved him. My beautiful boy. I ached to see him again, and yet I was afraid of what would happen the next time we were together. It would be so easy to accept his offer of marriage, but I did not want to give in to him. It was far too dangerous for us both. What hope was there when my dark powers had almost killed him the last time we kissed?

It would be much better for me to start a new life in Zurich and pray that George fell in love with someone more suitable for him, someone the empress would approve of. Such as a princess aligned with the Light Court. Someone I, with my dark powers, could never be.

CHAPTER TWO

~⊘~

The trip from Sevastopol to Yalta took us all day by carriage along the dusty, winding Vorontsov Road through the mountains. Aunt Zina complained for the entire trip, bemoaning everything from the state of the roads and the age of the carriage to the color of the horses pulling us. Even Maman was glad when the countess and Dariya left us at our villa and continued on to their own rental closer to town.

Maman's mother, Grand Duchess Maria Nikolayevna, had built our family dacha more than fifty years ago. The estate had been given to her by her father, Tsar Nicholas, as a wedding present. Grand-mère had died in 1876, and her many properties had been divided up among her children. Our villa nestled in the hills at Yalta was almost as grand as Livadia, the palace of the current tsar and his family.

We settled in, and later that evening, I opened the windows in my bedroom, stepping out onto the balcony. I could still smell the salt on the breeze, even though we were far from the sea. Here, the nights grew much darker than the summer white nights of St. Petersburg. There were more stars in the sky, more chances to make a wish.

I closed my eyes, breathing in the night, and wished the summer would hurry up and come to an end. I was eager to get started on my new life. For as long as I could remember, I'd wanted to be a doctor. I had never wished for a life at the Russian imperial court, which was full of empty-headed, gossiping women. Not to mention ambitious vampires and scheming fae.

"Katiya?" Maman found me out on the balcony. "Come downstairs with me. Aunt Zina has come and brought a spirit board. We are going to hold a séance in the parlor."

I shook my head. "Please, not tonight, Maman. I feel a migraine coming on."

"Oh, how dreadful!" Maman said. "We are planning to summon someone from the sixteenth century!"

It did not matter whose spirit they wished to bother this evening; I wanted no part of it. My mother still believed that spiritism and séances were simply innocent fun, amusing diversions for ladies of the aristocracy. I, of course, knew better. My ability to conjure up the long departed went far beyond summoning spirits.

I, Katerina Alexandra Maria, Duchess of Oldenburg, was a necromancer. And I hated it. Ever since I had been a little girl, I had been able to bring the dead back to life. Fortunately, only a few people close to the tsar knew my secret. His son, Grand Duke George Alexandrovich, was one of them. Unfortunately, there were several dangerous and powerful people in Russia who knew my secret as well. People such as Maman's friend Grand Duchess Miechen.

"Are you certain, dear?" Maman asked. "The Montenegrins have arrived at Yalta and promised to call this evening. You've missed the princesses Anastasia and Elena, haven't you?"

My head began to pound even worse. I had not missed them at all. The Montenegrin princesses had almost killed me last spring by casting a charm to make me fall in love with their brother, Crown Prince Danilo. Although I had broken off the engagement, Maman still retained hopes that I would reconsider my feelings for the wickedly handsome Danilo and become a crown princess.

No one had told her the crown prince was a blood drinker. Like most of the nobility, she lived her life bedazzled by the glamour of the light and dark faerie courts and believed that all the vampires had been driven from St. Petersburg many years ago. I hoped I was doing the right thing hiding the truth from her. My brother and father, however, knew that evil creatures roamed our city. And they knew about me.

"Please send my regrets," I said, taking Maman's hands. "I think I will go to bed early tonight. Tomorrow is the excursion to the caves, is it not?"

"*Mais oui!* Zina will never forgive me if we do not go!" She kissed me on the forehead. "Sleep well, Katiya. Should I send Anya up here with some tea?"

"That would be wonderful." I smiled. My maid would be happy to escape from the company downstairs. She feared the Montenegrin princesses as much as I did.

Maman left, and it was not long before Anya knocked on my door. "Duchess? Your mother said you were not feeling well."

"It's just a headache," I said, coming in from the balcony and locking the doors. "Thank you." I sank down into the chair and inhaled the steam from my cup. For some reason the tea in the Crimea always tasted better than the kind we drank at home.

"I heard the princesses asking about you," Anya said, fussing with the tea tray. She'd brought a plate of brown bread and butter, along with some cheese and fruit, to ensure that I did not go to bed hungry.

Not everyone knew that the Montenegrins were veshtiza witches, with the power to turn into bloodsucking moths, but rumors of their dark magic had spread throughout St. Petersburg. Now shunned by the empress and the Light Court, they were attempting to curry the favor of the Dark Court faerie, Grand Duchess Miechen. Her court rivaled the Light Court, and the empress knew it.

The tense power struggle between the light and dark faerie courts had not improved since the battle with the lich tsar at Peterhof. Their powers might not have been apparent to most inhabitants of St. Petersburg, but the aristocratic elite knew the rumors and the legends, mostly tales spun by the fae themselves. Behind a veil of glamour, the two dangerous faeries plotted and schemed for control of the fate of the empire. The empress, of course, blamed the Dark Court for the attack against her husband, the current tsar. Grand Duchess Miechen, who dreamed of the day when her own son would wear the imperial crown, had no love for the lich tsar Konstantin. Nor was she particularly fond of the blood-drinking Montenegrins, whose treachery had caused her to miscarry twins last month.

"What did the princesses say?" I asked as I reached for a

slice of bread. Anya loved to gossip, and I would not be allowed to rest until I'd been told everything she'd heard.

She sat down in the chair next to mine and lowered her voice. "They said their dear brother was still at home with his parents, languishing and heartsick over you, but that they hoped to see you at the grand duchess's birthday ball this week."

I rubbed my temples. I knew I'd have to see them in public eventually. There would be plenty of people at the ball, and hopefully any conversations the Montenegrins and I had would be brief. If I never saw the crown prince again, it would be too soon.

Anya helped me get ready for bed and then took the tea tray away, leaving me alone in the dark. I heard the sounds of laughter coming from Maman's séance in the parlor. And someone, probably Aunt Zina, singing a gypsy love song. I closed my eyes and listened to her rich, husky voice.

The metal bed was not as comfortable as my bed at home in St. Petersburg. It felt more like my old cot at Smolny. But the linens smelled like sunshine and sea air. As I fell asleep, I dreamed of paper-thin white wings, fluttering outside on my balcony.

CHAPTER THREE

⌒◠◯◠⌒

The next morning, we met Dariya and her stepmother for our excursion to the Massandra caves. Adjacent to the imperial estate of Livadia, the grounds of Massandra had recently been bought by the tsar, and a grand palace was being built. Some of the caves were open for excursions, and that was where we planned to spend the day.

Dariya grinned at me, holding her parasol up to protect her fair skin from the late-morning sunshine. Accepting the footman's arm for support, I climbed into the carriage next to her. It would be a short ride to Massandra, for the estate was very near to our villa, but we would have to walk across the beautifully cultivated vineyards to reach the caves. The servants had packed two large picnic baskets for us. I could smell the freshly baked baklava that had been wrapped up for later.

Maman and Aunt Zina seated themselves in the carriage

seat across from us. "What a glorious morning!" my aunt said. She smiled like a cat that had gotten into the cream.

Maman, however, looked a bit weak. "How did your séance go?" I asked with concern.

"It was so exciting!" the countess said, ignoring the fact that I'd addressed my mother. "We made contact with a servant of Empress Yelizaveta Petrovna! He shared the most delightful recipe for a raspberry sorbet."

"What a comfort to know that spiritism has such practical uses," I murmured. Dariya poked me in the arm and stifled a giggle. "Maman, are you feeling all right?" I asked, turning toward her. She seemed paler than usual.

My mother forced a laugh. "Of course, dear. It is just unbearably early for me. I'm not used to being out of bed before noon, you know."

But it was more than that. The cold light that shimmered around her, the light that only a necromancer can see, looked different this morning. Not brighter or dimmer necessarily, merely different. A person's cold light grows brighter the closer one is to death. A necromancer uses her own cold light to manipulate life and death, just as she can manipulate another person's cold light. I was still learning how dangerous my powers could be. I did not understand what the change to my mother's cold light meant, but I suspected it was related to the previous night's séance. Had one of the ghosts touched Maman?

Our carriage ride was pleasant, as the dirt road took us high into the hills where we could look down at the harbor. The Crimean Peninsula was very rocky, and full of mountains dotted with caves. The narrow strip of beach along the southeastern coast was known as the Riviera of Russia, and this was where all the palaces and dachas belonging to the nobility glittered like gems in the sun.

The carriage stopped at the gates of Massandra and we climbed out, taking our picnic baskets. Maman and Aunt Zina carried their parasols. It would not be a long hike, but I was thankful for the fresh air.

I hurried ahead to walk with Dariya. She was swinging her picnic basket and humming an aria from the opera *Iphigenia*. I wished we'd had more time to spend at the ruins in Khersones. We still planned to perform the Greek play before our holiday in the Crimea ended.

As we walked down the shady path leading to the caves, we came to a bridge that crossed a crystal clear stream. We could hear voices on the other side of the bridge.

"Georgi! No!" There was a splash, and then a young girl shrieked with laughter.

My heart pounded in my throat as I recognized the voice.

Dariya looked at me and shrugged. "The imperial family?"

It was their estate, even if they were staying at Livadia while Massandra Palace was being finished.

"Perhaps we should have chosen another day," I said, starting to turn around.

"Katerina Alexandrovna!" A pleased young female voice stopped me. The tsar's eldest daughter had already seen us. "And Dariya Yevgenievna! Georgi! Nicky! Look who it is!"

Grand Duchess Xenia was dripping wet. Her older brothers behind her looked as if they'd been swimming as well.

My skin felt as if it were on fire as George Alexandrovich's gaze swept over me. His hair was wet; a lone, limp curl fell over his forehead and my fingers itched to push it back off his beautiful face. He eyed me warily. His siblings obviously did not know he had proposed to me less than a month ago. Or that I had refused him. And I hoped he would never tell them. What good could ever come of it?

The eldest of the tsar's sons, Grand Duke Nicholas Alexandrovich, smiled his shy smile and gave us a polite bow. "What brings you two out here this morning?"

Just then, Maman and Aunt Zina caught up with us. They became excited when they saw the tsar's children. "Your Imperial Highnesses!" my mother said, bowing. "We did not mean to intrude, but we had hoped to visit the caves."

The tsarevitch took Maman's hand gallantly and clicked his heels together. "No intrusion at all," he said with a grin. "We were searching for a new fishing spot. Would you like for us to accompany you up the path to the main cave? It can be tricky to find."

George looked as unhappy as I was with the suggestion. It appeared, sadly, that his passionate regard for me had already cooled. Which was for the best, I realized. But even though I knew we could never be together, I also knew that I would never love another.

"You are most kind, Your Imperial Highness," Maman said with a slight nod.

George stepped closer to me; I could smell the sunshine and fresh air on his damp clothes. His shirt was unbuttoned at the top, his sleeves rolled up to reveal tan, muscular arms that glistened with beads of water. I blushed as soon as I realized I was staring.

"Allow me to carry your basket," he said, holding out his hand.

His fingers grazed mine as I handed the basket to him. It was like an electric current passing between us. "Of course I still feel the same," he said in a low voice, so the others couldn't hear. "How could you doubt that?"

My cheeks burned and I felt a strange, light fluttering in my stomach. "Forgive me, Your Imperial Highness. I had forgotten my thoughts were so transparent to you." His telepathy was one of his faerie gifts, courtesy of his mother.

He held my elbow gently, forcing me to stay until the rest of our party had gone on ahead. His touch sent shivers up and down my entire arm. I could see Dariya talking with Grand Duchess Xenia before they disappeared on the winding forest path. No one noticed our absence.

"How have you been, Your Imperial Highness?" I didn't know what else to say to him.

He smiled, and his face seemed to light up. "Terrible. And you?"

I didn't answer him. "How is the Order? How are your Koldun studies?"

He sighed. "I leave for Paris next week to study with a secret circle of wizards."

"Paris? For how long?"

"Several months, I'm afraid."

It had always been my and Dariya's dream to visit the City of Light. What beautiful sights the grand duke would see. "How exciting," I said, happy for him. But I could not help feeling sad that he would be so far away.

"And you leave for Zurich soon," he said.

I nodded and kept staring straight ahead as we walked. If I stopped to look at him now, would I change my mind about leaving?

21

"My father actually believes it is a good idea for you to go."

That caused me to stop in the middle of the path. "He does?"

George shrugged. "Normally, he does not believe women should have occupations, but he feels a university education would be beneficial for you as his imperial necromancer."

Of course. I was a valuable pawn to the tsar and his wife's Light Court. My education would depend solely upon my usefulness to the Crown.

"Is he feeling better?" I asked. The ritual at Peterhof that had transformed our tsar into the ancient warrior of legend, the bogatyr, had been draining. For the tsar as well as for me. But Tsar Alexander possessed an almost inhuman strength. His battle with the lich tsar Konstantin had been amazing to see. And frightening.

"He is much improved," the grand duke said. "But as a physician you may be able to discover ways for him to recover faster the next time the bogatyr is needed."

I sighed and shook my head. "But that's not why I want to be a doctor. I want to help all people. Not just the tsar."

"At least he is letting you leave, is he not?"

"He does not want me anywhere near you. Neither does the empress."

"I'm going to Paris. You wouldn't be near me even if you stayed in St. Petersburg." George stopped us again and grabbed my hand. "Katiya, I'm concerned for your safety. The Order has seen signs that there are other people working with Konstantin. We think someone else in St. Petersburg wants to finish what Princess Cantacuzene started. Even after all these years, there are still those who believe that

Konstantin Pavlovich was the rightful heir after Alexander the First."

"The Dekebristi, you mean." They were the undead minions of Konstantin's vampire clan, first raised by Princess Cantacuzene more than sixty years ago.

He nodded. "Among others."

"But we stopped him at Peterhof." The lich tsar had tried to defeat Tsar Alexander and had failed because I summoned the bogatyr to fight him. "He can't come back, can he?"

George looked me in the eye. "He simply vanished that day. I'm sure Konstantin Pavlovich has been hiding away somewhere, plotting his revenge. He's just waiting for someone else powerful enough to help him return from the dead."

The grand duke was right, of course. What on earth had given me the idea that a weak and silly sixteen-year-old girl like me could have defeated an undead wizard? He would be back. And he would certainly come for me. "What are we going to do?" I whispered.

George frowned. "You are going to be careful. I hate that you will be so far away in Zurich. Won't you please reconsider staying in St. Petersburg, where at least the Order will be able to look after you?"

It made sense that Konstantin would come after me. Most likely before he came after Tsar Alexander. I was the easier target. And once I was out of the way, the bogatyr could not be summoned to protect the people of St. Petersburg.

It hurt me to see the grand duke look so worried. It would be easy to choose the safer path and stay at home with my family. But there was no way I'd ever become a doctor if I remained in Russia. Our medical schools did not admit women.

No thanks to the tsar and his narrow-minded education ministers.

I shook my head sadly. "I can't live in fear. Whether he comes after me in St. Petersburg or in Zurich, nothing would be able to stop him. I want to go to medical school."

George's eyes narrowed. He was angry with me for being stubborn.

Without thinking, I reached for his hand and held it between both of mine. "Don't be mad. And please don't worry about me. The Order needs to keep the tsar safe. Konstantin is not concerned with me." Not much, I hoped.

George's breathing had changed when I touched his hand. He was still angry, but there was something else that flashed in his eyes as well. Something silvery and dangerous. His fae heritage. "God, Katiya," he murmured as he dropped the picnic basket and pulled me closer to him.

His lips brushed mine, and in a heartbeat, the rest of the world fell away. All my fears about the lich tsar, all my worries about medical school. I let go of his hand and put my arms around his neck. I knew the others weren't far ahead of us and would probably turn around if they noticed us missing. But I didn't care about anything at that moment. Nothing but being in that beautiful boy's arms. My beautiful boy.

The last time we'd kissed, my powers had been dangerously out of control. He'd almost been killed. I couldn't let myself lose control again.

And yet, I was so close. I could feel the tingling rising up from deep inside me as his kisses trailed across my cheek and his hands curled around my waist. My powers were beginning to uncoil as I felt his warm lips on my skin.

I heard a twig snap behind me and pushed away from him instantly. My sleeves and the front of my dress were damp from being pressed up against him and his wet clothes. My heart was pounding and my breath ragged.

It was his sister, Grand Duchess Xenia. But she just winked at us and shouted, "I don't see them anywhere!" before turning and skipping back toward the rest of the group.

George was breathing hard too, and he sighed as he let go of me. "I'm never going to hear the end of this from her."

"Will she tell the empress?" I asked. My cheeks felt hot with shame. What would I do the next time I saw Her Imperial Majesty? Could I hide from her forever?

"My sister won't say a word if she thinks I would get in trouble." He smiled, adding, "Xenia is a silly romantic." He gently lifted my chin, lightly touching my bottom lip with his thumb. When he looked at me with his ocean-blue eyes, the silver flash was gone, but I could still sense the fae power in his gaze. Everything inside me began to melt. Slowly. "I won't ever let my mother come between us, Katiya," he said. "I promise you."

"But—"

He placed a finger on my mouth to quiet my fears. My lips tingled from his touch. "You promised to give me a year, Katiya. One year to convince my parents that you and I belong together."

I remembered making that promise. I'd walked away from him that day at Peterhof, after my powers had risen up and almost suffocated him. *Mon Dieu*, what would have happened this time if the grand duchess hadn't found us?

I pulled away from him and reached for the picnic basket.

Praying that no one would ask me how my dress got damp, I self-consciously tucked a loose strand of hair behind my ear.

With a friendly growl, George took the picnic basket away from me. I couldn't help smiling. I tried to hurry us along. I knew that we needed to catch up with the others before they reached the entrance to the caves, but George deliberately slowed his walking. Proper etiquette dictated that I slow down as well and walk just slightly behind the tsar's son.

"A grand duke never skips," he said, a small smile at the corners of his lips.

CHAPTER FOUR

◦◦◦

The caves at Massandra were part of the larger cave system reaching across the Crimean Peninsula. Monks had created monasteries in the caves, and Tatars had built medieval cities inside of them. And we, a few silly Russian women, were going to have a picnic there.

These local caves would one day be used as a wine cellar for the palace. The land here was very fertile and there were already vineyards that had been producing fruit since the early eighteen hundreds.

The entrance was partially hidden under a thick canopy of trees. We would have had difficulty finding it without George and his siblings' help.

Aunt Zina and Maman thanked the tsarevitch for his escort. George handed me my picnic basket silently. I tried to look cheerful, and failed miserably. "Will we see you at the dance next week?" I asked.

He did not smile either. "I'm afraid I must leave for Paris before then."

I nodded, realizing I might not see him anytime soon. A lump welled up in my throat.

He leaned closer. "We'll be together again before long, Katiya. I won't leave without saying goodbye." Once more, he was reading my thoughts. No one noticed when he gave my hand the briefest squeeze. No one noticed my blush, or the way he made my fingers tremble.

I bowed to his brother and sister, then hurried into the cave after Maman before I could tear up. Dariya looked at me curiously, but said nothing.

Neither Maman nor Aunt Zina noticed my mood. They were fussing over the ribbons on the dress Xenia Alexandrovna had been wearing. "What on earth will her mother say when she comes home dripping wet like that?" Maman was asking.

"You would think they'd have more than just the grand duchess's governess out here to look after them," Aunt Zina said.

I was surprised to discover that the caves were several degrees cooler than the air outside. My sleeves had dried already, but the damp front of my dress made me shiver. We set the picnic baskets down in an alcove near the entrance and picked up the oil lanterns to light the darkness. Aunt Zina's oohs and aahs echoed against the smooth cold walls of the caves. Dariya and I raced on past our mothers into the shadows.

"Don't run too far ahead, girls," Maman said.

But we ignored her. There was so much to see. The caves

had obviously been occupied by humans before, but we did not know how long ago. We wandered from room to room, entering deeper and deeper into the belly of the cave.

"Are you going to tell me what happened out there?" Dariya asked quietly as we slid our hands over an old fresco painted on the stone wall. I raised my lantern higher to examine the figures. And so my cousin could not see me blushing. The fresco looked incredibly old. I took my hand away as some of the paint flaked off. I did not want to damage such priceless art.

I sighed finally. "There is nothing to tell. George Alexandrovich belongs to the Light Court, and I belong to the Dark. He is going to Paris and I am going to Zurich."

Dariya looked at me in shock. And then grinned. "Katiya! You are in love! I never would have guessed it! You with your cold medical journals and dull Latin textbooks!"

"And I don't suppose you've ever been in love, then?" I scowled at her.

"Oh, lots of times. But you!" She nearly knocked me over with one of her enthusiastic embraces. "Oh, I'm so happy for you, Cousin!" She pulled back to grin at me. "He's a much better choice than Danilo of Montenegro."

I snorted. "A toad would be a better choice than Crown Prince Danilo." I had to hold the lantern out so Dariya wouldn't knock it out of my hand or catch her hair on fire. "There will be no engagement," I added. "George Alexandrovich is the tsar's son."

"And you are a tsar's great-granddaughter."

I shook my head. "His mother would never approve. There is no hope for it."

"That's the best kind of love. Hopeless love." She shrugged as she let go of me. "Don't worry. You'll pine away and he'll pine away, and then you'll get over it and so will he."

I rolled my eyes. I was not in the mood for her teasing.

She turned around. "I'm famished. Do you think we could sneak some of those meat pies before our mothers notice?"

"You go ahead," I said. "I want to see the next room." I did not feel like eating. I just wanted to sulk.

"Are you sure?" my cousin asked.

"Go on. You won't tell anyone about the grand duke, will you?"

For a moment, Dariya looked as if she was going to tease me again, but something in my voice must have made her change her mind. She shook her head. "Katiya, a marriage could be secret, you know. Grand-mère married her second husband and kept it hidden from her father."

This was true. Grand Duchess Maria Nikolayevna married her lover, Count Stroganov, not long after her first husband died. If her father, Tsar Nicholas, had known about the unequal marriage, he could have sent Grand-mère to a convent and exiled the count to Siberia. Grand-mère lived in France and kept her marriage secret for two years until after the tsar died.

But I could not imagine marrying George and living in hiding from his father, counting the years until he died. I didn't wish for the tsar to die anyway. And George would surely grow to resent me.

And what of his mother, the empress? She would never forgive me if I took her son away from her.

Dariya gave me another friendly embrace. "Don't worry,

Katiya. I won't tell a soul. And if there's any hope of things working out, I'm sure they will."

Her quick, light footsteps echoed down the corridors as she hurried back toward the cave entrance and our picnic baskets. I could barely hear Maman's and Aunt Zina's voices, they were so far away from where Dariya and I had explored. I raised my lantern again, not sure which way I wanted to go next.

There were two archways to choose from. One looked as if it led back around toward the room we had just visited. The other sloped downward, as if it led deeper into the mountainside. I foolishly chose the latter passage.

I shivered as I passed through the archway. It was even colder in here than in all of the previous rooms. I wished my lantern gave off more warmth. But the dim light it provided allowed me a glimpse of a wondrous sight. The walls in this chamber were completely covered in gold-leafed icons of saints and angels. The paintings took my breath away.

A heavy and ornately carved chair sat at the back of the room, covered in gold leaf and brightly painted. It looked as if many years before there had been precious stones inlaid along the arms and back, but they had been long ago pried off. A faded and worn tapestry stretched across the seat. It looked like a throne for a king. Or a tsar. The familiar Maltese cross was embroidered on the back cushion. Held up on either side by what looked like two angels, it was the symbol of the Order of St. John of Jerusalem.

Carefully, almost reverently, I reached out to touch the tapestry weaving.

There were Greek words inscribed in gold lettering around

the back of the chair. Eager to stretch my Greek vocabulary, I tried to translate as I traced the letters with my finger:

"The path to the light travels straight through the darkness," I muttered.

The lightest breeze lifted the hair on the back of my neck. Something had stirred the air in the cave. I glanced around.

"Byzantium was to be mine . . . ," someone hissed in my ear.

With a gasp, I backed away from the throne and looked around the room. I saw no one. I turned, but was not graceful enough to keep my balance. I stumbled backward and fell into the seat.

The room began to spin. And grow even colder. Unnaturally cold. I could have hit myself for being so stupid. *Mon Dieu*, why had I strayed so far ahead of the others?

"Necromancer," a sickeningly familiar voice called out to me. The cold feeling intensified. "You are able to walk between the worlds of the living and the dead."

"Stay away from me!" I shouted as I jumped out of the chair and glanced around. I did not think I was in the cave's chamber anymore, but in some terrible limbo.

Strands of cold light snaked through the air, giving everything a bluish-white glow. A few of the strands seemed to be wrapped around a large, dark figure, but he was struggling against them.

"Necromancer, you must finish what the House of Bessaraba began. Restore me to life. It is my birthright to rule this land!"

I shrank back from him like a coward, with a cold, sick feeling in my stomach. I did not know what place this was, but I recognized the wicked voice. And his face. It was Konstantin Pavlovich, the lich tsar. The Montenegrins had foolishly brought the dead tsar back this summer with a ritual gone horribly wrong. This had definitely put a strain on relations between our two countries, even if they did try to help stop him afterward.

"You c-cannot hurt me," I stuttered, not completely believing my own words. "The bogatyr defeated you at Peterhof."

"Bah! You have the cold gift. I can smell it on you. You have the ability to perform the ritual."

He moved a little closer to me, although I cannot say he actually walked. "YOU!" With a sudden roar, he recognized me from the battle at Peterhof.

He lunged forward and I jumped back and hid behind the throne, escaping his touch by inches. The thick cold-light strands seemed to hold him back. For now.

"Witch! You will pay for everything you've done!"

I backed away even farther from him. Even if I didn't know where I was going. "I will never let you return," I said. "I won't let you harm the tsar, or anyone else."

"I AM THE TSAR!"

"No!" With my heart beating in my throat, I was too terrified and nowhere near foolish enough to try to attack the lich tsar on my own. The only thing I knew how to do was run.

And hide.

"*Sheult Anubis*," I whispered, calling upon the one Egyptian incantation I knew, the one that I'd found in the book Johanna had given me. Instantly I was engulfed in protective shadows. Konstantin Pavlovich roared again, almost like a wounded animal, but his bindings held him fast. He was a prisoner in this place unless he could find a necromancer to help him. And that necromancer would not be me.

It seemed as if I ran forever. There were no walls, no borders or edges that I could find. I was hopelessly lost. I fought down the panic rising up inside.

Completely wrapped in my cloak of shadows, I sank down to the floor, close to panic. My heart was pounding and my hands were shaking. How would I get out of here?

I'd seen no other person in this cold-light realm besides Konstantin Pavlovich. Why was the lich tsar here? Was this place physically in the Crimea? Or somewhere not quite connected to regular time and space? The more I thought about it, I realized that I had arrived here after touching the throne in the cave chamber.

Only minutes ago, I'd been laughing and behaving in a silly fashion with my cousin in the caves. Would I ever see her and the others again?

I let the shadowy cloak fade away as I began to search for a way out.

"What in the name of the Holy Ones are you doing here?" A man's voice startled me.

I jumped up and gasped, not having realized someone else was present. "Who are you?"

A dark robed figure stepped closer to me, holding out his hand. "I can take you back to the cave, but you must come with me now." It was a young man, dark-haired, with piercing dark eyes. He had a heavy French accent.

"Do you know me? How did you know I was in the cave?"

He sighed impatiently. "Mademoiselle, you have been poking into things which are not your business. Do you want to get back to your family or not?"

I nodded.

"Then come with me, quickly." Immediately, he began to mumble something in another language, definitely not French or Russian. His words caused the cold light to dissolve into a faint silvery mist.

I held my breath and watched as everything faded away slowly. I felt cold and nauseous. When the mist had completely cleared, we were back in the cave, standing next to the throne.

"Who are you?" I asked.

He bowed curtly. "You are most welcome, Mademoiselle." He turned around and hurried off silently, back toward the cave entrance.

"Please wait!" I started after him, and heard Maman's voice.

"Katiya?" Maman asked, approaching me from the same corridor the stranger had taken. "What is it?"

I looked past her, but the man had already vanished. "Did you see anyone else in the caves with us?" I asked.

"Of course not. We've been looking all over for you. It's time for luncheon." Maman held her lantern up to get a closer look at me. There was concern in her eyes. "Heavens, you're as pale as a ghost! Are you all right?"

"I'm fine, Maman. Just hungry." I had to find out who the stranger was, and what he was doing in that horrible place with Konstantin Pavlovich. Surely Tsar Alexander was not aware of the throne, or visitors would not be allowed to visit the cave. Did I need to tell George?

I forced a smile as I looked up at my mother. "I cannot wait to eat. Did Dariya leave us any meat pies?"

Maman followed me back through the twisting cave chambers until we arrived at the entrance. Dariya and Aunt Zina stood there, holding the picnic baskets. They were more than ready to leave the chilly caves as well.

We followed the shade-covered path until we returned to

the tiny stream where we'd seen their imperial highnesses that morning. "This looks like a perfect spot for lunch!" Maman said. She pulled a blanket out of the first picnic basket, spreading it out on the grass by the sunny bank.

We had cold deviled eggs and meat pies, and drank the cool lemonade our cook had prepared. I stared at the babbling stream and wished I could speak with George about the stranger. Perhaps the man had passed the imperial family as he left the caves to go to wherever he'd come from. I didn't know if I wanted to tell the grand duke about Konstantin Pavlovich, however. What could he do? And he would only worry about my safety even more. No, I would have to find out about the strange man on my own.

CHAPTER FIVE

〜◦〜

It was Aunt Zina who insisted we put on our Greek play at the dacha. We decided to perform in the garden room on a hot August afternoon. Maman and Aunt Zina had topiary columns and large potted palms moved to create a stage for us. Maman would not let us use the good sheets as togas, but she did give us an old length of gauze to cut up. Dariya made wreaths of ivy and laurel for our heads. We thought we looked like nymphs.

Dariya's father, Uncle Evgene, said we resembled patients who had escaped the lunatic asylum. He wisely decided to forgo the afternoon's entertainment and went riding with his friends.

We planned to perform one scene: Iphigenia's nightmare, the dream that leads her to believe that her brother Orestes is dead. I stood on a footstool in the middle of the garden, rehearsing my lines.

What notes, save notes of grief, can flow,
A harsh and unmelodious strain?
My soul domestic ills oppress with dread,
And bid me mourn a brother dead.
What visions did my sleeping sense appall
In the past dark and midnight hour!
'Tis ruin, ruin all.

Dariya, in her gauze toga, practiced her pity-filled gaze in the role of the chorus.

Turning pale, Anya whispered, "I think it is bad luck to speak of your brother's death, Duchess."

"It's not my own brother, but Orestes," I told her. "Iphigenia's brother. And he doesn't really die."

"Still," Anya said. "You shouldn't be speaking of such things."

Dariya shrugged. "The play really has a happy ending, despite the bloodstained altar and ghastly sacrifices."

I could not help shuddering. Perhaps this was not the best piece of Greek drama for two young ladies to perform. But before I could say anything, Maman called to us. Her guests had filled the garden room, taking their seats on the sofa and chairs in front of our stage.

Anya jumped up and darted off, too shy to be in front of so many people. I noticed Grand Duchess Miechen and Maman sitting down beside Aunt Zina. An older woman with white hair and enormous green eyes leaned forward to whisper in Maman's ear. She looked up at me and nodded. Surely they couldn't have been talking about me. I had never seen the woman before in my life.

"Katiya!" my cousin whispered. "Are you ready?" She held her harp out, eager to begin.

"Of course," I said, tearing my gaze away from my mother and the stranger. As Dariya plucked her harp, I began to recite my lines. Iphigenia was a Greek princess whose father, Agamemnon, had been told to sacrifice her in order for the Greeks to win the Trojan War. But the goddess Artemis rescued Iphigenia at the very last moment and hid her away in Tauris, the land now called the Crimea.

Iphigenia became the priestess in charge of ritually sacrificing to the bloodthirsty Artemis any foreigners who landed on the shores of Tauris. Then fate caused her brother Orestes to shipwreck at Tauris. Iphigenia was unknowingly about to sacrifice her last remaining sibling on the bloody altar. The Greeks loved irony in their plays.

The garden room was crowded and there was little breeze. I soon felt myself growing warm and faint. I heard a soft buzzing in my ears, but I couldn't let it distract me from my lines.

> But the strange visions which the night now past
> Brought with it, to the air, if that may soothe
> My troubled thought, I will relate.

I cast a quick glance at the small audience and saw them bathed in a faint light, but it wasn't cold, as it should have been. It seemed to be radiating white-hot. I tried to take a deep breath, praying for a soothing breeze. I felt a tightness in my chest. What had happened to everyone's cold light?

With relief, I finished the scene of Iphigenia's gloomy dream and curtsied to the crowd. Dariya ended her song on the harp with a flourish and joined me. Everyone stood up and clapped, but I only wanted to get out of the room. No one seemed to be in distress besides me. Grand Duchess Miechen fanned herself lazily with a delicate ivory fan, but did not seem to notice anything unusual happening. I half suspected her of being the cause.

"Katiya, what's wrong with you?" Dariya hissed in my ear. "You've gone completely pale."

"I need some fresh air," I said. After one last curtsy, I grabbed my cousin's hand and led her away from our makeshift stage and through the glass doors into the courtyard.

It was still hot under the late August sun, but at least there was a sea breeze outside. I closed my eyes and began to feel better immediately.

"What is it?" Dariya asked. "What's happening? Did the grand duchess do something?"

"And just what do you think I would be doing?" Miechen's voice startled both of us. The dark faerie had slipped out onto the terrace behind us without making a sound. Dariya sank into a brief but perfectly executed curtsy before escaping back inside. The coward.

My heart was pounding in my throat. "Your Imperial Highness, did you not feel the change in the air in the garden room?"

The grand duchess shrugged elegantly. "Such things happen when you invite a striga to your villa. Her name is Madame Elektra. She is a local witch, of sorts."

"A striga? And Maman invited her here?" I asked.

"Your mother and Madame Elektra have been friends

for many years, Katiya. It is strange that you two have never met."

"I think I would remember meeting her," I said, frowning. "She seems to suck the cold out of the room."

"Strigas are blood drinkers. More powerful than any veshtiza or upyr. But no danger to you."

"Does Maman know?" I asked, growing indignant. "She has told me repeatedly that vampires no longer exist!"

Miechen shook her head, smiling. "Elektra is not a vampire. She is much older and more powerful than Princess Cantacuzene ever was. If she truly wanted it, she could take the vampire seat of power away from Militza of Montenegro." The grand duchess flashed her fan and sighed. "It is a pity Elektra hates St. Petersburg."

"But what she did in that room," I said. "Surely she's causing harm to everyone in there."

"The heat was caused by the reaction of the cold light itself with her own powers. She does not steal cold light. It shrinks away from her."

"Where does it go?" I asked.

"It will come back, when she is gone. Most of the people in your mother's garden room did not even notice the change. They only felt a slight discomfort. And perhaps they will blame that on your cousin's atrocious harp playing."

I ignored the dark faerie's catty remark. "Does the empress know about the striga?"

"It's one of the reasons your mother and the empress are no longer as close as they used to be. Marie Feodorovna can be terribly narrow-minded sometimes."

I shuddered. "Why is my mother friends with such a creature?"

"Madame Elektra saved your mother's life many years ago. But perhaps this is a discussion you should have with your mother." Miechen continued fanning herself and turned to go back inside. "I can tell you this, Katerina Alexandrovna. You have nothing to fear from Madame Elektra."

CHAPTER SIX

~∽◦∽~

I could not help feeling nervous around Madame Elektra. She made the servants uneasy as well. Anya said our villa's cook had crossed herself and spit over her left shoulder when she heard Madame Elektra was attending the afternoon's entertainment.

"The local people think she's a witch," Anya whispered when she caught up with me in the garden. "They hide their children when she goes to the marketplace. The cook said she curdles the milk and keeps the bread from rising."

"How ridiculous," I whispered back.

"She was at your mother's séance last week," Anya pointed out. "I remember her pale green eyes."

I found it difficult to breathe around the striga. But Miechen had assured me it was safe. A striga only drinks the blood of other vampires. They cannot tolerate human blood.

"She can't hurt you, Anya," I told our maid. "She is not like the Montenegrins."

Anya shuddered. "Are you certain?"

I wasn't, but I had to believe Miechen. Maman had many friends in her social circle who were dangerous. Of course, she had a daughter who was dangerous as well. I bit my lip. "Perhaps it's best if you stay away from Madame Elektra."

"Of course, Duchess." Anya curtsied and hastily disappeared back upstairs.

Dariya found me and pulled me into the parlor. "Did you see Prince Kotchoubey? He said he liked the music I played! And he brought me the sweetest nosegay!" She held out a small bouquet of the palest pink roses.

I smiled at my cousin. "You really like the prince, don't you?"

She blushed prettily and held the roses up to her face to breathe in their scent. "Don't you think he was the most handsome young man at the dance the other night? And his grandmother is a friend of Miechen's. So my stepmother approves."

She pulled the flowers away from her face with a pout. "They are fading already. They don't live for very long, do they?" She laid the tiny bouquet down on the garden bench and left me to find her stepmother.

I picked up the bouquet and touched the brown edges of the petals. With only the faintest wish from me, the brown disappeared and the roses once again looked crisp and fresh. I could see faint slivers of cold light slipping away from my hands as I did so.

It was a foolish thing to have done.

"Such a waste of your talent." It was a voice I did not recognize.

I was so startled I almost dropped the flowers. "I'm so sorry, I was just . . ."

Madame Elektra stood in the doorway, her enormous green eyes glittering dangerously. Her snow-white hair was swept into a braided bun at the nape of her neck, but she lacked the fashionably short bangs favored by my mother and the St. Petersburg set. She was dressed in a simple gray gown, similar to those my instructors at Smolny had worn.

The old woman smiled at me, and I felt an oppressive heat rising up in the space between us. It stole my breath away. "I was just teasing, my girl. Sometimes it feels good to use your powers after hiding them for so long, yes?" she asked.

I didn't want to admit it to myself, but she spoke the truth. I frowned. "It doesn't seem like such a terrible gift just now."

She cackled. "It just might come in useful one day." She patted me on the arm like a kindly grandmother would. "Take care, Katerina Alexandrovna," she said before leaving the doorway and returning to Maman's parlor. The moment she left, I was able to breathe again.

I hurried to find my mother. But she was saying goodbye to Grand Duchess Miechen and Aunt Zina. Dariya was following behind them.

"You forgot your flowers," I said, holding out my cousin's bouquet.

"*Merci*, Katiya!" She snatched up the bouquet and embraced me.

"How lovely!" Maman said. "Were those from a beau?"

Dariya blushed as Aunt Zina told her about Prince Kotchoubey.

"If only Katiya had a beau." Maman sighed. "Someone to make her forget all about the crown prince of Montenegro."

Dariya glanced at me and tried not to giggle.

"It wasn't as if he jilted me, Maman," I said, glaring at my cousin. "I turned him down."

"Of course you cannot marry him now, dear," Maman said. "Besides, his mother is angling for Princess Hélène of Orléans."

"Really?" Miechen asked, her violet eyes glittering with interest. "But will her parents let her convert?"

"I wouldn't think so," Maman said as she went with the grand duchess and Aunt Zina to the front hall to see them out.

Dariya and I followed them. "Was that about the French princess having to convert from Catholicism to marry Danilo?" I asked her.

"No, silly, she'd have to transfer her allegiance from the Light Court." My cousin smirked. She gave me a quick kiss on the cheek before departing with her stepmother and the grand duchess in Miechen's carriage.

Dariya was learning so much about Dark Court and Light Court intrigues now that she was a lady-in-waiting. I only hoped she would be able to stay out of the intrigues herself.

CHAPTER SEVEN

≈

The next week there was to be a late-summer ball at the imperial palace of Livadia. It was held every August for Grand Duchess Ekaterina Mikhailovna's birthday. The ancient woman was a great-aunt of the tsar, and Dark and Light Court members were not invited; they were simply obligated to attend. Everyone, from the youngest maidens to the elderly matrons, wore dazzling white dresses and their most brilliant diamonds.

I had not seen George again, and I assumed glumly that he'd decided it would be better to leave without saying goodbye. I was not looking forward to the ball.

Dariya tried to cheer me, instructing Anya to fix my hair in a new style that night. My dull wheat-colored hair had a golden cast to it in the candlelight at the ball. Maman looked pleased. "All of the young men will be eager to dance with you!" She kissed me on the forehead.

Papa was still in St. Petersburg, so we were escorted by my uncle Evgene Maximilianovich. Aunt Zina fussed with the rose in his lapel during the entire carriage ride to the palace. "Those petals are faded around the edges! It looks so shabby! You must replace it with one of the empress's roses as soon as you can make your way to the gardens."

"Yes, dear," Uncle Evgene said meekly.

Dariya clutched my hand tightly as she stared out the window, eager to catch a glimpse of the rest of the aristocracy arriving at the palace. I tried to ignore the conversation between my aunt and uncle. I would not be so foolish as to meddle with dead flowers tonight.

"There's the princess of Greece!" my cousin whispered. "And I think her brother is with her. Do you think his parents are still planning to marry him to the Swedish princess? I know the families are related."

Most of Europe's royalty was related. We shared one large, twisted and tangled family tree. I could claim ties with most likely all of the people dancing inside the palace. I was related to witches and fae and, quite possibly, even a few wolf-folk. There was at least one other necromancer, if my cousin was to be believed. Dariya's mother, who died several years ago, had shared my talent.

. However, I knew of no blood drinkers in my family, thank God.

The Montenegrins were the first guests we ran into after we were announced in the Livadia ballroom. Princess Elena and her older sister, now Duchess Anastasia of Leuchtenberg, were whispering together when they spotted us. "Katerina Alexandrovna, what a wonderful surprise!" Anastasia said. She was my aunt now, after her marriage to Maman's youngest brother, but I refused to dutifully kiss her on the cheek.

"Stay away from me," I said as quietly as I could.

"No hug for a dear friend?" Elena said, reaching forward to embrace me. She made my skin crawl. I did not raise my arms to embrace her back, but instead waited for her to let go of me. "Danilo sends his love," she whispered in my ear.

"I have nothing to say to you, Elena. Or your brother." I just wanted the crown prince to leave me in peace. It would be nice if his sisters would do the same.

"Take a turn with us in the gardens?" Aunt Anastasia asked, her cold hand gripping my arm painfully. She would not be refused. I glanced around, torn between calling for help and not wishing to cause a scene.

Maman and Aunt Zina and Dariya had already been swept up into the dancing on the marble terrace. Aunt Zina was merrily waltzing with the tsar's youngest brother, the flirtatious Grand Duke Alexei Alexandrovich. Handsome young Prince Kotchoubey had claimed Dariya's hand. Uncle Evgene had quickly disappeared, either to steal one of the empress's roses or, much more likely, to join the other men in the card room.

Brightly lit luminarias dotted the grounds, and a string quartet played Tchaikovsky's latest waltz from the rose-covered gazebo. The sea breeze cooled the garden and carried the heavy scents of jasmine and roses across the night.

Anastasia and her sister steered me away from the dancing crowds, into the mazes of rosebushes. Hundreds of blossoms in every color bloomed with a vengeance. The perfume hung in the air, too sweet for me to breathe.

Far off in the darkness, we could hear the raspy call of an owl.

Elena grabbed her sister's arm, looking slightly panicked. Then she smiled at me sheepishly. "Did you know there are some blood drinkers that can turn into owls? They only drink the blood of other vampires."

"Indeed?" I asked, the hair on the back of my neck standing up. I wondered if they knew about Madame Elektra. I wondered why Miechen had not told me the green-eyed elderly woman could change shapes.

"You know that is only a rumor," Anastasia said. "Most likely."

"And where is Militza?" I asked, wondering why she hadn't been present to ambush me as well.

"She is still on her honeymoon with Grand Duke Peter Nikolayevich," Elena said. "They're visiting Egypt to see the pyramids."

"How wonderful," I said, truly thankful that she was not with us. Of all the daughters of the Montenegrin king, Militza, now a grand duchess and leader of the St. Petersburg vampires, frightened me the most. "And your parents are well?" I could be polite with the Montenegrins as long as they did not try to drink my blood in the empress's garden.

Anastasia stopped to inhale the scent of a dark-red damask rose. "The queen is well. She awaits the birth of her next child in the fall. Our father is ecstatic."

Of course. I'd noticed Queen Milena was pregnant when I was abducted to the Montenegrin palace earlier that year. The queen would be giving birth to one more blood drinker. I could not be any less happy for her.

"Your aunt was telling us that you visited the Massandra caves last week," Anastasia said. "Did you enjoy them?"

I did not wish to discuss the caves with the Montenegrins. "What do you want from me? Why have you brought me out here?"

Anastasia shuddered delicately, pulling her lace shawl over her shoulder. "Every time I've been to the Massandra estate, I have a terrible feeling, as if something very bad has happened there." She looked at me very intently. "Did you feel anything strange, Katerina?"

"Of course not," I lied. I wondered how many people knew of the throne room inside the caves. Did the Montenegrin princess know about the strange cold-light realm?

"Are you as anxious as I am to be returning to Smolny?" Elena asked. "I have missed everyone so."

I shook my head and smiled. "I will not be returning this fall." I was so thankful I would be safe from Elena's mischief. I was filled with relief that I would no longer have to sleep in the same room with her. "I will be attending medical school in Zurich."

Anastasia rolled her eyes and stopped to sit down on a marble bench. "Why on earth would you want to do such a thing?"

Elena looked at me with reproach. "That is terrible news. You and your cousin will both be gone, then." She sighed and glanced at a moth that was fluttering around one of the luminarias. "Oh well, I shall still have the Bavarian princesses to talk to."

"Please give them my regards," I said. They would continue to be vulnerable to Elena and her veshtiza poison. But surely the empress had some way to protect the students since she was allowing Elena to return to Smolny. I could not find it in my heart to forgive the Montenegrins for kidnapping me and using me in their brother's blood ritual. Or for poisoning my cousin.

I was almost certain there was nothing they could do to me here, at the empress's palace, but still I felt anxious and did not want to be alone with them any longer than necessary. I wished I could escape from the princesses and return to the ball. Not that there was anyone there that I wished to dance with. Where could George Alexandrovich be? What was so important that he was allowed to miss his great-aunt's birthday party?

Anastasia sighed. "If only Marija were still alive, my darling. She would have still been at Smolny with you."

Elena grabbed my hands and squeezed. Very tightly. "You remember our sister Marija, do you not?"

The Montenegrin princess had died several years ago, when Elena and I were only twelve. "Of course," I said, pulling my hands away. "She was beautiful, and very shy." The very opposite in temperament to the rest of her sisters. But she'd been a veshtiza as well. Had she ever stolen blood from me? I repressed a shudder.

"Heavens, we must return to the dancing!" Anastasia said, as she stood back up. "Elena was hoping the tsarevitch would be here this evening."

"Is he?" I asked halfheartedly. My mood lightened somewhat when the princesses turned around on the garden path and we headed back to the palace.

"I heard Princess Kotchoubey say the tsarevitch and his

brother would be joining us later. The empress is looking splendid tonight, don't you think?"

Was George still here in the Crimea? My spirits lifted a little. I wanted to race to the ballroom and search for him.

"If you will please excuse me, I just remembered I have promised a polonaise to one of my brother's friends. I'd better hurry along." I nodded and almost skipped off, before they could detain me any longer.

There was, of course, no sign of the tsarevitch or his brother. But I did see the empress, in a beautiful snow-white gown embroidered with so many diamonds she shimmered. She was wearing her favorite tiara, the one made for Katerina the Great. Grand Duchess Xenia was at her side, wearing a sweet white dress and a pearl-encrusted *kokoshnik* on her head. The grand duchess smiled when she saw me. The empress did not.

I knew it was impossible to hope that she might one day change her mind about me. And I really couldn't blame her. I wouldn't want my child to marry a necromancer either.

I did end up dancing with two young gentlemen, especially after my mother remarked that I was behaving like a wall-flower. But neither the grand duke nor his brother showed up at the palace that night.

The ball ended with a grand display of fireworks out over the water. They lit the sky as bright as day with sunbursts of rainbow-colored lights. All of the guests clapped enthusiastically.

Dariya came out on the terrace with me to watch the fireworks. She leaned over the railing, out of breath from dancing so much. "It's a pity you can't make a wish on them, like falling stars."

I turned to look at her. "What would you wish for?"

Her face lit up with the explosion of another burst of fire in the sky. She was looking across the lawn at the young Prince Kotchoubey. He was dancing with one of the empress's ladies-in-waiting, but glanced over at us and gave Dariya a shy smile. She sighed. "That this night would never have to end."

The fireworks were dazzling, but the air was soon smoky and smelled of sulfur. I stared at the last dying bursts of light in the sky with an odd, vaguely ominous feeling in my stomach. I squeezed my eyes shut, making a wish of my own, trying to ward off any evil.

We returned home long after midnight, with Aunt Zina complaining of her bleeding feet. I couldn't see why, as a married woman, she had needed to dance with all of those men, especially the tsar's brother, but I kept my thoughts to myself. Uncle Evgene did not seem to mind.

Dariya looked happy, but tired as well. Even Maman appeared to have had a good time. I was the only person who seemed glad the birthday ball was over.

CHAPTER EIGHT

~⁂~

Anya's frantic voice woke me the next morning. "Duchess! The tsar's men are here! They are asking for you!"

I sat up in bed slowly, my head thick and my eyes bleary. "What time is it?"

"After ten, Duchess. You must hurry and get dressed. Your mother is waiting for you in the parlor." I climbed out of bed and started to open my armoire, but Anya shook her head. "There is no time for that! Here!" she said, holding up one of my pretty but faded blue dresses from the previous summer. I struggled into my underthings as she threw the dress over my head. It smelled as if it had been freshly laundered. Anya briskly spun me around and buttoned up the front before I was completely awake. "Is there tea?" I asked, trying not to yawn in my maid's face.

"You have no time for tea," she said, grimacing as she brought me my stockings and boots. She tapped her foot impatiently while I buttoned up my shoes. But she still insisted on twisting my hair up into a presentable knot before allowing me to go downstairs. She fussed with the curls until she was satisfied, and then shooed me out the door.

The men in Maman's parlor were not just any of the tsar's men. It was George Alexandrovich. And the strange man from the caves was with him. *Mon Dieu*, how did they know each other?

I curtsied politely to the grand duke, thanking Anya silently for insisting that I wear the blue dress. It matched the grand duke's eyes. "Your Imperial Highness, we missed you at the ball yesterday evening."

"Forgive me, Duchess." Both he and the strange Frenchman were frowning. "It was not my intention to miss my mother's dance. We had business to attend to for the tsar."

I could tell Maman was upset. She was sitting in her favorite chair, twisting her handkerchief into pieces. "Katiya, please listen to the grand duke. He says you would be in great danger if you went to Zurich. The tsar has decided not to let you go."

"What?" I turned on George. "What have you done? What did you tell the tsar?"

The stranger spoke up as I heard Maman gasp at my impudence. "I believe you know why you cannot leave the country unprotected right now, Duchess. It would be beyond foolish for you to think you are safe on your own."

"Who are you?" I asked, too mad to ask any other questions.

The Frenchman bowed his head slightly. "Forgive me. I am called Papus. I am . . . a student from Paris."

I did not need George's faerie sight to understand. I realized this man must be one of the sorcerers sent to accompany

George back to Paris. "What were you doing in the cave last week?" I asked him.

He looked the slightest bit uncomfortable. "As I have already told the grand duke, I was searching for an ancient manuscript that was rumored to be buried in the caves."

I lowered my voice, so Maman could not hear. "And what were you doing in that other place?"

He drew in his breath sharply but did not answer.

"Where I saw Konstantin. In the cold-light realm."

George folded his arms, the space between his eyebrows crinkling unhappily. He ignored me and looked at my mother. "Duchess, would you be so kind as to get some tea for your daughter? She looks as if she could use something hot to drink."

Maman stood up quickly. "Of course, Your Imperial Highness. Katiya, I'll be right back, darling." Normally my mother would ring for a servant to bring tea, but something in the fae grand duke's request made Maman suddenly eager to leave the room.

He waited until she was gone before speaking again. "It does not matter what purpose Papus had, but you had absolutely no reason to be there with no one knowing where you'd gone."

"But I don't know how I got there. I touched the throne, and the next thing I knew I was someplace strange, and then I saw swirls of cold light flying all around the lich tsar's head."

"And Papus said you trapped yourself in the Graylands." George looked angry. At me.

"I am sure I would have found my way out of these Graylands eventually." I was thankful, at least, to finally learn the name of the frightening place. "We should warn the tsar."

George was growing angrier by the minute. He seemed to

be struggling with his self-control. "My father already knows. But you," he said softly. "You are too reckless to look after yourself. The tsar cannot risk losing his only necromancer." He took a deep breath and drew himself up regally. "Katerina Alexandrovna, you are hereby ordered to return to the Smolny Institute for the coming school term."

I could not believe it. He knew how much going to Zurich meant to me. "No! You must be teasing me!"

The scowl on his face told me he was not teasing.

"You cannot do this!" I forced back angry tears, refusing to accept this quietly. I would write to Papa immediately.

Reading my thoughts, the grand duke shook his head. "Your father has already been informed of this by the tsar himself. There is nothing you can do, Katiya. You know your parents would feel safer with you in St. Petersburg anyway."

I glared at George. "Your Imperial Highness, I beg you to rethink your decision. I will not be exploring any more caves this summer or at any time after that. There is truly no need—"

"Katiya, it is the tsar's decision. Not mine. The Smolny Institute will be protected by one of my mother's spells. A spell that will also prevent the veshtiza from harming the students. It is the safest place for you."

Papus nodded. "I am confident you will be safe under the empress's protection, Duchess. You need not worry."

I wanted to scream. I did not want to go back to Smolny. Not now, when all my childhood hopes and dreams of being a doctor were within my grasp. But I could not throw a temper tantrum. I took a deep breath and attempted to calm down. Papa would understand me. I knew he would be able to talk to the tsar. At least he would try. "The only reason I stumbled across Konstantin Pavlovich was because I read the words inscribed upon the old throne," I told them.

"What throne?" Papus asked suspiciously.

"What do you mean, what throne? How did *you* get to the Graylands?"

Papus and the tsar's son frowned at each other before the grand duke sighed. "She should know," he said. "She serves the tsar just as we do."

Papus nodded. "As magicians, we can call upon higher powers to help us travel between dimensions," the Frenchman said. "Are you sure you saw a throne?"

"Of course I saw a throne. I touched the throne. I read the Greek words: 'The path to the light travels straight to the darkness.'"

Papus said nothing, but he and George shared a grim look.

I rubbed my pounding temples and looked back up at the French wizard. "Wait a minute. You're talking about demons. *Mon Dieu*, that's who you called upon to assist you."

Papus's face drew up into a sneer. "Demons? *Mais non*, Mademoiselle."

"Katerina Alexandrovna, listen to me," George said, grabbing me by the shoulders gently. "They're not demons. I would never call upon a demon." He looked me in the eye and lowered his voice. "Do you trust me?"

"Your Imperial Highness—"

His voice was low and calming. "Katiya." Was he casting a glamour on me? The whole world could fall away and I would be safe as long as I was looking into his eyes. "Do you trust me?" he repeated.

The blue in his eyes deepened, and almost glowed. Finally, I nodded.

Papus was sitting on the arm of Maman's favorite chair. "Duchess, could you describe the throne that you saw?"

"You honestly did not see it?"

He shook his head.

I sighed. "It was old, with faded and chipped paint. But dazzling. And it had the Maltese cross embroidered on the back, with two angels on either side of the cross. It must have been breathtaking to see in its day." Not to mention the ruler who had sat upon the throne. I hesitated, not wanting to admit that I'd heard voices there, but finally I added, "The lich tsar mentioned Byzantium."

"Of course," George said, nodding thoughtfully. "Katerina the Great was Konstantin Pavlovich's grandmother, and he was her favorite grandson. She had him named Konstantin with the hope that Russia would reclaim this area from the Turks and her grandson would rule the reclaimed Orthodox kingdom."

"What about the throne I saw?"

"I don't know what to tell you," Papus said. "It could have been the throne of the Byzantine emperor, but why would it be here?"

George frowned. "My father just recently bought the Massandra property from the Vorontsov family. It belonged to a Polish count before then."

George and I looked at each other. "Johanna," we said at the same time. The vampire princess who had turned Konstantin into a lich had belonged to well-known Bessarabian nobility, but had been previously married to a Polish count.

Papus shook his head. "It could have been her family's

property. She probably kept the throne hidden in the caves all these years, believing no one would find it. And it must have been disguised with some sort of magic, since I couldn't see it." He looked at me thoughtfully. "Perhaps you could because you are a necromancer. You can walk easily between this world and the next."

"But I couldn't return on my own," I said. "I don't know if I would have discovered a way to escape eventually or not. How did you get me out of that place? You say you use magical guardians, but I saw no one else there other than you and Konstantin Pavlovich."

"It's . . . complicated," Papus murmured. "A secret knowledge we are bound under oath not to reveal to the uninitiated."

"But the throne . . . ," George mused. "If the Grigori are involved . . ."

"Let us hope for the tsar's sake that they are not," Papus said.

I had no idea who the Grigori were, but I was still fuming at the idea of returning to Smolny. And Elena. *Mon Dieu.* It took all of the good breeding and proper manners that I possessed not to stomp my feet in anger. *Merde.* "What makes you believe that the empress's protective spell over Smolny will keep me safe from Konstantin? We don't even know how I stumbled across him in the caves."

George shook his head. "Do not worry. My mother's spell is more than just a faerie glamour. It casts a protective shield over the entire institute. Nothing supernatural can get in. Or out. Once you are back at Smolny, you will not be able to leave."

This made me like the idea even less. "I'll be trapped! I cannot believe you would do this to me."

George sighed. "Katiya, I want to know that you are safe. Why must you be so stubborn?"

"You don't know that it will help at all, and what if the lich tsar gets in and I can't get out?"

Papus stood up. "I am certain you will be safe, Duchess. And the members of the Order will be on guard outside of the institute. The Order of St. Lazarus."

My eyebrows rose at that, and I repressed a shudder. Several members of the Order of St. John of Jerusalem, the elite imperial guard, had been turned into the walking dead by Princess Johanna. She'd been building an army of undead soldiers for Konstantin. Thanks to me, the unfortunate creatures were now sworn to protect Tsar Alexander as the Order of St. Lazarus. "The tsar is aware of this?"

"The tsar is the one who commands it." George took my hand. "And he will command you to report to Smolny, if you do not go willingly."

I stared at him angrily, trying very hard not to let the tears leak out. I jerked my hand out of his and turned toward the window.

"To the devil with this!" George muttered with an exasperated sigh. He stomped out of the parlor. The door slammed, rattling Maman's china figures on the curio shelf.

"Duchess?" Papus said softly. "It is not difficult to see that he cares for you a very great deal."

"He is being unreasonable. I cannot hide behind the empress's magic spells. And why isn't everyone more concerned with protecting the tsar? He is Konstantin's main enemy. Not I."

"The Order is protecting the tsar as well. The empress cannot, unfortunately, cast a protective spell around the tsar. But—"

"And why not?" I interrupted. "Why won't her spells work on him?"

"She is forbidden by the church to cast any spell over the sovereign. But he is well protected nevertheless."

At that moment, Maman came hurrying in with Anya, behind her, carrying a tea tray. "Katiya? We heard loud noises! Is everything all right? Where is the grand duke?"

I had no idea where George had gone. Surely he wouldn't leave the French sorcerer here alone. I looked out the window into the street. George was standing next to the imperial carriage. He still looked angry.

"Perhaps I should go down to him," I said, hesitating. I was afraid this would be the last time I would see him before he left for Paris.

I could have sworn Papus winked at me as he nodded slightly. "I am going to sit here and drink my tea, if you do not mind." He settled himself in the stuffed chair and smiled at Anya and my mother.

I flew down the staircase and out the door before my mother could protest.

The grand duke turned around as I approached him. His glare softened. "I was expecting Papus to follow me," he said.

I shook my head. "He is taking tea with Maman. I wanted to apologize to you. I should never have made you angry."

"Don't you understand how much I wish I could stay here and protect you myself?"

I sighed. I wished he would hold me, but there was no way we could touch, not here in front of my family's dacha. The unhappy look in his eyes told me he'd read my mind and felt the same way. "Will you leave soon?" I asked.

"Tonight." His smile was sad. "Please let me leave with some peace of mind, knowing you will soon be safe at Smolny?"

There was no way I could avoid it, so I finally nodded, blinking back tears. "The tsar's men will not have to drag me kicking and screaming. I will go quietly."

His sigh was heavy with relief. "Thank you. The imperial guard will be posted around your mother's dacha until you return to St. Petersburg."

Papus joined us just then. "So sorry to keep you waiting, Your Imperial Highness. Shall we go? It was an honor to formally meet you, Duchess."

George took my hand and bowed over it. I felt his lips touch the back of my hand just barely. "At your service, Duchess."

"And I am at yours, Your Imperial Highness," I said. "Please take care of yourself."

"Always." With a grim smile he turned and climbed into the imperial carriage after Papus. I stood there and watched the carriage pull off toward the winding mountain road that would take them to the harbor in Yalta. A ship would take them to Varna, on the Bulgarian coast, and from there they would travel by train to Paris. The journey would last the better part of a week.

And I would be returning to St. Petersburg with Maman within the next few days. By the time the grand duke reached Paris, I would be back at the Smolny Institute for Young Noble Maidens.

CHAPTER NINE

❧

The following morning, we left the family dacha and returned to Sevastopol, where the train waited for our long journey back to St. Petersburg. Our private railcar was comfortable, and the trip would have been pleasant if not for Aunt Zina's nervous dog. The tiny bichon frise shed almost all of its hair and vomited every half hour from nervousness.

Dariya had already abandoned me and was traveling back to St. Petersburg with Miechen's entourage. Maman was kind enough to let me sit by the window, and I stared out at the vast fields as we raced north through the Crimea. The mountains stretched out before us, the rich farmlands disappearing into the distance.

When night fell and the view outside the window darkened, everyone climbed into their sleeping berths. The swaying of the train lulled me to sleep and I dreamed I was back at the Livadia Ball. I dreamed that I was searching the ballroom for George Alexandrovich. I wandered in and out between hundreds of dancing couples as the orchestra played a polonaise from the opera *A Life for the Tsar*. But I could not find George anywhere.

A man grabbed my arm, digging his fingers painfully into my skin. I turned around but the man was wearing a black mask. He was much taller than George, but nowhere near as tall as the tsar.

"Who are you?" I asked.

The man smiled; his white teeth were dazzling and sharp. "Your life will be in less danger if you do not know, Duchess. You have been poking around where you should not be."

The man had a French accent, but did not look like the wizard Papus. He was much taller and his movements were far too graceful and quick. Almost unnatural. Before I realized what he was doing, he had swept me up into the crowd and we were dancing the polonaise. "The Koldun is keeping his eye on you," he said. "He believes you are a danger to the tsar."

I was confused. The Koldun was the tsar's own wizard. George was in training to replace the existing one. Who that was, I did not know.

I raised my chin and stared into his black eyes. "I can assure you, and you can assure your Koldun, I will give my life to protect the tsar."

He chuckled. "That would be a terrible waste, *ma petite*."

A sudden chill gripped my heart. "What do you mean?"

The masked man did not answer but instead spun me away from him as the music swelled. I found myself unable to stop spinning. The ballroom turned into a huge blur.

I woke up with a gasp. The train was rocking gently as it

66

raced through the dark Crimean night. My mother was asleep in the berth next to me. At some point she had covered me with a thin blanket, but I was shivering. I could still hear the masked man's laughter in my ears.

Maman shifted and moaned softly in her sleep. The train berths were small and cramped, but our car was much more comfortable than others. I had no right to complain. Taking my blanket and wrapping it around my shoulders, I climbed out of my berth and stood at the window. The sky was beginning to lighten, and by sunrise, we would be passing through Kharkov. I dressed quietly and slipped out of our compartment and headed to the dining car. A cup of hot tea would clear my head.

It was near Kharkov that the imperial train had run off the track last autumn. Twenty-one people on the train had died in the crash, and many more than that had been injured. Officially, the train had been going too fast and the engineer had lost control.

I'd heard whispers from the Dark Court that the train had been sabotaged by vampires. But even an army of vampires could not have accomplished such destruction. In my heart, I suspected dark magic, and remembered Grand Duchess Miechen's express disappointment when the imperial family survived. She did not hide the fact that she wished for her husband, the brother of the tsar, Vladimir Alexandrovich, to inherit the throne of all the Russias. Was she cruel enough to plot the murders of her own nieces and nephews?

It would have taken much more than any man-made explosive to blow the imperial train completely off its track. The tsar had been forced to tear the crumpled metal roof with his own hands to free the empress and their children. The empress had a sprained hand, and Grand Duchess Xenia had had cuts and scratches on her face and arms. The youngest, Grand Duchess Olga, had been thrown clear through a broken window. The young grand dukes had been badly bruised but were all right. I'd seen the faint scar on George's hand where the glass had cut him.

Shaking the awful images from my head, I slipped into the dining car. It was empty except for a woman close to Maman's age. She was wearing a plain black dress and sat reading a book while her tea grew cold.

As I sat down a few tables away from her, the waiter hurried up to me. "Your Highness, we would have been more than happy to bring breakfast to the Oldenburg car. There is no need for you to sit here with other passengers." He nodded to the woman in black dismissively.

"It is quite all right," I said. "I did not want to disturb my mother or my aunt. And I won't be any trouble to you. If you would just bring me tea, please. With lemon."

As the waiter bowed and left, I looked up to see the woman staring at me. She saw me looking back and quickly glanced again at her book.

The sun was beginning to peek over the horizon. I put my hand flat against the cold window as we rolled slowly past the scene of the accident. A cathedral was being built on the site to give thanks for the imperial family's safety. Imperial guards stood before the building site, their pale faces stony and grim. The Order of St. Lazarus.

The woman was staring out the window at the guards as well. And she was frowning.

"Is something the matter?" I asked.

She seemed surprise that I had addressed her. "Those men. There is something dreadfully wrong with them. I have seen the same sickness in St. Petersburg."

I felt my stomach sink. "You have?" How many other people had noticed the walking dead in St. Petersburg?

She gestured to the open book on the table in front of her. "I've been researching their symptoms but cannot find any known diseases that correlate."

"Are you a doctor?" I asked. When she nodded, the anxious feeling I'd had was mixed with excitement and curiosity. I was almost giddy. A female doctor! "I would be honored if you joined me. My name is Katerina Alexandrovna of Oldenburg."

Recognition showed in her face. "Your father is Duke Alexander Petrovich, then. I am Maria Bokova. I have recently agreed to work in the Oldenburg Hospital for Infants." She stood and curtsied to me, stiffly.

"How exciting! Please sit with me," I said, waving my hand at the empty seat at my table. "I plan to attend medical school myself and have many questions I would love to ask you!"

As she sat down carefully, she folded her hands primly in front of her. "And your father agrees to your plans? Why would he allow his daughter to be subjected to such misery?"

"Misery?"

"It is not a life for a pampered young girl, Highness. Why would you throw away the life you have for one such as mine?"

"I want to help people. I want to find cures for diseases." I'd always known that it would be hard, but I had not expected a female doctor to be so hostile. I had expected more camaraderie. More support. "And I am not a pampered young girl," I said, unable to ignore her bitter remark.

"Don't believe for a moment that your father's money and imperial ties will make it easy for you," she continued. "It's bad enough if the instructors and the fellow students believe you have received special favors for being a woman. Whether you actually received those special favors or not. And if they believe your papa bought your admission to the university, it will be a thousand times worse."

"I passed the entrance examination to Zurich on my own," I said coolly.

She nodded, but did not seem very impressed. "Perhaps you think it will get easier once you hold your diploma in your hand, but that is rubbish. There are more political and bureaucratic hoops to jump through in order to practice here in Russia as a doctor."

"And yet you intend to practice in St. Petersburg, and not in the country," I pointed out. "Surely the problems with bureaucracy are greater in the city."

Dr. Bokova sighed. "Yes, and I am very grateful to his highness, your father, for this opportunity. I am willing to risk the headaches and heartache. There are so many poor women and children in the city that need medical care."

"I hope the other doctors at the hospital will not make your work difficult," I said. Secretly, I worried if Papa could do anything about it if they did.

Dr. Bokova shook her head. "That is neither here nor there. There are always trials and struggles." She actually smiled a little, the lines around her eyes softening. "It builds character, you see."

I smiled back, hoping that she might be warming toward me. But as she glanced back at the unfinished cathedral, now fast disappearing from our view, my apprehension returned. "Those men out there," I asked warily, "you said you saw others with the same symptoms in St. Petersburg?"

"Yes. And before that, in Paris." She looked back at me and started to stand up. "I am sorry, Your Highness, but I should return to my research."

"In Paris? Can you tell me when this was?"

"Last month," she said, nodding. "Do not be alarmed, Your Highness. I don't feel this mysterious disease is contagious, whatever it is. But I do hope to continue my research when we reach St. Petersburg. Rest assured it will not interfere with my duties at the hospital."

"Of course."

Dr. Bokova smiled again, stiffly. "Best of luck to you with your studies, Duchess. Are you headed for Zurich now?"

"Unfortunately, no. My parents wish for me to delay my studies one more year and continue at the Smolny Institute this fall."

Her smile grew warmer. "Do not be impatient. Perhaps the tsar and his ministers will reopen the women's courses at the Medical and Surgical Academy in St. Petersburg."

"That would be wonderful, but my father has his doubts." I stood up, realizing the sun was coming up and my mother might be awake and wondering where I'd gone. "It has been such an honor to meet you. Please don't let me keep you from your research."

"Thank you, Duchess." With a curtsy she returned to her table and her book. And I returned to the Oldenburg car.

Maman was just beginning to stir. She fussed as she climbed out of her berth. "Good heavens, you're awake early, Katiya. And that sun is so bright. Do draw the curtains for me, dear."

I had wanted to go back to sleep after my strange dream. However, if I had not gotten up and visited the dining car, I would not have met Dr. Bokova. I realized how fortunate I was to have had that nightmare.

After closing the curtains, I turned around to kiss my mother on the cheek. "Good morning, Maman."

"*Mon Dieu*, are we in Kharkov yet? By this time tomorrow, we should be almost home. I shall be so happy to see St. Petersburg again." She grabbed my hand and squeezed it. "And I'm truly glad you will not be going to Zurich this fall."

I smiled back at her, choking on the bitter taste in my mouth. I still intended to go to medical school. One day.

CHAPTER TEN

❧

Two weeks later, I discovered my grand duke had been true to his word. As my parents' black carriage pulled inside the courtyard of the Smolny Institute for Young Noble Maidens, I saw several members of the Order of St. Lazarus standing stiffly at their posts at the front gates. Waxy and expressionless, they stared straight ahead and did not move. They wore the same dark-green and gold uniform as the Order of St. John, except for the medals on their chests. The familiar Maltese cross had been replaced by an oval medal showing a green hand holding a sword. Curious. I couldn't remember St. Lazarus using a sword. Or having a green hand, for that matter. But the members of the undead order did have a sort of greenish tinge to their pale skin.

Maman did not even notice them. I could not decide whether their presence made me feel safer.

Thankfully, I was able to persuade my mother not to

accompany me inside the building. "Do take care of yourself, Katiya," she said, squeezing my hands in hers as we stood at the front door. "And give my regards to Madame Tomilov. Your aunt Zina and I will be spending the next few weeks in Biarritz. We will come by to visit you when we arrive back in St. Petersburg."

I kissed her on both cheeks. "You be careful too, Maman." I did not want the life my mother lived, constantly following the imperial court in its travels endlessly seeking pleasure. Denmark, Finland, France, Peterhof, the Crimea, Tsarskoe Selo. Only the coldest and darkest part of the winter, the social season, was spent in St. Petersburg by the aristocracy.

There were many old friends who were happy to see me at Smolny. Madame Tomilov, the headmistress, was pleased that I'd decided to return. "Some girls do well without the extra year here at the institute, but I always encourage them to make the most of the education we have to offer. Students who complete our entire program leave more polished. You will learn extra court etiquette and gain knowledge about the nuances of St. Petersburg court society. You'll also acquire a deeper appreciation for our culture."

I wanted to point out that I probably knew more secrets and nuances about the Dark and Light Courts than Madame Tomilov ever dreamed and, furthermore, that I did not need to know these nuances to succeed in medical school, but I kept silent. I wanted the school year to pass by quickly so I could continue with my own plans.

"In addition," Madame Tomilov continued, "you will teach two classes a week to one of the lower forms. I realize you did not intend to receive a teaching certificate, but it is traditional that students taking an additional year of the White

74

Form learn pedagogy and begin teaching simple subjects to the younger girls."

"Pedagogy?" I asked. It was a term I'd never heard before.

"The science of education," Madame said. "We shall teach you how to teach properly."

"Of course, Madame," I said, curtsying and wondering what course I would be required to instruct. I suspected it would not be Practical Necromancy. And I hoped it would not be Geometry.

My favorite instructor, Madame Orbellani, hugged me when she saw me. "We will continue with the Greek and Latin lessons, Katerina Alexandrovna. The more you know, the easier it will be when you do go to university."

The Bavarian princesses were delighted that I'd returned. Erzsebet embraced me and spun me around before letting me go. "We will have so much fun this year! Augusta and I are finally old enough to attend the Smolny Ball in November!" I smiled at both of the curly blond princesses. At least there was the ball to look forward to. Perhaps George Alexandrovich would be back from Paris by then, and we would dance the mazurka as we had last year.

Elena did not show any surprise when I brought my things into our old room. I looked over at the empty cot where Dariya had slept. I would miss my cousin, even though I was glad she was now safe, far away from Elena. I wondered how my cousin liked being a lady-in-waiting for Grand Duchess Miechen.

A fourth cot stood in the far corner of our room, and I wondered if the Bavarian sisters were moving in with us from the younger girls' room. It was rather crowded in their dormitory.

"I knew you would not leave us," the Montenegrin princess

said. "Too many wonderful things will be happening this year. Especially all the balls, where I will dance with the tsarevitch and you will dance with my brother!"

I could not tell her anything. I could not even mention the spell over the institute, since it was because of her that the spell had been cast in the first place. With a bit of malice, I wondered what the empress's spell would do to her the first time Elena tried any of her dark-magic tricks or tried to sneak off the school grounds.

I decided not to offer any explanation for my change in plans. I couldn't tell her the tsar wouldn't let me leave the country because Konstantin Pavlovich might reappear. Nor could I tell her why this school was the safest place in St. Petersburg.

There was a soft knock on the door. "Excuse me, I believe this is my room?" A pretty young girl with dark-blond hair swept up in a neat bun entered.

I recognized her immediately. "Princess Alix?" It was the German princess, sister of the Grand Duchess Ella Feodorovna.

She smiled shyly, but said nothing.

An older girl brushed past her and sashayed in. "I was told this would be my room this year as well," said Princess Aurora Demidova.

Elena rose regally from her cot. She was not happy to see Princess Alix. "I'm Elena of Montenegro. And I take it you already know Katerina of Oldenburg."

Alix did not curtsy, but instead moved quickly to put away her things. "I am honored to be here." She took a small black box out of her trunk and carefully slid it under her cot.

Aurora Demidova looked at all of us before turning her back to us and disdainfully examining the bed linens. "I've heard there are new rules this year because someone here was disobedient. Is it true we are not allowed to leave the school premises at all?"

No one knew of the empress's spell, but the headmistress had mentioned that she would be very strict this year about permitting students to leave.

Elena looked at Princess Aurora warily. She did not approve of either of our new roommates. I had a sinking feeling that the school year was going to be very difficult. Elena did not like it when she was not the center of attention.

I sat down on Alix's cot, careful not to disturb her neatly folded pile of white school uniforms. "And what has brought you here?"

Alix frowned. "My sister wanted me in St. Petersburg, closer to her. And my father wished for my education to be polished. He distrusted the English nanny my grandmother had sent to us."

"A nanny? At our age?" Aurora Demidova snorted and turned back to her unpacking. Elena snickered, deciding to side with Aurora over the German princess. Aurora was no rival to Elena for the tsarevitch's affections. But the tsar's son had been extremely attentive to Princess Alix during her visit to St. Petersburg last year. I wondered which princess he would dance with at the upcoming Smolny Ball this year.

At that moment, the Bavarian princesses, Erzsebet and Augusta, burst in. "You'll never guess what has happened! Madame Metcherskey has left! We don't know why. But isn't that wonderful?"

"Thank goodness," Elena said as she poked through Aurora's basket of hair ribbons. "That skulking bat was horrible. I know you must be ecstatic, Katiya. She was always scolding you for something."

I said nothing, but smiled at Alix and shrugged. It was true that the pinch-faced Madame Metcherskey had made my life miserable last year. Despite the facts that I really wished to be somewhere else, that I was again sleeping in the same room with a bloodsucking witch, and that there were undead soldiers outside our front gates, the prospects for the coming school year suddenly became just a tiny bit brighter.

CHAPTER ELEVEN

❧

I did not mean to test the empress's enchantment. The next afternoon, I was walking in the courtyard with the Bavarian princesses when they decided to race out to the cluster of birch trees by the front gates. The leaves had turned from deep green to blazing yellow and were beginning to fall to the ground. Augusta wanted to collect a few of the leaves to press inside her journal.

I had no idea the empress's spell did not stretch across the entire school campus. We reached the boundaries of the spell before we could have left the courtyard.

My body reacted violently. I was repelled backward, with bone-jarring vibrations racking my limbs. My ears were ringing. I fell to the ground, out of breath and feeling bruised and sore all over.

My friends turned around and stared at me in fright. They had passed through the invisible barrier without noticing a thing. There was nothing unnatural about the Bavarian princesses.

"Mon Dieu, Katerina!" Augusta hurried back to me and helped me to stand.

"I must have tripped over a stone or something," I said unsteadily. Every inch of my body throbbed. How powerful was the empress's magic? Could it actually kill me?

"Did you twist your ankle?" Erzsebet asked with concern.

"I just . . . I think I need to go inside and lie down," I said. I was shaking with both fright and anger. I hated the idea of being trapped. Even if it was for my own protection.

"If you aren't feeling well by dinnertime, we'll be happy to sneak some food to you," Augusta said. "There will be mushroom soup tonight! And mutton pie!"

I thanked them, but by the time I reached our room, the effects of the spell were beginning to fade. I was still shaken and had a lingering headache, but I was otherwise unhurt. I really just needed a quiet, empty room in which to collect my thoughts, and I realized that my dormitory room, with Alix and Elena and Aurora all sniping at each other, would not be quiet enough.

I wandered the halls until I found myself in the library, which was nothing more than a drafty parlor with one small bookcase stacked with books. I'd read the hundred or so books over and over again in the years since I'd begun attending Smolny. It was not a large collection, but then, ladies of the aristocracy were not generally encouraged to read too much. Or to improve their minds. There were plenty of the classics here for Madame Tomilov to ensure we were exposed to fine literature, but that was enough for her.

I passed over the poems and stories of Alexander Pushkin, which I had read so often I could quote them by heart, and settled down in the chair with the tattered copy of Euripides's plays to reread *Iphigenia in Tauris*. I wondered if Madame Orbellani could find a copy of the play in its original Greek for me. I was anxious to practice my Greek and Latin once more. Especially after meeting Dr. Bokova. I'd always known the medical courses would be difficult, but I did not want to be remiss in any of my preparations. And since I had a year to wait, I decided I was going to make the most of it.

> And steep in tears the mournful song,
> Notes, which to the dead belong;
> Dismal notes, attuned to woe,
> By Pluto in the realms below.

I heard a whisper, or maybe it was just the exhalation of a breath behind me. The hairs stood up on the back of my neck. I jumped up out of my chair, and looked around the room. No one was there with me. And yet I could feel a presence. The person was very close. Too close. I shut the book and placed it back on the shelf, feeling compelled to leave.

Was it the empress's spell? Did she know that I had tested her magical barrier? I felt a horrible sense of guilt, but the presence did not feel like fae. It felt cold, like death. But ever since returning to Smolny, I could no longer see anyone's cold light.

The moment I stepped into the hallway, the strange feeling passed. I looked into the empty library again, almost curious enough to reenter the room, but I felt a strong resistance.

There was something in that room that did not want me in there.

In all my years at the Smolny Institute, I had never encountered anything like this before. It was a presence, but did not seem like a person. It was cold, but gave off no cold light that I could see. My heart started to pound in my chest. I wondered if Konstantin had been able to get past the empress's spell somehow. What could I do?

As I hurried away down the hall, I felt a little bit foolish. There was no reason for the lich tsar to come looking for me here. And no reason for the empress's spell not to hold fast. Still, I was spooked, and did not want to be alone anymore. I decided to join the others for dinner.

I noticed Princess Alix limping slightly as she headed toward the dining hall. "Are you all right?" I asked.

"It's nothing," she said. "I'm fine. I was just taking a walk on the grounds. I think I overtired myself."

"I'd be happy to help—"

"I said I'm fine. Please forget it."

I took my seat next to Elena at the dinner table without another word to Alix.

Alix sat down across from us and began eating in silence. The Bavarian sisters joined us as well. Augusta dug into her food as Erzsebet leaned over toward Aurora.

"May I borrow your notes for the Domestic Arts examination?" she asked.

"Why must they test us after only one day of class?" Elena moaned.

Domestic Arts had been my least favorite class last year. Who knew there could be so much to learn about running a household? It seemed ridiculous to me to be examined on the most efficient way to manage servants or how to plan a menu.

"Of course you may." Aurora nodded haughtily to the Bavarian princess, her spoon poised over her mushroom soup. "I do not have many notes, however. My grandmother taught me everything I shall need to know."

Elena rolled her eyes. In a low voice, she whispered to me. "I hope her grandmother taught her how to survive a veshtiza's kiss. I am looking forward to the next full moon."

The gleeful malice in Elena's voice alarmed me. Even if she was a little snobbish, Princess Aurora had done nothing to Elena. "You mustn't," I whispered back. "You'll get into trouble."

"No one will ever know. Unless you tell them, Katiya."

I fretted. What would Elena do at the next full moon when she discovered she could not change? At least Aurora and Alix and the rest of the Smolny students would be safe from veshtiza poison.

That night, I had a chance to speak with Elena alone. "Must you change into a moth every month? What happens if you do not turn?"

Elena's eyes narrowed. "You know many of my family's secrets, but I will not tell you all of them. Not until you are one of us."

I sighed. "That will never happen. I will never marry your brother. Ever. And my family supports my decision." At least, my father did. Maman would have been delighted to see me as the crown princess of Montenegro. She had dreams of seeing one of her children sitting on a European throne one day.

"But you and Danilo are already bound. Your blood is a part

of him now. You cannot ever break that bond." Elena smiled. "Don't you see?"

I could not fall asleep that night, and I laid awake for hours worrying about what she had said. The bond I had with the crown prince was indeed still there, just as it had been ever since the ritual in the Black Mountain temple. That was the night when the crown prince drank my blood. The night when the lich tsar was released by the Montenegrins.

At times, I could swear that I felt Danilo's mind reaching for mine. It was frightening, being connected in such an intimate way to someone so dangerous. To someone I loathed. I wondered if he could read my mind just as George could. I needed to find a way to be completely free of the crown prince. Only then would I be safe from the rest of the Montenegrins as well.

CHAPTER TWELVE

I slept fitfully that night, and the next morning felt horrible as I dressed and dragged myself downstairs with the other girls to breakfast. The sleep I had managed to get had been full of strange, tiring dreams that I could not even remember. Just annoying wisps and fragments that made no sense remained.

Madame Orbellani passed out our mail in the dining hall that morning, and I received a letter from my brother, Petya. He had written to me from Moscow, where his regiment was training. There was no news from him of the Order of St. John of Jerusalem, and I knew I should not have even expected any. My brother would not think it proper to tell me what went on inside the ancient order assigned to protect the tsar.

I sighed. It was a letter full of brotherly duty, saying he missed me, and our parents, had experienced treacherous weather during his train ride, had seen a pair of gloves in a Moscow shop that he thought I would like, and that he looked forward to seeing me at Christmas. My brother was not the letter-writing type. It was strange to receive such a long, rambling note from him.

There was an odd scribbling at the bottom of the letter—a hastily written number three next to a symbol that looked like the Maltese cross. The symbol of the Order of St. John. Had he wanted to tell me something but changed his mind? Had the Order found the lich tsar? I felt so frustrated not knowing what was going on outside the walls of Smolny.

Augusta looked as sleep-deprived as I did. Her pretty blue eyes looked sunken and her face was paler than usual. "Are you feeling well?" I asked her. Pushing her bowl of oatmeal aside, she put her head down on the table.

Her sister Erzsebet looked worried. "She was awake moaning and tossing restlessly all last night."

Madame Tomilov hurried over. "Augusta, are you ill? Get up and see the nurse at once." She looked around at the rest of us. "Is there anyone else who is not feeling well? The nurse has already seen several girls this morning."

I looked at Elena, accusingly. *Mon Dieu*, not again. It was not the full moon, and she did not look any pinker than usual. Surely she could not have turned into a veshtiza last night? She looked at me with an innocent, questioning look.

"Katerina, you do not look well either," Elena said, sounding terribly concerned. "Madame Tomilov, perhaps she should also go and see the nurse."

Madame nodded in agreement. Before last year, the headmistress would not have been so quick to monitor our health. We would have been told that suffering builds character and not to complain. But a number of parents threatened to pull their daughters out of Smolny after many girls had been mysteriously poisoned.

No one knew the true story, of course. Who would accuse a king's daughter of turning into a poisonous, blood-sucking moth? I had no idea what the doctors told Madame Tomilov. Did she know the truth about Elena? The empress knew, and surely she would have sent Elena back to Montenegro if she felt the princess was still a danger. But the empress believed her spell was strong enough to protect us all.

I helped Augusta stand up and together we went to visit Sister Anna, a nun who had been sent to Smolny by the empress to minister to the sick girls. Sister Anna had little medical training, and instead believed that all illnesses could be cured by fasting and prayer. I worried that Augusta would not be strong enough for any fasting. Or for kneeling on the cold floor for any length of time. What we both needed, in my opinion, was either some strong tea or a long nap.

Sister Anna was sitting at her plain wooden desk, writing in a large journal. She smiled when she saw us. "Good morning, girls. What brings you to see me this beautiful day?" She was a small woman, dwarfed in her white woolen habit. She wore a very severe black wimple that hid all of her hair.

"Madame Tomilov sent us, Sister. She said there are many of us that have been feeling poorly today."

Sister Anna shook her head, her thin lips pinched together. "A bunch of nothing, I believe," she said with a heavy peasant accent. "Let me have a look at you." She gestured toward the hard wooden chair next to hers.

I nodded at Augusta to sit down first. I was already starting to feel a little better. Not quite so achy and tired anymore.

"Hmmm," the sister said, as she felt Augusta's wrist for a pulse. "Open your mouth." Augusta did so obediently, with a bewildered glance up at me.

"Nothing more than a guilty conscience, my dear. What have you done?"

Augusta looked frightened. "I am so sorry, Sister. Please forgive me."

Sister Anna nodded and patted her hands, encouraging her. "What do you wish to confess?"

Augusta's shoulders sagged. "I sneaked into the kitchen last night and found the basket of cherries meant for today's dessert. I ate half of the basket all by myself."

I sighed. No wonder Augusta looked awful. She'd been up all night, overeating.

"Gluttony is a terrible thing, Augusta. I want you to go to the chapel and pray for two hours." Sister Anna turned to me. "And now, let me look at you."

I took the tiniest of steps backward. "I am feeling much better already, Sister. I thank you so much."

"Wonderful. Off with both of you, then." She picked up her pen and returned to her writing.

I walked with Augusta to the chapel. "Are you really feeling better?" she asked me as we turned the corner and got out of the sister's hearing.

"I'm just tired," I said. "I had difficulty sleeping last night."

The Bavarian princess grabbed my sleeve. "Me too! That's why I went to the kitchen to begin with! I kept being awakened by something. And it wasn't Erzsebet's snoring."

That strange, cold prickle on the back of my neck returned. "Did you find out what it was?"

"No. It must have been hunger. Oh Katiya, those cherries were delicious. I hope the cook has more. I hope there is pie for dessert tonight!"

Augusta went off happily to the chapel to pray for her bellyache, and I hurried on to arithmetic class.

In class, I took the letter from Petya out of my pinafore pocket and carefully placed it in my textbook, rereading it instead of listening to Madame Orbellani's lecture. I stared at the number three at the bottom of the page. Was it a key to a code? Petya had always been interested in secret codes when he was younger. I overheard Papa discussing it with him one day, saying that the Order would have a perfect use for his talent. I glanced up at the front of the classroom, at Madame Orbellani. She had written several numbers on the board in an equation and was crossing out digits on both sides of the equal sign.

It gave me an idea. Starting with *My Dearest Katiya*, I crossed out every third word in my brother's letter. I hoped that it looked like I was doing my arithmetic problems diligently. It worked perfectly. The words I crossed out sent a chill down my spine when I read them together:

Katiya, there is treachery within the Inner Circle.
The tsar is in danger. It is not safe for me to send
word directly. Warn the tsar, Sister.

Mon Dieu, what kind of danger threatened the tsar? I'd never even heard of the Order having an Inner Circle. I gasped out loud.

"Katerina Alexandrovna, do you wish to share your

answer?" Madame Orbellani asked. "Please remember to raise your hand first."

My mouth went dry. My brother did not realize I was trapped at Smolny behind the empress's spell. He was hoping I would be able to slip away and send word discreetly to the tsar. What could I do?

"What is the answer, Katerina?" Madame Orbellani asked again patiently.

I was not in the mood for mathematics. "Forgive me, Madame, but I am still unwell. May I return to Sister Anna?"

Madame Orbellani sighed. "Of course. I shall expect to see your mathematics problems correctly answered in the morning."

"*Oui*, Madame." I hurriedly closed my books and gathered them up. I hated lying to my favorite teacher. But perhaps in the quiet of my room I would be able to send a warning to George. I knew he was thousands of miles away in Paris, but hopefully he would still be able to pick up on my thoughts. It was the only way I knew to discreetly inform the tsar of my brother's warning. I had to try.

CHAPTER THIRTEEN

A urora and Elena had French lessons at this hour, and
then they would be going to lunch. Alix was in music
class. Our room would be empty for hours, I hoped.

I had tried listening for George's voice many times at night,
while I lay in bed, but there was never any message from him.
As I did not share his faerie gift for telepathy, I really did not
expect it. Perhaps today would be different. Even if I could not
receive a reply from him, I hoped he would hear my thoughts,
and at least become aware of the danger Petya mentioned in
his letter.

I crawled into bed and slipped under the covers, knowing
that if anyone did come in, they'd assume I was feeling poorly.
I really wanted to be left alone. I desperately needed the sleep,
anyway. I only hoped I could stay awake long enough to get
my message to George. I closed my eyes and concentrated on
the grand duke's beautiful face. *George Alexandrovich, Your*

Imperial Highness, I have urgent news for you. My brother, Pyotr of Oldenburg, sends this message. There is treachery within the Order. He says the tsar is in danger. I hesitated, then added, *Please be careful.*

There was, of course, no reply. I heard nothing but the distant clanging of the chapel bells. Even the halls of Smolny were quiet. I felt a little foolish, but I continued. *George Alexandrovich, Your Imperial Highness—*

"He cannot hear you, my love."

My blood turned cold. I bolted up straight in bed, looking around my room in terror. The voice in my head was not that of George. But it was familiar just the same. *Get out of my head, Danilo.*

The Montenegrin crown prince's laugh made me shiver with disgust. *"The empress was very wise when she cast the spell over your school. Do you think she knew it would prevent you from communicating with her son?"*

I sighed. *You know no such thing. Why is it that you can hear me, then? And that I can hear you?*

"A Vladiki's blood bond is more powerful than any other magic, my dear. Even your empress's fae charms. And now you cannot warn your dear grand duke of the danger his family is in. I'm sure of it. And at a time when the threat is far worse than your brother realizes." His voice was taunting. He enjoyed telling me this news.

I wanted to scream. *What do you know of the Order? I don't believe anything you say to me, Danilo.*

"I know much more than you do. Much more than you ever will. Not all of the wizards in the Order are loyal to the tsar."

Who is the traitor? You must tell the tsar this!

"Why should I?" Danilo asked lazily.

Your parents are still allies of His Imperial Majesty, are they not? Who are the wizards working for?

He laughed again, filling me with frustration. "*Like my sister, I still have my secrets, Katerina. Even after we are married, you will not be allowed to know everything.*"

I was desperate and decided to ignore his last remark. *Danilo, please warn the tsar. You must find a way to get word to the grand duke. Or help me find a way to break through the empress's spell.*

"*As much as I love chatting with you, I must go, Katerina Alexandrovna.*"

Danilo, please! I could not believe I was begging him for anything.

But he was gone. There was nothing left but the silence of my room, only the sound of the soft rustle of my bedcovers as I sat up. It frightened me to realize just how powerful the blood bond between us must be. I could not trust him to seek out the grand duke and deliver my warning. I would have to find another way.

"*Mon Dieu!* I cannot take it anymore!" Elena's voice shouted over the stomping of her shoes.

The door to our room burst open, slamming into the dresser beside it. Elena rushed in and threw her books on her bed. She stopped and stared at me. "What are you doing here?"

"I was not feeling well. Must you shriek like that? The headmistress can probably hear you from her office."

Elena sighed as she flopped down on her bed. "Princess Aurora drives me insane with the superior airs that she puts on! She got the highest mark on our French exam this morning, and Madame Tomilov gave her a bonbon!"

"And what is wrong with that?"

Elena lowered her voice. "And Alix is even worse."

"She is just shy."

Elena snorted. "No, she is a snob. Just because her grand-mother is the queen of England. Bah! Katiya, you know as well as I do that the Hessian princess is . . . different. She will never be like us."

I looked at Elena with disbelief. I hated it when she likened my powers to hers. "I don't see that as a bad thing. Erzsebet and Augusta are not like us either."

Elena stood up and paced back and forth. "But the Bavar-ians do not count. They are blissfully ignorant of the things that go on in the dark of St. Petersburg. They know nothing of vampires or faeries. They will live happy lives never aware of the creatures that live alongside of them."

"And you are saying that Alix of Hesse-Darmstadt is one of these . . . creatures?"

Elena stopped pacing and sat down again on her cot. "I'm saying there is something not right about her. She is always watching me. Judging me, as if she knows my secrets. She knows and she is not afraid."

"Are you certain?" It occurred to me now that Princess Alix had often looked at me in a similar fashion. "How could she know our secrets if she was not . . . unnatural as well?" I could not believe Elena had become my confidante.

Elena shrugged. "We must be on our guard around her. Per-haps we can find out more about her and her family."

Besides the fact that she came from Germany and her sister was married to one of the tsar's brothers, I knew little about Princess Alix. I'd been invited on an ice-skating outing with her and her sister and the imperial children last winter, but she'd been very shy. I knew she did not speak much French or Russian, but spoke fluent English. She was also secretly in love with the tsarevitch.

My own undead creature, Count Chermenensky, had called her a monster, I remembered. The memory of the day I'd met the undead count made me blink back angry tears. Why had he reacted so strangely to Princess Alix? She was not a ghoul like the count. Whatever she was, surely she was not a danger to any of us, trapped behind the empress's spell.

⦿

I woke up that night to hear Elena restless and muttering in her sleep. Her moaning did not wake Aurora or Alix, thankfully. The silvery light of the full moon brightened up our room, and I snuggled down deeper in my blankets, glad that she was not able to turn into a moth. I worried, though, what would happen to her without a transformation. Would she still need to get blood in her human form? Would she seek it from one of her roommates?

"The veshtizas are not true vampires, as the Vladiki are." Again, the crown prince's thoughts floated into my head strong and clear. I wondered if it was due to the full moon that it was so much easier to hear him now.

What does that mean? I hated to encourage Danilo, but I wanted to know more about his sister's powers.

"It is not necessary for her survival to drink blood. A veshtiza gains her magic powers from blood, which she can only gather at the full moon in moth form. But it does not harm her if she does not change." Danilo's laugh was low and velvety in my head.

"Of course, it does not make her a happy person when she does not get to change. The empress's spell will make my sister a difficult person to live with."

Does she know? How are you aware of the empress's spell?

His laugh sickened my stomach. "Duchess, I know most of your secrets. We are bound, remember?"

I shuddered, wishing once again there was a way to remove the blood bond between us. I could not let the crown prince know all of my secrets. But how could I undo the fact that he had drunk my blood in order to complete his own ascension ritual? It had all been part of his parents' plan to make him as powerful a blood drinker as his father, the Montenegrin king. The king had received his own powers from drinking the queen's blood. Queen Milena had spent years searching for a necromancer bride for her eldest son. Unfortunately, the bride she had chosen was me.

"And no, Elena does not know of the empress's spell." Danilo's thoughts continued to invade my head. "I would not tell her if I were you."

I breathed a small sigh of relief. Thank you, Danilo.

He laughed again and I tried to ignore the way it made the hair on the back of my neck tingle. "Pleasant dreams, my love."

CHAPTER FOURTEEN

❧

The first full moon had come and gone and most of the students seemed unusually restless. Elena in particular. And the German princess as well. She seemed to spend more and more time in the library, and would glare at me if I tried to enter the room while she was there.

"Alix, what is wrong with you?" Aurora Demidova snarled the next morning as Alix stomped around trying to get dressed for breakfast.

Princess Alix glared at her but said nothing. I wanted to stay out of it. Elena was exceptionally grumpy that morning too. I followed them down to the dining room and ate my cold porridge in silence, trying to avoid the nasty looks my roommates were casting at each other throughout the meal.

The next night was even worse, as all three of my roommates were vicious and snapping at each other. Aurora accused Elena of stealing her favorite slippers. Alix accused

Aurora of stealing her red hair ribbon. Everyone went to bed fuming, but no one slept. As the waning moon filled our dark room with its dim silvery light, I breathed a sigh of relief that the empress's spell was keeping everyone safe from Elena's blood thirst.

I tried to pay closer attention to Princess Alix in the coming days. I had not noticed anything besides her shy façade, but perhaps Elena had been right. The princess had seemed more agitated than usual in the past week. She still did not fit in with the rest of us. I laughed to myself, realizing that I did not really fit in here either.

The nights had continued to bring broken sleep, with loud howling noises that woke me up and then disappeared. I could not tell if it was a dream or something real. I noticed several other girls at the breakfast table were looking hollow-eyed and fatigued as well.

Erzsebet was whispering with the girls at her table, but suddenly stopped as Elena and I sat down. I caught Augusta sneaking glances at Elena several times during breakfast. Aurora took her plate and sat at the head of the table, close to the table where the headmistress and Madame Orbellani ate. Alix ate her food quietly and ignored everyone. She did not seem to be suffering quite as much as the rest of us.

"Alix, did you sleep well?" I asked. "I hope my tossing and turning did not disturb you."

She shook her head, but kept on eating daintily. Elena kicked my foot under the table. I ignored her.

Augusta was staring at her plate. Elena yawned. "You definitely kept me up."

Alix glanced at Elena, her eyebrow raised slightly. "Perhaps you should pay a visit to Sister Anna. I am sure she could find a way to help you sleep easily."

Erzsebet threw her fork down, and the clattering noise silenced every other girl in the dining room. "Why isn't the headmistress doing anything?" she cried, getting up hastily and running out.

Augusta looked horrified. She glanced toward the headmistress's table, not sure if she should go after her sister or not. Madame Tomilov's face showed no emotion as she rose calmly from her seat and left after Erzsebet. "Do you think she'll be expelled?" Augusta whispered. She was blinking back tears.

I grabbed her hand and squeezed it. "I don't think this is serious enough for that." I had never heard of anyone being expelled from Smolny.

"Finish eating, girls. It will be time for class soon." Madame Orbellani's voice was soothing, but firm. She looked a little tired as well. I wondered how much sleep she had gotten lately.

Whether it was something Elena or Alix was doing, I needed to find out what was happening at Smolny. I remembered the presence I'd sensed in the library the past week. A chill went down my spine. Was the school haunted by a ghost? We'd never felt such a presence before. Why now, when the empress's spell was supposed to be keeping us all safe from anything supernatural?

CHAPTER FIFTEEN

❧

My class in pedagogy was small—only three other girls and myself—in a tiny classroom with Madame Fredericks, an elderly German woman who was more interested in reading Marie Corelli romances than teaching us how to teach others. And I was to begin with a French grammar lesson. That morning was my first class with the Blue Form girls, the form between the youngest Browns and the oldest Whites.

Seventeen girls, ages twelve to fourteen, in royal-blue uniforms sat in a stuffy classroom, staring at me expectantly. My stomach was twisting into knots, even though I'd prepared my notes and reviewed them over and over in bed the night before. I gave them all a brave smile. "Good morning," I said.

The blank looks on their faces reminded me of the members of the Order of St. Lazarus standing guard outside our school gates. It took everything I had to repress a shudder. It didn't help that Madame Fredericks was sitting at the back of the room to review my progress. I spoke up a little louder this time, smiling an even braver smile. "Good morning."

"How do you answer your teacher?" Madame Fredericks said in a gruff, booming voice. She was writing notes in a journal. So much for taking control of my students right from the beginning.

"Good morning, Mademoiselle," the girls said obediently. *Mon Dieu*, they even sounded like the undead soldiers. I chose to believe it was because it was so early in the morning.

"My name is Mademoiselle Katerina, and today we are going to study French verbs." I turned around and picked up a piece of chalk. "Let's start with one of the easier ones," I said as I wrote the word *aimer* on the dusty board. I heard several giggles behind me and smiled to myself. At least they were paying attention. I turned around. "Now we will all say the verb together, and one of you will come up to the front and write it on the board."

Their voices chanted low and unsteadily. *"J'aime, tu aimes, il aime, nous aimons, vous aimez, ils aiment . . ."*

"Excellent," I said, trying to encourage them. I walked between the aisles of wooden desks, which were probably older than I, and stopped in front of a dark-haired girl with bright-green eyes. In French I asked her name, and then placed the chalk in her hand. "Charlotte, will you write the verbs as we speak them again?"

"Oui, Mademoiselle," she said, standing up from her desk.

Madame Fredericks was no longer paying attention to the class. She was absorbed in her romance novel. As long as the class continued according to my lesson plan, she would not bother me and I would receive a passing grade.

Charlotte stepped up to the board and raised her chalk, ready for the class to recite their verbs. But before anyone could say anything, her hand moved with a jerk and she began to scrawl across the board, in Russian: *STAY OUT OF THE LIBRARY.*

The girls gasped. I moved quickly toward Charlotte, who was now standing with a blank stare in front of the board. "Thank you, dear," I said, erasing the board swiftly. I took the chalk from her hand and guided her gently back to her seat. The temperature had dropped dramatically in the classroom, and I saw several of the students begin to shiver.

Madame Fredericks did not raise her head from her book once. Charlotte still looked a little dazed, so I asked another girl at the desk closest to her to please take her to the nurse.

"Shall we repeat our verbs again?" I asked, praying that I'd erased the message so quickly, no one would remember it. The sudden chill was gone, but I was shaking myself. What had happened to Charlotte? Had she been possessed by the ghost? Was the ghost trying to communicate through her?

A sea of hands shot up. "Mademoiselle Katerina? What is in the library? Did Madame Tomilov make it off-limits? Is it off-limits to the Browns and the Whites as well? Why did Charlotte write that?"

I sighed. I had once again lost control of my class. "I do not know. But I would like to return to the topic of French verbs. Let's try another one." I turned around and wrote *embrasser* on the board. To kiss. Let them giggle at that one. I faced the class again. "Let's conjugate this one together. *J'embrasse, tu embrasses, il embrasse, nous embrassons . . .*"

I made it through the last fifteen minutes of the lesson with no more strange disruptions. After the students filed out into the hall and headed for their next class, Madame Fredericks stood up and handed my evaluation to me. "Next time, do not allow the students to write on the board," she told me. "They will do anything to get out of class."

"Of course, Madame," I said. I should have been glad that she hadn't noticed the chill in the room, or the haunted look on Charlotte's face. But the only emotion I felt at that moment was dull rage. And fear. How could this be happening in spite of the empress's spell? And why couldn't I see the ghost? When Madame Fredericks dismissed me, I went straight to Sister Anne to check on Charlotte.

Charlotte's color was much improved. She was reading her French textbook but looked up and smiled when she saw me. "*Bonjour,* Mademoiselle Katerina," she said.

"You look as if you're feeling better," I said.

Sister Anne seemed pleased. "You may return to your classes now, Charlotte."

I walked with the young Blue Form girl on my way to my own classes. "Do you remember what happened this morning?"

Charlotte frowned. "A little. I was standing in front of the chalkboard and the next thing I knew, I felt cold and dizzy. Did I pass out?"

"No," I assured her. "But you did look as if you might. Do you remember what you wrote on the board?"

She looked up at me, her face full of guilt. "I didn't write anything. I was supposed to write the French verbs but I never did. Am I in trouble?"

"No, Charlotte. Of course you're not in trouble. You should probably hurry on to class now."

A ghost. There was no way I could see its cold light as long as the empress's spell was in place. I felt helpless. As much as I dreaded it, I realized I would have to return to the library to investigate. The school day dragged on endlessly, through Mathematics, and French, and Domestic Arts, and Music, but at last my classes were over and I headed for the library.

"Katerina, are you coming with us?" Elena and Augusta were headed outside to get fresh air in the courtyard.

"I'll catch up with you. There is something in the library that I need."

Elena rolled her eyes. "You and your books! Augusta, come along."

I hurried alone to the library, not sure what I could actually do. The empress's spell had rendered me powerless. If there was a ghost, what would I be able to do about it?

Princess Alix was in the library, reading a volume of English poetry. I was not expecting to see anyone there, and I know I looked startled. "Excuse me," I said. "I'm . . . just getting a book and I'll leave you in peace."

"You're not bothering me."

"That's good." What else was I supposed to say? I stared at the bookshelves, not sure what to do. Would the ghost come back if there was more than one person here? Had Alix felt its presence already? She seemed so calm. It was unlikely she had noticed anything. The presence I'd felt was not really evil, but it was mean. And it definitely did not want me in the library.

"Is something wrong?" Alix asked. "Why are you staring at me?"

"I'm sorry," I said. "May I ask you something? The noises at night have not bothered you at all?"

The princess stared at me with her clear blue eyes. "If you are wondering whether the ghost is disturbing me, then no. If you are asking whether the moaning of my roommates is keeping me awake, then yes."

We stared at each other in silence for a long time. She knew of the ghost, and yet was not afraid of it. Finally, I said, "I felt the presence in here last week."

Alix closed her eyes and was perfectly still. "Yes, but she is not here now."

"She? Do you know who she is? She has not tried to harm you?"

But the German princess was not interested in chatting with me anymore. Alix stood up abruptly and gathered her things. "If you will excuse me, I must be somewhere." She brushed past me, and I wished more than anything that I could see her cold light. She was most definitely a good person, which was probably why she irritated Elena so. There was no evil lingering around her, but there was a sense of grimness in her blue eyes. No sense of joy at all. She was the strangest girl I'd ever met.

❧

I tried to find Erzsebet next. I wanted to know how she was doing after her outburst that morning. She was resting in her room.

"Come sit with me, Katerina," she said. "Please don't go."

"How are you feeling?" I asked, sitting down on the bed beside her.

"Better," she said with a heavy sigh. "Madame Tomilov was kind. She only gave me a five-page essay to write."

"Why were you so upset this morning? Was it the lack of sleep or was it something else?"

"I don't know," Erzsebet mumbled, staring down at her quilt. She seemed to be debating whether or not to tell me. "Everyone will think I'm crazy."

"Erzsebet, what are you talking about? You know I wouldn't think that."

"I heard voices last night." She sniffled and shook her head. "Well, one voice, actually. A girl laughing. I thought it was Augusta, but she was sleeping. The girl sounded like she was in the hallway, but when I opened my door, the laughing stopped. It's like she just vanished."

I took a deep breath. I couldn't tell her what Alix had said, but I could tell her what I'd experienced. "I think I've heard her too. In the library last week." Erzsebet gasped and grasped my hand, squeezing it tight. "Who do you think it is?"

The Bavarian princess looked at me like I was insane. "Isn't it obvious? It's Marija of Montenegro. Elena's sister."

No wonder the girls had been whispering about Elena that morning. "Are you sure?" I asked. "Do you know anyone else who's actually seen her?"

Erzsebet shook her head. "Madame Tomilov told me not to discuss it with any of the other girls. I shouldn't have said anything to you, Katerina, but you won't tell anyone, will you? Especially not Elena. It's her fault somehow. I'm sure of it."

"We can't be certain of that," I said. "Or even that it's truly Elena's dead sister haunting us."

Erzsebet shrugged. "I don't know, Katerina, but there has been a lot of gossip around the school that Elena was responsible for the strange illnesses last year. I've heard she knows some kind of folk magic from the Black Mountains."

The glamours of the Light and Dark Courts could only hide so much from everyone. Of course there were always rumors and hints that something more sinister lurked in the shadows. If only I could've told her about the empress's spell, I think she would've felt safer. Then again, not many people in St. Petersburg knew the empress was a faerie. "But why would Elena make her sister's ghost haunt Smolny?" I asked. "And why now and not sooner? She could have appeared years ago."

"I don't know, Katerina." Erzsebet shook her head, her blond curls swinging. She was not quite old enough to wear her hair up. "I'm probably being ridiculous. But you've heard the ghost too, right? I'm not going insane?"

"I can't promise you that you're not insane," I said, teasing her gently. "But yes, I've heard something that I can't easily explain. But I don't know what to do about it."

"We have to tell Sister Anna. She'll know what to do." Erzsebet sat up. "Let me put my uniform back on, and we can speak to her right now."

I hesitated. "What if she doesn't believe us? I think we need some kind of proof before we bother any of the staff with this. Otherwise, she might punish us for lying."

Erzsebet slumped back down against her pillow and sighed unhappily. "What does one do to get rid of a ghost?"

There were a thousand other questions I would have rather

asked first, like who she was, and why was she here. After all those years of watching Maman's séances, I knew how to properly conjure a ghost, and the polite way to dismiss one. But I had a feeling this ghost would not leave politely. And without being able to see cold light, I was stumbling around in the dark.

CHAPTER SIXTEEN

⟨⟩

A few weeks later, Alix fell ill and was bedridden for several days. She lay pale and damp with sweat, clenching her bed linens in stoic suffering. She was not able to get up from her bed to go to class with us, and at night, I listened to her tossing and turning. She whimpered in her sleep as if in pain. I asked Sister Anna to check on her, but the woman would only agree to say prayers for Alix.

Those prayers were useless. I crawled out of my own bed to check on the German princess several times during the night. She always woke up before I could cross the room. Sitting straight up in bed, she whispered in alarm, "What are you doing?"

"Can I get you some water?" I asked, reaching for the pitcher at Aurora's bed stand.

"No!" Alix cried, but her voice was strange, as if she weren't even talking to me. With an anguished moan, she fell back against her pillow again. She was drifting in and out of consciousness and her fever seemed to grow worse as the nights went on. Ignoring her weak protests, I put damp washcloths on her forehead and coaxed her to take sips of water.

Her sister, Grand Duchess Ella, arrived the day of the full moon and insisted upon taking Alix away from Smolny and to her St. Petersburg palace to recuperate. At first our headmistress forbade it, but the grand duchess was adamant. Sister Anna sided with the grand duchess, suggesting that Alix would feel better in her dear sister's care.

Madame Tomilov looked very displeased that anyone, including a grand duchess, would dare oppose her, but in the end instructed me to help Alix pack her things. The German princess seemed unsteady on her feet.

"Is it time for your monthly course?" I whispered as we reached our room. I knew that would not cause her to have a fever, but it could be exacerbating her problem.

Alix blushed, but only shook her head. She pulled a small suitcase out from under her neatly made cot and laid it open on top of the blankets. The first thing she placed inside was her German Bible.

"Has the fever returned? Do you have any aches or pains?" I could not help asking.

"No. Please, Katerina. I do not wish to discuss my illness with anyone." She dropped down on her hands and knees, searching for something else under her cot. Her small, dark wooden box, which she slid out and placed in her suitcase.

"Is it your digestion?" Alix had been teased by Aurora and some of the other girls for having a weak stomach. But the food at Smolny truly left something to be desired. Especially the boiled mutton they'd served to us every night that week. "I am sure Sister Anna or I could persuade the cook to make a nice broth for you."

Grand Duchess Ella stood in the doorway and watched as Alix gathered her things. "You won't need most of those," she said impatiently. "Sunny, we really must hurry and get you home."

Alix finished packing and fastened the lid on her suitcase. She turned and glared at me, but then her face relaxed, and she was civil as she answered me. "I thank you for your concern. I hope I will be able to return to Smolny soon."

I smiled at her. It was just her extreme shyness that caused her to act so stiffly. She must have been quite a different person at home to be called Sunny by her family. "I am sure you will," I said. "Your sister will take excellent care of you."

"Yes, she worries constantly about all of her sisters," she answered as she and the grand duchess exchanged glances.

"May God bless and protect you, Katerina," Grand Duchess Ella said to me. "Thank you for looking after Alix."

I watched from the tiny window in the stairwell as Alix climbed into the imperial carriage. The carriage stopped suddenly at the archway leading from the inner courtyard, and then just as suddenly lurched forward. The horses galloped off, pulling the carriage in a hurry, as if they'd been spooked. It was almost as if the empress's spell did not want to let the German princess leave Smolny.

CHAPTER SEVENTEEN

◦⦿◦

Alix was still gone a few weeks later when I celebrated my seventeenth birthday. The headmistress discouraged extravagant celebrations for student birthdays, but allowed us to receive notes and small packages from relatives. My parents, who were still in Biarritz on the French coast, had sent a large package of cakes and fruits for me to share with my friends. I received letters from my brother and a mysterious parcel of Swiss chocolates in a heart-shaped tin. Elena smiled. "They are from Danilo, of course."

I was almost afraid to try them, worried they would be laced with some sort of Vladiki poison. But Elena sampled one without asking, and was kind enough to even offer some to Erzsebet and Augusta as well. I decided the candies were probably safe and chose one before Elena had given them all away.

It was delicious. I vowed to find more Swiss chocolates at

Christmastime to give as gifts. Dariya and Countess Zina would adore them. So would my father.

Madame Orbellani had managed to find me a copy of the latest medical journal from Berlin. "This is to help you study your German," she said with a wink.

"*Danke*, Madame," I said, giving her a hug.

Sister Anna said a prayer for me and gave me a tiny icon of St. Katerina in a golden frame.

"*Merci*, Sister," I said, dutifully hugging her as well. I tried not to think about my namesake saint, the fourth-century virgin of Alexandria, who was beheaded at age eighteen for refusing to make sacrifices to the emperor's pagan gods. The daughter of nobility, she was one of the most highly educated young women of her time, which made her the patron saint of female students everywhere.

Dariya surprised me with a visit that afternoon, and we strolled in the garden, which was covered with fallen brown leaves. They crackled under our boots as we walked arm in arm just like we had for years together before, sharing secrets and gossip.

"How do you like being a lady-in-waiting?" I asked.

"It's dreadfully boring!" Dariya said. "Nothing to do but stand around in a scratchy old gown and wait."

"Wait for what?" I asked distractedly. A toad was hopping out from beneath the decaying leaves.

"Nothing, or anything!" Dariya said with a long sigh. "I go to balls and stand behind Grand Duchess Miechen waiting in case she needs a shawl, or waiting to see if she needs tea."

"But that is what the pages are for," I said. It was an honor reserved for only the brightest young men of the Corps de

Pages, who studied at Vorontsov Palace, to be chosen to serve as a page to one of the imperial family members. It often sparked a brilliant diplomatic or military career.

My cousin shook her head. "Miechen likes to be surrounded by handsome young men in their smart uniforms, but she doesn't trust them to make the tea the way she likes it."

I'd had no idea the dark faerie was so particular about her tea. My cousin giggled when she saw the dubious look I gave her.

"Two sugars," she said, mimicking the grand duchess's faintly German accent. "And just a hint of cream."

"Cream?"

Dariya shrugged. "It is the English way," she said. "Perhaps one of the children's nannies introduced it to her."

Russians loved their tea, and we swarmed around the hissing samovar found in every house and every café or bakery to warm our hands and bellies with the strong drink. Some people liked it very sweet, and I'd seen my grandmother drink it in the ancient fashionable style with the sugar cube held between her teeth. I myself liked more lemon than sugar in mine. But to defile one's tea with cream? I couldn't help shuddering.

"I prefer raspberry jelly," Dariya said. "But I did try adding cream once, and really, Katiya, it wasn't bad."

I shook my head and looked at her in what I hoped would be stern reproach. "What would your stepmother say?"

She giggled. "My stepmother has already taken to drinking her tea exactly like the grand duchess. I don't think she likes it that way, but she pretends she does!"

It really did not matter to me how the dark faerie drank her tea. Or how the rest of the Dark Court drank theirs, for that matter. "Have you heard any news of the Light Court?"

Dariya narrowed her eyes at me shrewdly. "I've heard lots of news. Especially about a particular grand duke who is all the rage in Paris."

I blushed as she gave me a friendly nudge. "I was curious about Grand Duchess Xenia," I protested. "She is always kind to me."

"But she is not in Paris," Dariya teased. "I have heard that George Alexandrovich has found himself a new set of fast friends. Dangerous magicians," she added in a lower, less teasing voice. A group of younger girls wearing brown uniforms passed us on their way to afternoon music lessons.

The fact that George was destined to become the next Koldun was a secret I could not share with Dariya. Especially since she now owed her allegiance to Miechen. What damage could the dark faerie do if she knew the name of the Koldun who protected the tsar? Even if she did know who the current Koldun was, I would protect George's secret all the way to the grave.

Dariya went on, "There are several young officers in the Order of St. John who dabble in ceremonial magic. I hear they have secret gatherings in London and Paris as well."

"To do what?" I asked. This must be what Petya had written to warn me about. I prayed he wasn't involved.

My cousin shrugged. "I expect it's mostly for entertainment, just like séances. But I'm sure there are a few magicians who perform real spells and rituals."

I stopped walking to look at her. "Dariya. Have you forgotten how dangerous it can be when people 'dabble'?"

She was not teasing anymore. "Of course not. This is why I wanted you to know about your grand duke. It's not safe for him in Paris."

"What exactly have you heard?" I asked.

"That he has fallen in with a group of powerful dark wizards. That he is enjoying Paris and all that it has to offer."

"And what would you have me do about it?" I felt helpless, trapped here at Smolny. "I cannot leave."

"Why not? I honestly can't understand why you chose to return here in the first place, Katiya. I didn't understand your desire to go to Zurich either, but what on earth made you change your mind?"

I couldn't trust Dariya and tell her the truth. She knew about my powers, and she knew about Elena. But anything I confided to her now could be passed along to Grand Duchess Miechen. She couldn't learn about the empress's spell around Smolny, or that I was being held a prisoner here for my own safety. As well as for the tsar's. He needed me close by, and safe, in case Konstantin returned. I was certain that the empress did not want the grand duchess knowing of the threat to the tsar.

"I'm really too young," I said finally. "I only just turned seventeen, Dariya. Next year I will be ready." The tsar could not make me stay at Smolny longer than that.

"That is true," Dariya said, nodding sympathetically. "You'd probably be the youngest student at the university, and you would hate all the attention that drew. But tell me, how is teaching? I would imagine that the Blue Form girls are just as silly as ever."

I smiled. "They are. And yet, they seem so bright and eager

to learn. I don't remember being so intelligent when we were in the Blue Form classes."

"Speaking of silly girls," Dariya said, "I did hear one piece of Light Court gossip that will amuse you. Grand Duchess Ella made the empress furious when she insisted on taking Alix from Smolny. She said Alix was very ill." Dariya's liveliness disappeared and she looked at me anxiously. "It wasn't the veshtiza, was it?" she asked.

"No," I assured her. "I'm positive it wasn't." I suspected it had to do with the empress's spell around the school. But if Alix was some sort of supernatural creature, like Elena and myself, how had Ella convinced the empress to release Alix? I remembered the way the carriage had passed through the spell's barrier with extreme difficulty. "How do you know the empress was angry?"

My cousin shrugged again. "Grand Duchess Ella has not been invited to dinner at the Winter Palace since. But I'm sure the empress will forgive her soon."

I wondered just how much magic was required for maintaining the spell around Smolny. The empress must have been more powerful than anyone suspected. Or she had someone or something helping her.

We were coming to the end of the path and Grand Duchess Miechen's carriage was waiting for Dariya. I embraced her when we got to the carriage. "Thank you so much for coming to visit. It would not have been the same if I'd had to spend my birthday here alone."

"We've been celebrating your birthday together out here in the courtyard for six years. Under this same birch tree! Since you would not leave Smolny, I had to come to you." Dariya smiled. "The grand duchess sends her birthday wishes for you as well. As does my stepmaman."

"Give them both my thanks," I said.

She turned around to look at me. "What are you going to do about your grand duke?"

"Worry." I could think of nothing else. It was not proper for me to write to him. And whom could I trust to send a message for me? Not Dariya.

Dariya sighed. "Then I wish I hadn't distressed you with the news. I would not have told you if I did not think you could do something about it. I thought you and the grand duke had an understanding."

I shook my head. "The only understanding we have is that he has his path to follow and I have mine."

My cousin crushed me in her arms. "I'm so sorry, Katiya. Perhaps it is for the best. You belong in the Dark Court, after all. With us. You deserve a proper Dark Court marriage."

I shivered at her words. Why was she so ready to claim her alliance with Miechen? Of course, it was the court we'd both grown up in, whether we were aware of it as children or not. I pulled away and stared at her. "What if I don't want a marriage at all?"

"That's ridiculous. You can study medicine if you wish and still be married. I've learned that there are girls who marry male students just so they can attend the university. Without their father's or guardian's permission, they simply find husbands of convenience. Usually for a large amount of money, of course."

"That is not what I want at all," I said. I remembered Dr. Bokova, the woman I'd met on the train. Did she have to marry a stranger in order to get her education? No wonder she thought I was privileged and spoiled.

Dariya smiled. "I believe you can create the life you want, Katiya. You are strong enough to make all of your dreams come true."

"And what about you? What about your dreams?"

My cousin shrugged. "I want the rich and handsome husband and the grand palace. That is enough for me, I think." She glanced around and, seeing we were still alone, she smiled. "And there are several rich and handsome young men that attend Miechen's court. Being a lady-in-waiting has its advantages. The grand duchess has been so kind to me. She's pointed out several eligible young princes."

I wondered if Miechen kept Dariya close because of her relationship with me. Was the grand duchess spying on me through my cousin? Surely she had other methods. "Don't be in such a hurry to get married," I said. "Enjoy your time at Miechen's court. Within reason, of course."

Dariya grinned. "It would be so much more enjoyable if you were there too. Perhaps I will see you at one of the balls soon?" Her eyes lit up. "The Smolny Ball is coming up!"

I brightened up at the thought, remembering my dance with the grand duke. Would the empress allow me to leave the school for the ball? Surely the Winter Palace would be protected from Konstantin and his magic.

I stood there at the gate and watched the horses pull Dariya's carriage away, taking my cousin with them. The carriage passed through the spell barrier easily. I hadn't felt lonely before, but now I felt incredibly alone. And cold.

The wind had picked up as the sun had begun to sink

behind the birch trees. Shivering, I made my way back inside the institute. I had a nice bowl of borscht for supper, and a fruit tart. After dinner, Elena brought out a deck of cards she kept hidden underneath her pillow.

Erzsebet threw herself down on Elena's cot. "Are you going to tell Katiya's fortune?" she asked.

Elena looked up at me and smiled. It made my blood run cold. "I'd rather you did not," I began, but she interrupted me.

"Katerina, it is your birthday! Don't you want to know what the next year holds for you?" She shuffled the cards in her deck delicately before handing the pack to me. "You only have to pick one card."

Erzsebet and Augusta were looking up at me expectantly. Even Aurora, who was writing a letter on her own cot, glanced over at us with curiosity. Elena sighed sadly. "What if the cards can warn you of something before it's too late? Or prepare you for something exciting?"

I sighed and took the cards from her hand. I shuffled them again, knowing from watching Maman all these years that the cards would not read properly unless I'd touched them myself. I closed my eyes, willing the cards to say something benign about my future. Please, no Death card or Hanged Man, or anything else that would frighten the Bavarian princesses or cause them to whisper about me in the halls. And Aurora would be sure to tell Princess Alix if my cards foretold of evil and misery.

I held my breath as I handed the cards back to Elena. I pulled the card on the top of the deck and laid it down, faceup, on her quilt. The Queen of Swords. An elegant but unsmiling woman riding a horse, her sword held up like Joan of Arc. It was the same card the Montenegrins had sent me last year at Christmas. Fear made my stomach clench into knots.

"Oooh, how pretty!" Erzsebet said, shoving her sister aside to get a better look.

"Is she going to win a lot of money gambling, like the old woman in that Pushkin story?" Aurora asked.

Elena's face showed no surprise. "No." She picked the card up and examined it more closely. "But she will be taking dangerous risks, just the same." She looked up at me. "Every queen has her king. And Danilo is waiting for you to realize fate wants the two of you together."

I rolled my eyes, pretending the card had not spooked me. "Fate has nothing to do with it. Your ambitious mother wants the two of us together. But it's not going to happen."

She sighed as she wrapped her cards up in a silk cloth and tucked them back under her pillow. "Sometimes I do not understand you, Katerina Alexandrovna. You throw away happiness at every chance you get."

I went to sleep that night a little sad that I had not received any card or birthday token from the grand duke. Of course, it would not have been appropriate for him to send me anything, but social propriety had not stopped Danilo. I closed my eyes, wondering if George Alexandrovich even knew when my birthday was. Everyone knew the birth dates and saint days of the imperial family, for all of Russia prayed for each and every one of them. So all my life I'd been saying prayers for His Imperial Highness Grand Duke George Alexandrovich Romanov of Russia. Every April and every May, long before I'd ever met him.

I thought of his arms around me in the Crimea, his soft

lips on mine, and hugged myself in the dark. The recently full moon was shining through our tiny window, illuminating the sleeping bodies of Elena and Aurora. I wiped the silent tears off my face, and made an attempt to quit feeling sorry for myself. Somehow, I did not think my blue-eyed grand duke, somewhere in the moonlit streets of Paris with his secret wizards, was saying any prayers for me. But I could still pray for him. I prayed that he would return safely to me soon.

CHAPTER EIGHTEEN

❧

The fall days grew chillier and shorter, the nights longer. Alix had returned to Smolny the day after my birthday, looking much healthier than before. But she remained as shy and aloof as ever. Elena and Aurora ignored her, but the Bavarian princesses and I still tried to draw her out of her shell.

Soon it was almost time for the annual Smolny Ball, where the eldest students were invited to dance at the Winter Palace. One Monday morning, the empress herself arrived at the institute with her oldest daughter, Grand Duchess Xenia, to issue our invitations. It seemed she was planning to lift the charm and allow us to go to the ball.

All the students of the White Form, the eldest class, assembled in the dining room to see the empress. In the room hung a large portrait of the empress's predecessor, Marie Feodorovna, who was Tsar Alexander the Second's wife and our present tsar's mother. I was only ten when she died, but I remembered the scandal caused when the tsar married his longtime mistress and tried to make her the new empress. It had shocked and horrified the rest of the imperial family. Marie Feodorovna had been a sweet and kind, but sickly, woman. When Alexander the Second was assassinated only a few months later, his widow took their children and moved to Paris.

The current empress was wearing a pale-rose gown with a cameo at her neck. Grand Duchess Xenia followed behind her in a dress of pink and white stripes, carrying a matching parasol. She smiled shyly and winked as soon as she spotted me in the line of students.

Elena stood at one side of me, and Princess Alix on the other. We curtsied low, as we'd over and over again been taught. The empress slowly walked down the line, nodding at each girl as she passed her. She stopped as she came to the three of us. I felt the familiar shimmering feeling, as her faerie sight washed over me. I did not know if she was looking for anything specific, or if she was trying to intimidate me, her husband's Dark Court necromancer. The girl who loved her son.

"Katerina Alexandrovna." The empress was addressing me. I was allowed to raise my head.

"Yes, Your Imperial Majesty."

"How is your mother?" she asked. "Does she still have that atrocious-looking old cat?"

"She is well, from the last letter I received from her. It has been several months since I saw her. And her cat, Sasha, is the same, Your Imperial Majesty." Was this some sort of test? Surely she did not really care about my mother, or her unfortunate and undead cat. The empress had not exchanged any such pleasantries with anyone else.

"That is good to hear. And how do your studies go?"

"Very well, Your Imperial Majesty."

"That is also good to hear." Suddenly the shimmering feeling was gone and the empress continued her progress down the line of students. Why had she chosen to speak with me? Did she know the truth about Sasha? That I had raised the poor cat from the dead when I was little just so my mother would not be sad?

Princess Alix looked pale. Perhaps she was sensing the empress's power for the first time. The empress frowned a little as she looked at Alix with the faerie sight as well. What did she see in the Hessian princess? Had she looked at Elena too?

When the empress had made her way to the end of our line, she turned to us all and said, "Madame Tomilov has told me how proud she is of everyone. I'm looking forward to seeing you at the Winter Palace next week. I hope it will be a night to remember."

We all curtsied in unison. The grand duchess did not say anything, but instead presented us with a box of medical supplies for our small infirmary. She gave us all a shy wave before turning to follow her mother out.

As soon as the empress and the grand duchess left, we had to return to our classes. Madame Orbellani handed me the box of medical supplies and asked me to take them to Sister Anna.

On my way to the nurse's office, I passed the headmistress's parlor and overheard two women's voices.

"See to it that she does not leave the school grounds again, not even when the spell is lifted for the ball next week."

"Of course, Your Imperial Majesty."

The empress spotted me. "Katerina Alexandrovna, I wish to speak to you. Madame Tomilov, you may leave us."

The headmistress's voice shook slightly. "Yes, Your Imperial Majesty."

Willing myself not to show any fear, I entered the parlor and curtsied. The empress was a short woman, but there was nothing petite about her. Her power radiated off of her, filling the whole room with her presence. Her dark-brown eyes bore into me before she spoke. "My wish is that every student here at Smolny remains safe."

"Of course, Your Imperial Majesty."

"The spell was tried severely when Ella took her foolish sister Alix through with only the protection of a family heirloom. If she thinks she can pull that stunt every full moon, she is very much mistaken."

Before I could even begin to wonder what she meant by "every full moon," she continued. "I will be lifting the spell for the Smolny Ball, but you are to remain here, Katerina. The Order of St. Lazarus has requested that you stay."

I felt like I'd been kicked in the chest. "The Order?"

"Your creatures are here to protect you, of course. From the lich tsar. Their commander feels they can keep you safer here than anywhere else in St. Petersburg."

"They are not my creatures, Your Imperial Majesty." I was shocked at myself for speaking in such a way to my empress, but all I could think of was not being able to see George.

"They serve the tsar, of course," she replied with a hint of disdain in her voice. "But they protect you because you are the rightful owner of the talisman."

I'd surrendered the Talisman of Isis to the tsar at Peterhof. I wanted nothing more to do with it or its dark powers of necromancy. "I cannot attend the Smolny Ball?" I asked. I could not believe the Order of St. Lazarus had anything to do with her decision.

"Not this year," the empress said, her face softening only a little. "You must agree that it's for the best. You are a danger to him, as well as to yourself."

George. She would do everything she could to keep us apart. And she was right. I was a danger to him. But I wasn't the only danger. "Your Imperial Majesty, I've heard alarming stories about the grand duke in Paris. Is he safe?"

The empress narrowed her eyes at my familiarity. "The grand duke is doing important work for the tsar," she said. "The Light Court has allies guarding him closely while he finishes his work there."

I was able to breathe a little easier, knowing this. Even if I would not be able to see him. Perhaps it was for the best. But I hated it all the same.

The empress swiftly dismissed me, and I was allowed to return to my errand. I delivered my package to Sister Anna and hurried back to class.

As I slid into my seat next to Elena in Madame Orbellani's room, the Montenegrin princess whispered, "I hope the tsarevitch dances with me again. Do you know he has not answered any of my letters since the first one?"

I could not believe Elena would do something so foolish. "You wrote to the tsarevitch? How could you be sure the letter would reach him? The imperial guard has probably given your letters to the tsar. Or the empress."

"She does not like me," Elena muttered. "But she will. I know she will, once she sees how happy I can make Nicholas Alexandrovich."

"*Ecoutez*, mesdemoiselles," Madame Orbellani warned.

I wanted to tell Elena she was deluding herself, but what could I say? I'd been deluding myself as well. The empress had no love for me either. Neither of us would ever be welcome in the Light Court. I grasped her hand and gave it a friendly squeeze. "I think one day soon you will find someone else that suits you better."

"But my parents have been hoping for a match between me and the tsarevitch for years. I have dreamed about my wedding for so long I cannot imagine anyone else as my groom."

I didn't know what to say. I wasn't sure if Elena loved Nicholas because she wanted to be the next empress or because it would please her parents. Elena was a romantic who believed in the power of true love, but she was also the daughter of a blood drinker, and a shape-shifting witch. I was scared of her, but couldn't help feeling a little sorry for her at the same time.

CHAPTER NINETEEN

I was summoned into the headmistress's parlor that evening. Madame Tomilov looked up at me sternly. "Katerina Alexandrovna, I have heard some troublesome news, young lady. One of the staff has told me that you tried to leave the institute grounds last night."

Mon Dieu! Who on earth would lie to the headmistress about me? "Of course not, Madame. Any of my roommates can tell you the truth. I was asleep all night."

"And why wouldn't this person speak the truth?" Madame Tomilov glared at me. I had never seen her mad before. Especially not at me. "Katerina, I know you were having some difficulty adjusting at the beginning of the school term, but you cannot break the Smolny rules. These rules have been put in place for your safety. I have decided your punishment will be forbidding you from attending the Smolny Ball."

This was part of the empress's plan. She had told the

headmistress to punish me, and this is what my classmates would be told when they found out I was not going to the ball. I clasped my hands in defeat. "Of course, Madame," I whispered, trying very hard not to cry in front of her. I was too old for such displays of emotion. No matter how upset I was.

"Very well." Madame Tomilov picked up a pen and began writing in her ledger. "You may return to your class now."

I stood up, wiping my eyes with the back of my hand.

Madame Tomilov glanced up at me. "It's for your own protection, Katerina."

I nodded and turned to go. She knew the empress had forbidden me to leave the institute. Madame also knew I had not tried to leave the grounds last night. That was small comfort. I still felt as if I'd been betrayed.

CHAPTER TWENTY

❧

It was humiliating when Elena and the others found out I was not attending the ball. I could not tell anyone the truth, so I shrugged and scowled and pouted a lot. I hoped I would be able to spend the evening looking for the ghost again. I sat on my bed and pretended to read my Greek poetry while Alix, Elena, and Aurora got dressed.

"And where did you think you needed to sneak out to?" Elena hadn't stopped fussing at me all day. "Of all the stupid things to do, Katerina! Missing the ball!"

"Perhaps she does not enjoy parading around in front of thousands of strangers," Alix said. She was calmly pinning up her hair, but I could see she looked a little pale. I knew she was nervous about her first Smolny Ball.

"My dear Hessian princess," Elena said, twirling around in her white dress and looking at herself in the tiny mirror, "that is the best part."

I rolled my eyes. I wanted to get a message to Grand Duchess Xenia, but there was no one I trusted to deliver it. Not Alix and definitely not Elena. I had considered sneaking out to the ball anyway, but what would I accomplish? I would only anger the empress even more, and for what? Petya should have been able to get word to George by now. I had sent my brother a letter written in the same code as his, begging for more information, but had heard nothing from him. In the end, I decided it was better for me to use my time at Smolny alone to investigate the ghost in the library.

I pretended to yawn. "I hope you three do not wake me when you come home."

"I suppose we'll have to tell you all about the festivities in the morning," Elena said. "Sweet dreams, Katerina."

"Have a wonderful time," I said.

I heard Elena say "Hmmph!" as she stomped off down the hallway, with a definitely nervous Alix and an excited Aurora following along behind her. I snuggled down under my covers and read until I was sure everyone had left for the ball.

When the school was silent, I slid back out of bed and headed for the library. I could hear people talking in the kitchen.

"It came out of nowhere, Madame," said Masha, the school cook.

"Don't be ridiculous. It's a frying pan. It had to come from somewhere." It was the headmistress's voice. Something very bad must have happened for her to be up this late.

"Olga was washing the pots. The frying pan came at her from the other side. There was no one else here with us."

"Get someone to clean this mess up. Olga, can you stand up?" I heard the kitchen girl moan in reply. Madame Tomilov sighed. "Masha, can you fetch Sister Anna?"

If the ghost was throwing frying pans at people, she was becoming dangerous. I slipped past the kitchen and hurried on to the library before Masha came out and the headmistress could see me.

The library was one of the few rooms in the entire institute that had an electric light. I flipped the switch, and the room was flooded with a dim glow. It was empty, of course. All of the younger girls had gone to bed hours earlier. Everything was in its place, the books lined up neatly on the shelves, the cushion sitting perfectly on the chair, the magazines in a neat stack on the end table. I sat down in the chair and closed my eyes, wondering if the ghost was finished with her hauntings for the night. The forbidding presence I'd felt last week was gone. "Marija?" I whispered, afraid the headmistress would hear me. "Are you in here with me?"

Silence.

"Marija?"

There was a soft sound, like someone exhaling. A heavy breath. The forbidding feeling was coming back. The impulse to get up and leave the room. She was definitely here.

I had no idea what to do with a ghost, especially when I could not see the cold light. "Marija, I'd like to talk with you. You need to stop frightening the girls. You can't stay here anymore."

The soft hissing sound grew louder. She was becoming angry. I shook my head. "I can't leave until we're finished talking, Marija. Why did you hurt the kitchen girl tonight?"

133

Suddenly, I was struck across the face with a force that knocked me back in the chair. I yelled out.

My cheek stung. I scrambled up out of the chair. I could still see nothing else in the room with me. The forbidding presence was overwhelming. I felt it closing in around me, as if trying to smother me. I backed away toward the door. "You cannot keep hurting people, Marija! You have to leave!"

"What in the name of the saints is going on here?" I heard Madame Tomilov's voice as she stomped down the hallway toward the library.

The pressure on me did not let up as I reached the doorway and backed into the headmistress.

"Katerina Alexandrovna! What is the meaning of this?"

Sister Anna arrived right behind Madame Tomilov. "Child, what happened to your face?" she asked. She looked frightened as she stared at me.

I put my hand up to my cheek. "Did she leave a mark?"

"Who did this to you?" Madame's voice was stern. She grabbed my chin and tilted my head up so she could examine my face more closely.

"I . . ." What could I say? "I think it was the ghost."

Madame closed her eyes as she sighed. Behind her I heard Sister Anna gasp, *"Mon Dieu!"* and she crossed herself.

"What did you think you were doing in here?" the headmistress asked.

"I just wanted to get a book. I couldn't sleep." Part of what I told her was true, at least.

"Go back to bed, Katerina. I'm sure this will all seem like a terrible dream in morning."

She was not going to admit that I'd been attacked by the

ghost. Which meant that all of the girls at Smolny were in danger. I turned around and took one last look in the library. The presence still seemed to be in there, waiting. But I had no desire to communicate with her again.

"*Oui*, Madame," I said finally to the headmistress, and went back to my bedroom.

The ghost had not stayed in the library. When I reached my room, there was a message from her, in neat black letters on the floor in front of my bed. It was not in French but in Russian.

ΠΥ ΗΔΠΣ IS ΗΩΤ ΠΔЯIJΔ.

I traced the lettering with my hand. The words had been burned or scorched into the wooden floor. I shuddered. I got a rag and tried to rub the words out but they would not budge. I pulled a throw rug over the letters and got ready for bed. I glanced in the mirror and saw the red handprint still stinging my cheek. She had definitely left her mark.

I lay awake in bed for several hours, fretting over the ghost. If she wasn't Elena's sister, then who was she?

"*Marija died of consumption when she was fifteen. Her body was carried back to the Black Mountain for her burial.*" It was the crown prince.

I rubbed my eyes. I was too tired to argue with him. *Why are you bothering me again, Your Highness?*

"*You have accused my family of terrible things. Of course my sister's body is properly buried in Cetinje. There is no way Marija's spirit could be restless. Or imprisoned at your beloved Smolny.*"

Forgive me, Your Highness. I did not mean to imply any such thing. There must have been other girls who had died at

Smolny Institute over the years. There had to be a way to find out who they were. But I was certain Madame Tomilov would not tell me.

"I had hoped to see you at the ball this evening, my beloved. There was another who was searching for you."

My heart leapt. "George?" I whispered.

The crown prince's laugh was cruel. "No. He was not in attendance this evening. It was your brother, the young Oldenburg. He was very upset when he heard that you had gotten into trouble at Smolny."

I sighed, overwhelmed with disappointment. I knew Petya would not have mentioned anything about the Order to Danilo. I wondered if he'd been able to get in touch with George.

"Do not feel too bad, my dear. I have heard news of your Romanov friend. He is still in Paris, with the Black Magi."

"Who are the Black Magi?" I demanded. "And how do you know this?"

"They are a secret sect of magicians in Paris who conjure spirits to do their bidding. Your friend is learning many new things as he studies with these men. Dark things."

"There is a specific reason that he is studying with them. Some special knowledge he needs for the tsar," I said, trying to defend George, and trying to make sense of this news myself. Was the tsar aware of the true nature of the Black Magi? What if the traitor within the Order had sent George to see these magi? "How do you know all of this?" I repeated. "And when was the last time you saw George Alexandrovich?"

"I?" Danilo laughed. "If I never see the tsar's son again it will be too soon. I have many friends in Paris, however. Loyal friends."

I took a deep breath, and tried to calm down. My heart was pounding out of my chest. "Danilo, would you warn me if the grand duke was in any specific danger?"

His soft laughter made me nauseous. *"I know many grand dukes, Katerina. How can I possibly keep up with them all?"*

"You know I am speaking of George Alexandrovich. Is he in danger right now?"

"It depends on what you consider danger, Duchess. I am beginning to believe the other magi are in more danger from him and his growing powers. He has started down a dark path, my dear."

"You are lying to me." I rolled over in my bed, putting the pillow over my head as if it would shut out the crown prince. Of course, it did not.

"Katerina, why would I lie to you? It matters not to me what the grand duke does. He is not bound to you like I am."

"The blood bond means nothing, Danilo. I will never marry you."

"We shall see, Katerina. We shall see."

There was no way on earth that George would use dark magic. He belonged to the Court of Light. He was half fae. And half whatever the tsar was. The rumors that our sovereign was a shape shifter had dwindled in the previous years, but according to Maman he'd been called Sasha the Bear when he was younger. And not just for his size. But none of the tsar's children were shifters. And none of them were as powerful in fae magic as their mother. But what if George had received the gifts from both of his parents, and with the occult knowledge he was learning in Paris, all of it had somehow changed him?

Suddenly, I felt sick to my stomach. What if I had been

the cause? Had my dark powers changed him in any way? I wanted to cry. I could never live with myself if I had somehow tainted the grand duke's soul.

"*Such a guilty conscience,*" Danilo said. I'd forgotten all about him. His laughter mocked my pain.

"Please leave me in peace," I whispered, tears rolling onto my pillow.

"*Do not cry, Duchess,*" he said. "*There may be some hope for your grand duke after all.*"

"Leave me be!"

The silence was immediate. I was alone with my pain and my tortured thoughts. I did not know if I'd pushed him away on my own, or if he'd just decided he'd had enough of taunting me. Either way, I was glad. I was exhausted and wanted nothing more than to sleep the rest of the night away. With no dreams.

But I did wake up when the girls returned from the ball. They stumbled in late, just hours before dawn. I had no interest in hearing their tales. I already knew what I'd wanted most to know. George had not been there. And the ghost that was haunting Smolny was not Elena's sister Marija.

CHAPTER TWENTY-ONE

"And the empress's dress was exquisite! Ice-blue silk embroidered in silver with sapphires and diamonds! Oh Katerina, I wish you could have seen it!" Erzsebet could not stop talking about the ball over breakfast the next morning.

Even Princess Alix seemed to have enjoyed herself. She blushed a little when I asked if she liked the dancing. "Of course. It was an honor to represent Smolny Institute in front of everyone at the Winter Palace."

Elena and Augusta rolled their eyes. I glanced up and saw an older woman following Madame Tomilov across the dining hall to the kitchen. It was Dr. Bokova. I wondered if she'd been summoned to attend the kitchen girl, Olga. I hoped the poor girl's head was feeling better that morning. I could not understand how Olga had provoked the ghost into causing such harm.

Elena leaned closer to me and whispered, "Danilo was most

disappointed he did not get to dance with you last night. He came all the way from Cetinje to see you."

It was my turn to blush. "I'm sorry he wasted his time."

Elena shrugged. "Perhaps Madame Tomilov will let him visit us here. Surely she cannot begrudge a sister a visit from her brother. And if he happens to see you at the same time, all the better."

I set my spoon down on the table beside my bowl. "Elena, please get it into your head that I am not going to marry your brother. He needs to get it into his head as well."

"He is taking me back home to Cetinje for the Christmas holidays. Perhaps you would like to come and spend Christmas with us?"

I glared at her. "You know I do not." I would never willingly set foot in Montenegro again. It had not been willingly the first time I visited.

"You are no fun, Katerina. I don't know what Dani sees in you."

"Power. Untapped, beautiful power." The crown prince had been listening to our conversation through me all morning. Before losing my temper, I closed my eyes and counted to ten. *"Of course I've been listening. My name was mentioned. I had hopes you were thinking wicked thoughts of me."*

I reached ten and then continued counting to twenty.

"Do not be angry, Duchess. They will only think you are insane." He laughed. He knew he was the reason for my apparent nervous breakdown. I had to find a way to get him out of my head. I wondered if an exorcism would work.

The wicked thoughts I was having of the crown prince were not the ones he had in mind. I smiled, imagining him tied up and dragged behind a horse, or thrown into the Black Sea.

"Katerina? Are you all right?" Augusta asked. All the girls at the table were looking at me curiously.

The voice in my head was silent again. I smiled even more. "Perfectly," I said, and finished my porridge.

❦

The girls in my Blue Form class would not stop whispering about the gossip they'd heard regarding the ball, and some of them seemed to know about the kitchen incident. But I was not interested in listening to them.

"Focus on your lessons, *mes petites*," I told them. "We have several weeks left of class before the Christmas holiday begins. Open your textbooks to page one hundred fifty-four." I turned around to write a sentence on the blackboard.

"But Mademoiselle Katerina," Charlotte asked, "is it true they served pineapple sherbet sprinkled with gold dust at the Winter Palace?"

"Did you really dance with the tsar's son?" asked Sarah, another student.

I turned around and looked as stern as I could. Madame Fredericks was sitting in the back of the room, absorbed in a Marie Corelli romance. But I knew she was listening to everything that happened. "I will only answer questions that you ask *en français*," I told the students.

The girls were happy to comply and I spent the rest of the hour regaling them with stories of the Smolny Ball. From the previous year.

I was counting down the days until the end of the school term. I missed my parents, not to mention my brother, Petya. And I was certain that George Alexandrovich would have to return to St. Petersburg to spend the holidays with his family. We had much to discuss. Surely the empress could not expect me to stay at Smolny during Christmas? Would she be that cruel?

CHAPTER TWENTY-TWO

In the end, the empress was not that cruel at all. The spell was lifted, and my mother and brother arrived at Smolny to pick me up the day the Christmas holidays began. Maman seemed nervous as she came to my room to oversee my packing. "It is freezing in here, Katiya! How do you sleep at night?"

I didn't know if she was sensing anything supernatural or not. I decided not to mention the ghost to her, for surely she would want to hold a séance. Petya was waiting in our family carriage at the gates. I gathered up my belongings and hurried downstairs. We had almost made it to the door when I saw Elena's brother and sister in the hallway.

"My lovely duchess, Katerina Alexandrovna," Crown Prince Danilo said, taking my hand. His warm lips lingered on my skin. I tugged my hand away. "And your beautiful mother is with you."

Maman curtsied. "Your Highness." He did not take her hand, I noticed.

Anastasia of Montenegro, now the duchess of Leuchtenberg after her marriage to my uncle George, smiled at Maman. "Our mother is anxious to see us all home. She delivered a healthy baby boy last month, Prince Petar."

"Please give both of your parents our warmest congratulations," Maman said.

My brother took my bag when we reached the carriage and helped me and Maman into our seats. It was good to see them both. Petya looked as if he'd aged years since I'd seen him last. He was thinner, with several lines etched in his face that I had never noticed before. I hoped he would have time to talk to me about the Order. Maman babbled the whole ride home about the servants and Papa's ongoing plans for his Institute of Experimental Medicine. I leaned against the window and stared out at the snow-covered streets. It had been months since I'd been outside of the school. It felt wonderful. And strange.

"I suppose you will not want to attend Miechen's Children's Ball," Maman said with a sigh. "She was so looking forward to seeing you. But I told her you would probably think you were too old."

"That's fine, Maman. I'll go," I said, still gazing out the window at St. Petersburg. My city was beautiful in the winter. A new snow had fallen overnight and blanketed everything in white.

"Wonderful! You'll have the chance to see all of your cousins," she said, not pausing to breathe. "Of course, you'll need some new dresses made. For evenings at the ballet too."

Petya was staring out the window as well, and did not seem to be paying attention to a word Maman was saying. We passed a patrol of imperial soldiers. I glanced at my brother. I was dying for a chance to talk to him alone.

Betskoi House looked the same as it always had. Papa came to the door to meet us, along with several servants. Anya was there and gave me a hug before Papa could. "Duchess! It's so good to have you back!"

"I've missed you too," I said, even though I thought she was safer here at home with my parents than she would have been at Smolny.

"How's my girl?" Papa said, embracing me in his strong arms. His mustache tickled my cheek. He smelled wonderful, like fine tobacco and old books. "I'm so sorry things did not work out this year the way we'd planned," he whispered.

"I'm fine, Papa. It's all right." I didn't want him feeling guilty about anything. It had not been his fault. "I'll make it to medical school one day."

He gave me a tender squeeze before letting me go.

"Anya, is the tea ready?" Maman asked. "We are freezing to death."

Everyone hurried inside, and I finally got Petya to myself as we lingered in the front hall. "Have you heard from George Alexandrovich?"

He frowned. "No, but I have heard several stories about him and the Order's Inner Circle. Katerina, I wish I'd not involved you with any of this."

"With any of what?"

"I fear you have grown too close to the grand duke, Katerina. No doubt our parents would be pleased with such a match, but I do not want to see you get hurt." He frowned before adding, "I worry that he is too dangerous for you."

I had to laugh. I was much more dangerous to George than he was to me. "I thank you for your concern. But what stories have you heard?"

"Katiya? Petya? Where did both of you go? The tea is ready!" Maman called to us from the top of the stairs.

I grabbed my brother's arm as he turned to go up. "Tell me, please."

He shook his head. "Later. I promise. But please stay away from the grand duke if you can."

There was no way I would stay away from George. If he was in the city, I had to see him. I needed to know what the Paris wizards had done to him. If it meant endangering myself, then I didn't care.

CHAPTER TWENTY-THREE

I was almost finished getting dressed for Miechen's ball that Friday night when I heard Maman's voice.

"Mon Dieu!" She cried from her boudoir. I rushed in to see her fretting over her tarot cards.

"Maman, please do not get upset. It's just a silly card game." But even as I was saying this, I knew it wasn't true.

"No!" she wailed. "He returns again and again in my readings!"

"Who does?" I sat down at the side of her chaise lounge and peeked at her cards.

"La Mort." She looked up at me, her face pale. "Death."

"Maman, please put the cards away. I think you just need your rest."

"Mais non, I am sure he is stalking this family."

I looked at her more carefully. I had not seen the cold light in so long, it was strange to see the pale glow that my mother gave off. Her cold light looked normal; I could not see anything wrong with her. "Maman, the Death card can mean so many more things than just death. It is a symbol of change." The cards could say many different things to many different people. Even I had picked up some of the symbolism over the years. Maman tended to see the worst in her cards.

"He follows the Knight of Cups. A young man. I fear for Petya!"

I looked at the card. The young man rode a white horse. It was not my brother, but George I feared for. A clammy feeling clenched my stomach. I couldn't wait to get to Miechen's ball. "Maman, are you feeling well enough to go out tonight?"

"Of course, dear. Let me pull myself together." She grabbed my hand and squeezed it. "Thank you, Katiya."

"For what?" As I looked at her more closely, I realized she too seemed years older than when I had seen her last. I was suddenly aware how warm it was in Maman's boudoir. I wanted to open the window and let the icy breeze off the Neva River sweep through the room. Maman always did like to have her bedroom cozy to the point of suffocating. I had to have fresh air.

"You always seem to calm me down. I've missed you so much." She looked up at me and smiled, and I saw that her cold light had indeed changed a little. I never could see auras, so I had no idea what color surrounded her, but I remembered what Dr. Badmaev had told me long ago. And what Princess Cantacuzene had said to me as well. Maman had dabbled in the occult for so long, her protective glamour had worn thin. It would not take much for her to see the truth about the Dark and Light Courts. How hysterical would she become if she learned that vampires and dark lich tsars had already returned to St. Petersburg? That her own daughter had the power to raise the dead? I wanted to put off her knowing that for as long as possible. Never would be fine with me.

CHAPTER TWENTY-FOUR

❧

The Children's Ball held at the Vladimir Palace was the signature event of the Christmas season for the Dark Court. The imperial family was always invited as a courtesy, but they knew they were not totally welcome. Nevertheless, the empress delighted in stealing the spotlight from Grand Duchess Miechen every chance she could.

The enormous ballroom was ablaze with candlelight. A string quartet in the middle of the room played selections from Tchaikovsky's ballet, *Swan Lake*. I looked all over the ballroom for signs the imperial family had arrived.

Maman had engaged the famed dressmaker Madame Olga to come to Betskoi House and fit me for a new gown. It was a dark-blue velvet dress the color of midnight. Pearls had been sewn into the bodice, in the same teardrop shapes that adorned my *kokoshnik*. This was the lowest-cut neckline Maman had ever let me wear.

Petya escorted both Maman and myself up the curving

marble staircase at the Vladimir Palace, warning me softly that the grand duke would probably be in attendance. I shivered, partly from the bareness of my shoulders as my wrap was taken at the front door and partly from excitement. Even with the formal pearly-white kidskin gloves that covered my arms, I was still cold. My heart beat faster. I could not wait to see him. To hear his voice again.

I wondered if he could hear my thoughts, now that I was no longer hidden away at Smolny. Surely, he could, if he were close by. But what if he had not returned to St. Petersburg after all?

"George?" I whispered to myself, as I searched through the twirling young people. I was stopped by Miechen's eldest son, the young Grand Duke Kyril.

He bowed very seriously. "Katerina Alexandrovna, my mother has been asking for you. Will you come with me?"

I smiled politely at him, wishing he hadn't spotted me so soon. "Of course." There was no sign of the imperial family. What if the empress had decided not to make an appearance at the Dark Court gathering tonight?

Grand Duchess Miechen was talking with Aunt Zina. At a nod of Miechen's head, my aunt curtsied to her and left. "Young Duchess, it is good to see you again."

I curtsied low. "I have been at Smolny these last few months."

Her blue-violet eyes narrowed at me. "I am aware of the empress's spell. It was I who convinced her to let you return to your mother for Christmas holidays."

"I am extremely grateful, Your Imperial Highness. I have missed my family very much."

"And how are your studies going?"

151

I did not know if she was merely being polite, as the empress had been when she asked me at Smolny, or if she was truly interested. I took a deep breath and decided to confide in the grand duchess. "Your Imperial Highness, it is not safe at the institute. For the past few months, the girls have been terrorized by a ghost. We thought it was Marija of Montenegro until recently."

The grand duchess frowned. "How did the ghost get past the empress's spell?"

"She has probably been at the institute for many years, but perhaps the spell agitated her."

"I suppose that is possible," the grand duchess said, deep in her own thoughts.

I quickly explained all the incidents with the ghost over the past few months.

The grand duchess shook her head. "How intriguing. I wish I'd known about the ghost sooner."

"I hoped to do something about her myself, but the empress's spell prevents me from seeing the cold light. I am helpless."

"Then the ghost should be helpless as well. She must be incredibly powerful if the empress's spell does not affect her." Miechen smiled maliciously. "Or the empress is not as powerful as she claims?"

I shivered.

"How many people know about the ghost?" Grand Duchess Miechen asked.

"The instructors deny that she exists, but most of the girls have seen or heard her. The servants as well. I wish I knew who she was. Maybe I would be able to reason with her."

The grand duchess shook her head. "I would advise against that, Katerina. I will make my own inquiries about the ghost. Meanwhile, I am responsible for your safety while you are home these next few weeks. My spells are not quite as powerful as those of the empress, so I expect that you will not go looking for danger to test my protection." She looked as if she would have rather eaten dirt than admit to any such weakness.

"Of course, Your Imperial Highness."

"And now, you will owe me a favor, for I have bestowed this gift upon you."

"I understand, Your Imperial Highness," I said, curtsying again unhappily. A debt owed to the Dark Court was not a good thing. She knew she could not ask me to deliberately betray the tsar or the empress, but she could do any number of things to make their lives difficult. And mine in the process.

"Do not worry, Katerina. I will not call upon this favor this evening. I believe there is a handsome young gentleman waiting to speak with you in the winter garden." Her needle-sharp teeth flashed as she smiled at me.

She knew. She knew that George was seeing me in secret without his mother's knowledge. "You should probably hurry, before anyone else decides to take a walk in the garden room this evening." The Dark Court faerie was actually encouraging us. That could not be a good thing.

I curtsied one last time and tried not to look like I was rushing toward her tropical indoor garden room. I would have run if I could.

"George?" I whispered as loud as I dared. And he was there, sitting on a stone bench beneath two very large palm trees, partially hidden from view. No one would find us in here unless they knew where to look. "George!"

He stood up as soon as he saw me. "Katiya." He gathered me up in his arms, kissing me as if his life depended on it. Now I was truly home. Where I belonged.

I could feel the cold light rising within me, though. I gasped and tried to pull away.

"Shhh," George whispered as he held me against him. "It's all right. I'm fine."

"But it will kill you." I was frightened for him. I struggled to fight back against the cold light.

"No, Katiya. I'm much stronger now," he murmured as his lips pressed against my temple.

I made one more halfhearted attempt to push him away, but did not succeed. "What do you mean? Why haven't you written me? Where have you been?"

"Shhh" was all he said, his hands slowly moving up from my waist, sliding up my back and caressing my shoulders. "I don't want to talk about that right now, Katiya. Please."

I couldn't help sighing. His fingers on the back of my neck were casting their own magic spell over me. I didn't want to talk anymore either. I wanted the rest of the world to melt away and leave us alone forever. I kissed him back as my hands slid under his arms and up his back, pressing him closer to me. His fingers traced lightly down the sides of my dress's bodice, causing me to arch my back and shiver in pleasure.

His passion frightened me, but I didn't want him to stop. I knew there was much we needed to talk about, but at that moment, I needed his kisses more than anything. The mages in France, Konstantin, the Smolny ghost: none of them mattered right now. It had been months since we had seen each other. A lifetime since I'd felt his touch.

"I've missed you so," I whispered.

His breathing was ragged as he rested his forehead against mine. He was smiling. "You don't know what it means to hear you say that. I've missed you as well."

I put my hand on his chest. Surely I only imagined that I could feel his heart pounding beneath my fingertips. It was beating just as fast as my own. I'd never been so deliriously happy in my life.

If the boy had asked me to run away with him that very moment I would not have been able to say no.

"Katiya, there is so much I want to tell you, but I cannot." His voice was weary, as if his struggle to control his passion was exhausting him.

"What do you mean?" I did not pull away from him. I was scared to let go.

"Please go back to Smolny where you are safe. I don't know what I would do if something happened to you." He led me toward the stone bench, where we sat down.

I wanted to laugh at him but I couldn't. "No. I can't go back. Not now. Talk to me. Tell me about the mages and the Inner Circle. Are you in danger?"

He shook his head and frowned. "Don't be ridiculous. And don't worry about me. I told you. I'm stronger than I ever was before."

"But you won't tell me about the mages."

"I'm sorry, Katiya, but I'm bound by oath not to talk about them. I cannot."

I shuddered. The grand duke had joined their brotherhood. Danilo had been right.

George mistook my movement, thinking I was cold. He slid his hands up and down my gloved arms to warm them. "You look so beautiful tonight."

I blushed. His touch was setting my skin on fire. I had missed him so much. I gazed up into his dark eyes, and was frightened to see his cold light, spiraling around him in a dim coil. I reached out and held him close to me, as if I could keep his light safe. What had he been doing in Paris? It could not be anything good. "My brother believes there is a traitor within the Order," I told him. "That you and your family are in danger."

"Yes, I've heard. I'm sure your brother and his soldiers will find the traitor. My father is safe, thanks to the Order. And thanks to you."

"What about Konstantin? Has no one heard anything about him? Is he still imprisoned in the Graylands?"

"No one knows, Katiya. That is why I want you safe at Smolny under my mother's protection." He hugged me close to him, his breath warm on my hair. "Please promise me you will not do anything foolish."

"George, I am more worried for you. What are the wizards teaching you? What do you plan to do with that knowledge?"

He sighed, his hands caressing my back comfortingly. "I cannot discuss it. And there is so much I wish to tell you." His smile was grim. "I think you would actually enjoy attending some of the lectures I've had to endure."

"Such as?" I leaned my head against his shoulder and closed my eyes. As long as he kept talking, he wouldn't let me go.

"Alchemy, auras, even the history of ritual magic." His finger toyed with a fallen curl at the back of my neck.

"Is it all so boring for you?" I asked.

He laughed quietly. "I do like the astrology lectures. Not the casting of horoscopes, but the study of the planets. I prefer the more rational astronomy. They assigned me Nicky's chart, as he is the future tsar, and it is full of malign stars. But I spend my nights at the Paris Observatory, using their telescope instead of ancient star charts. It's so beautiful, Katiya. I wish you could see it."

"One day you will show me," I said, smiling up at him.

"Perhaps." He did not smile back.

I pulled away to examine him more closely. He looked sad. And he looked thinner than when I had seen him in the Crimea. I touched his cheek with the palm of my hand. "Tell me more about Paris."

He closed his eyes. "I shouldn't. I've probably said too much."

I sighed. This was getting us nowhere. If George wouldn't, or couldn't, tell me about the French wizards, then who would?

George stood up and began to pace. He ran his fingers through his hair. "Maybe seeing you here tonight wasn't a good idea. I've probably put you in more danger."

I stood up too. "From whom? Konstantin? Or the wizards?"

"I should go." His face was troubled. He seemed to be fighting with himself.

"No!" I grabbed his arm as he tried to turn away. He might have lost weight, but his arms were still muscular. I could not imagine what he'd been doing in Paris to build up such strength.

Gently, he took my hand and raised it to his lips. "I will not endanger you, Katiya. You mean too much to me." With another gentle kiss, this time on my forehead, he said, "Please be careful. Stay close to your brother until you return to Smolny."

"Wait. When will I see you again?" I was trying hard not to cry. My eyes were stinging, and my throat was sore.

"When it's not dangerous anymore. I promise." With a sad smile, he turned and walked off.

I held out until I no longer heard his footsteps, then sank back down onto the bench and gave in to the tears. Each time he left me, I was afraid it would be the last time I would see him.

To the devil with His Imperial Highness, I thought with an unladylike sniffle. I would find out what the Inner Circle was doing without his help.

I heard someone enter the winter garden. I could tell it was a woman by the swishing of her heavy skirts.

"Katerina Alexandrovna?" someone whispered. It was Aunt Zina.

"Yes?" I hurriedly wiped the tears from my face.

"Your mother is frantic! She's been looking all over for you. *Mon Dieu*, what is wrong, dearest?"

"I'm fine," I said, standing quickly.

Aunt Zina eyed me suspiciously. "It's a boy, isn't it? Has someone broken your heart?" She sat down and leaned forward, a greedy look on her face. "Tell me all about it, Katerina. I promise I won't tell your mother."

I forced myself to laugh. "Oh no, it's nothing like that. Let's go back to the ball."

"Are you certain? I think you could use some air first. Perhaps just a quick walk outside in the courtyard?"

I started to open the glass door, and stopped. I remembered what had happened the year before, when George and Count Chermenensky had saved me from Princess Cantacuzene's undead soldier. It pained me to think of it. I turned away from the door. "I think I'd rather have something warm to drink. Will you come with me?"

"Of course, dearest." She rose with a small, half-feral smile. I knew she belonged completely to Miechen's court. The glamour was no longer hiding her fae eyes from me. I sighed. One more person in St. Petersburg I had to watch closely.

CHAPTER TWENTY-FIVE

❧

I followed Petya around the house like a puppy, waiting for a chance to talk to him about the Inner Circle of the Order. He was keeping odd hours, sleeping all day and staying out past the early hours of the morning. I did not know if he was working on things related to the Order or just having fun with his friends. It was the holiday season, after all. He was evasive when I asked him.

Dariya and her father and stepmother came to our house for Christmas dinner after the mass. Aunt Zina smiled at me over the dinner table and kindly asked how my heart was. Maman and Papa both looked at me curiously. Dariya too.

"It's as healthy as ever." I did not look at her again for the whole meal.

My uncle discussed the plans for the new medical institute with my father. They had begun construction on the building, and Papa hoped to have the Oldenburg Institute of

Experimental Medicine open sometime in the coming year. I sighed, poking at my Christmas pudding halfheartedly. I wished I could be one of the physicians working at his institute. I wanted to treat patients as well, but researching cures for deadly diseases would be fascinating.

After dessert we went into the drawing room and opened presents. Papa had given me a set of Greek and Latin books, and from Maman I received another Marie Corelli romance. I gave them each a scarf that I had knitted.

Maman gasped with delight when she opened Aunt Zina's present: a book written in French on communicating with spirits. As if my mother needed any more information on that subject. I glanced at Dariya, who shrugged as she stroked Sasha's ragged ears. The cat purred even as it glared at me. Dariya did not seem to notice anything wrong with the rotting animal that was purring unsteadily in her lap. She had never been interested in the spiritism parties my mother held before, but now that she was considered a young woman, she was admitted to all the best social gatherings in St. Petersburg, and she'd been to several of Maman's séances. With Aunt Zina.

I'd received several letters from Dariya over the past few months while I was at Smolny, and they'd all described fancy dinner parties and séances that she'd attended. Dariya was now obsessed with finding a rich and handsome husband. Aunt Zina was attempting to keep her allied with the Dark Court and Grand Duchess Miechen. I hoped that my cousin would find a handsome, foreign prince and move far away to somewhere much safer.

"Oh, Katiya, look at this! What a treasure!" Maman

exclaimed, smoothing the black leather cover of her book. It looked ancient, but well cared for. I would have loved to know where Aunt Zina had gotten her hands on such a volume. And why was she so interested in Maman's séances?

"This gift is for you, dearest," Aunt Zina said, handing me a brightly wrapped package.

"*Merci*," I said, unwrapping it warily. It was a book about magical orders: *L'histoire de l'ordre du Lis Noir. The History of the Order of the Black Lily.* "You are too kind," I said, wondering how she knew I would be interested in such things.

"I hope you enjoy it. The Grand Duchess Miechen and I were shopping for Christmas presents, and she said it looked like something you would appreciate."

A chill slid down the back of my neck. Miechen. It made me nervous that I could not guess the dark faerie's motives. I knew I owed her a debt for my Christmas holiday. Would I owe her another debt for this book? Or was it somehow linked to the way I was to repay the grand duchess? I would read it as soon as everyone left.

My brother prepared to leave not long after we finished opening presents. "Where on earth are you headed?" Maman asked. "Petya, it's Christmas!"

He was dressed in his regiment uniform. "I have to go, Maman. I'm sorry." He kissed her on the cheek and then bowed to the rest of us in the room. "Happy Christmas, everyone."

I was disappointed. Each night I had tried to stay awake and catch him when he came home, but I kept falling asleep. My holiday would be over soon and I would have to return to Smolny. I would never get a chance to talk to my brother about the Order of St. John.

Aunt Zina and the others left not long after Petya. Dariya gave me a hug, thanking me for the diary I'd given her. "I hope to see you when the winter season begins. Will your mother let you come home from school to attend a few of the balls? And the ballet?"

"We shall see," I said, giving her an optimistic smile. I had no doubts that the empress wanted me locked up at Smolny as soon as possible. But when would she be willing to release me again? When the tsar needed me to summon the bogatyr? I could not wish for such a thing.

As soon as our guests left, I kissed my parents goodnight and took my Christmas gifts back to my room. I curled up with the book from Aunt Zina, not even bothering to change into my nightclothes.

I read about the first Russian grand master of the Order, Tsar Pavel, and his ties with a society of magicians in Paris. Pavel had allowed the magicians a safe haven in Russia after the terrors of the French Revolution. The court magicians of St. Petersburg learned much from their French counterparts and reorganized their coven based on the French order. The Russians called their grand master the Koldun, or the Sorcerer, who was the leader of the innermost circle of the Order. The outermost circle was made up of the tsar's most elite soldiers, who did not learn magic. Their mission was to protect the inner circle and its secrets. The middle circle consisted of several wizards who aided the Koldun. They studied alchemy and other forms of magic, all supposedly for the glory and advancement of Russia.

Surely it could not be the same group after all of these years. Unless some of the magicians were immortal. I shuddered, wondering what kind of power Konstantin would have had if he'd studied the secrets of the Order after his father. He would have been able to easily take the tsar's crown away from his brother Nicholas. Especially with a vampire as his consort.

The text was tedious, and despite wanting to learn all I could about the Order, I found myself nodding off again and again. With a sigh, I regretfully put the book away and prepared myself for bed. Anya came in with the hot-water bottle as I crawled into bed. She blew out the lamp as she withdrew, leaving me in the dark.

I had snuggled down into the warmth under the blankets when an odd thought popped into my head. If George was studying to be the tsar's sorcerer one day, who was the Koldun now? Suddenly, it seemed important to know.

The question kept me awake for hours. I hoped I would hear Petya returning home, so I could ask him. It had to be a member of the imperial family, a Romanov. One who was gifted in magic, like George. Whoever it was, he kept his magic a well-guarded secret.

It was long after midnight when I heard my brother's soft footsteps in the hall. I had drifted off to sleep and had been dreaming about Vorontsov Palace, the headquarters of the Order. I had dreamed I was dancing with George in the Great Hall in front of the portrait of the Tsar Pavel.

I jumped out of bed and threw on my dressing gown before opening my door. "Petya?" I whispered.

I had surprised him. It took a while for his eyes to focus on me in the dark hallway. "What the devil are you doing awake?"

He smelled like wine. Which surprised me. "Petya, are you all right? I need to talk to you. You promised."

He shook his head. "Please leave me in peace, Katiya. I don't want to talk about the Order. I don't even want to think about the blasted Order."

"Petya, just tell me one thing."

He opened his bedroom door. "Not tonight, Katiya. My head is killing me."

I put my hand on his coat sleeve. "Who is the Koldun?"

Petya stopped. He turned to me, his eyes flashing angrily. "Katiya, why do you ask me such forbidden questions? It would be dangerous for me to know, and even more so for you. Do not try to find out on your own either."

"But—"

"Good night, Katiya." He entered his bedroom and shut the door.

I should have realized Petya was not high enough in the Order to know these types of secrets. He was an officer in the imperial guard. Part of me was thankful he knew nothing of the Inner Circle's ceremonial magic and alchemy. But I was still worried for George. It meant that he needed to keep his own magic training a secret from the rest of St. Petersburg. How many people knew he was a wizard? Who was he training to replace? And what kind of awful magic were the wizards in Paris teaching him?

CHAPTER TWENTY-SIX

❧

The next morning, I accompanied my father on his visit to the Oldenburg Hospital, where he needed to drop off some paperwork for Dr. Ostrev, Anya's brother. Dr. Ostrev had worked hard to fill Dr. Kruglevski's shoes at the hospital, but he was still young and did not have Dr. Kruglevski's years of experience. I knew my father missed his old friend even more than I did.

Dr. Ostrev looked weary. Gray hairs had already begun to invade his head. He shook Papa's hand warmly and bowed to me. "I hope you have had a blessed Christmas, Your Highness," he said to Papa. "My sincerest thanks for the books you sent."

Papa smiled. "Not at all, Doctor. I was hoping to discuss the latest on the new institute with you. We have highest hopes for our laboratory. Have you heard about Dr. Koch's experiments?"

"With tubercle bacilli. Of course."

"I am hoping he is close to discovering a cure."

"That would be wonderful news indeed."

Just as their conversation had grown interesting, they drifted into more mundane topics, such as administration and bureaucracy. One of the kind nurses took our coats and another entered the doctor's office with a tea tray. It was Sister Anna, from Smolny. She smiled sincerely. "It is wonderful to see you, Katerina Alexandrovna. Is your family well?"

"Yes, Sister. Do you spend all of your holidays here at the hospital?"

She nodded, folding her hands humbly. "Of course. It is the Lord's work. Would you like to accompany me on my rounds? I think it would be an enlightening experience for you, dear."

I'd followed the nurses around the hospital too many times to count. I knew everything they did, from bathing patients to feeding them and redressing wounds. And it was a noble job. I was very grateful for the work these tireless sisters performed. But I wanted to do so much more for the sick. I wanted to heal their diseases. I wanted to find cures for the worst illnesses. I wanted to perform surgery and prescribe medicine. To research and discover new medicines. With a smile, I nodded and took the stark white apron that Sister Anna offered me.

"A good nurse provides comfort for her patients, as well as cleanliness." The sister handed me a bowl of water and some clean rags. "We should start with the young man on the end, there. Captain Troubetsky."

The captain had been hospitalized after falling from his horse in a training accident. I could not help being reminded of Count Chermenensky. The young man shivered with a fever, and moaned in a restless sleep. He was in severe pain.

I took the captain's pale hand gently. I could see his cold

light unwrapping, rapidly slipping from around him. The young man was dying. What if it had been Petya there in the bed? I would not let anything happen to him. Slowly, I uncoiled my own cold light and used it to grab hold of the young man's. I had to bind his cold light back to his body, or he would be gone. He moaned softly, and began to tremble.

I panicked. What was I doing? In all of my medical journals, Latin books, the literature of esoteric mysticism, I had never come across any sort of information that offered enlightenment regarding my dark ability. Princess Cantacuzene could have taught me, I'm certain, if I'd been willing to be her pupil. And Dr. Badmaev had hinted once before of a more academic, if unorthodox method of harnessing my powers. No matter how desperately I wanted to help this patient, I knew experimenting on him was dangerous. And very, very wrong. With a sigh, I placed his hand back on his chest. I crossed myself and said a prayer for mercy to be granted him. I took a wet rag and dabbed his forehead, hoping the fever would break soon.

His moaning increased. Sister Anna came over to the bed and poured out a teaspoon of laudanum for him. "Give this to the captain," she said, handing the medicine to me.

"Take this; it will help you rest," I said, coaxing the soldier to take the elixir. The thick green liquid smelled like anise, but he swallowed it without complaint. The patient fell back to sleep almost immediately.

"You would make an excellent nurse, Katerina Alexandrovna," Sister Anna said.

"That would be a waste of her talents," Papa said as he and the doctor reached the patient's bed. "She will be a brilliant doctor someday. Think of the discoveries she will make in her lifetime!"

Sister Anna scowled. "'Tis not natural for a lady to learn such things. An overeducated mind is open to too many temptations."

"There are lots of women who have become wonderful doctors, Sister," I said.

"Witches and harlots," she hissed. Sister Anna grabbed the washrag away from me and began roughly wiping down the soldier.

Dr. Ostrev tried to spare me the older woman's lecture. "Will you see to the dirty linens, Sister Anna?"

"Of course, Doctor," she said, bowing graciously. With a swish of her skirts, she and the bundle of bed linens were gone.

"I apologize for that," Dr. Ostrev said. "But if you are serious about becoming a doctor, you must get used to hearing such sentiments. I knew a young woman from Odessa who gave up on her dreams because she couldn't bear the way the older nurses treated her as a young female doctor."

Papa looked at me and nodded. "He has a point, Katiya. Sister Anna is not the only one who will try to discourage you."

"I understand. It truly does not bother me," I said with a smile. But I wondered how long my dedication would last if I had to continually endure such negativity.

I took the basket of fruit that Maman had sent and followed Sister Elizabeth, who was much kinder than Sister Anna, into the women's ward. At the end of the long row of beds, I was startled to see a familiar but sad face: Madame Metcherskey.

She had lost weight and looked even paler and more severe than before. I gasped.

"Poor dear," Sister Elizabeth said, straightening her blankets. Madame Metcherskey coughed, but did not open her eyes. "She has a failing heart. She is dying."

"Dying?" I whispered. I could not imagine anything ever striking down the indomitable and strong woman. This was not the same woman who had terrorized the girls of Smolny into studying their history. This was only a hollow shell of the woman she used to be.

Slowly, Madame Metcherskey opened her eyes, fixing her stare on me. Her wits were still with her. She recognized me immediately. "Katerina Alexandrovna. The troublemaker," she croaked.

When I took her cold hand in mine, her fingers clutched mine instantly. Her grip was still strong. "Madame. I'm so sorry for causing you such grief."

"Never mind about that." She tried to pull me closer to her. Her voice was raspy and hoarse. "Don't let the other girls repeat your mistakes."

"Which mistakes?" I whispered. Goodness knows I'd made too many over the years. Especially in her eyes.

"All light is not good, Katerina Alexandrovna," she said, letting go of my hand and closing her eyes. "And all shadows are not evil."

"Madame?" I looked up at the nurse in alarm as she checked Madame's pulse. "Is she dead?" I whispered. Her cold light was blinding white and stinging my fingers.

Sister Elizabeth shook her head. "She's just sleeping again."

Madame Metcherskey drew in a rattly breath just then, as

if to prove to me it was true. Her breathing became shallow, but steady. Sister Elizabeth smiled kindly at me. "She needs her rest now, dear."

Madame's words frightened me. *All light is not good.* Could she have seen her own cold light? I'd never known anyone who was able to see it. But I'd never known anyone who was dying either. I reached down and gave Madame's fingers one last squeeze and left her to rejoin my father.

How much simpler my life had been years ago when Madame Metcherskey, glaring at me for running in the halls, was my worst nightmare. Now the nightmares were so much worse.

CHAPTER TWENTY-SEVEN

~◈~

It was not long before the end of the holidays was upon us. I was to return to Smolny the day after the Blessing of the Waters, an annual tradition that brought all of St. Petersburg to the frozen Neva River. Since it was to be my last day of freedom, I planned to make the best of it. I dressed warmly, with an extra layer of stockings and petticoats under my woolen dress. Anya looked at me suspiciously as she fixed my hair. "Don't go looking for any danger, Duchess."

"I promise I'll be careful, Anya. But there are some things I must take care of before I go back to school."

I rode with Maman in our handsome black carriage. Papa and Petya would be there already with their respective regiments. This was a military as well as a religious ceremony, where the tsar cut out a piece of the frozen Neva River and lifted up a cup of water from below for the metropolitan of St. Petersburg to bless. There would be thousands of people there, and I hoped for a chance to slip away without Maman realizing I'd left.

The sky was gray and mournful, as if in memory of the tragedy surrounding last year's blessing, when Count Chermenensky had been thrown from his horse. Every year we prayed the running of the troops would be free of accidents. I worried most for my father and brother.

Aunt Zina and Dariya were waiting under a fur-lined tent that was close to the Imperial Pavilion. I did not see George standing up there with his family. My heart sank a little. I wanted to ask him about the current leadership of the Order, and wasn't sure who else would know. The membership of the Inner Circle of the Order was a closely guarded secret. Not all of St. Petersburg was aware the Koldun existed.

Aunt Zina waved to attract Maman's attention. Thousands of troops were assembled smartly across the river, their horses stomping in the snow impatiently.

"Hurry!" Aunt Zina called. "The ceremony is about to start!"

I could see Grand Duchess Miechen standing opposite the empress under her own pavilion, draped in midnight-blue silk. She did not usually attend the blessing. I wondered what had drawn the Dark Court to make an appearance on such a dismal and cold day? Grand Duke Vladimir, the grand duchess's husband, and brother to the tsar, stood with her. His steely gray eyes looked colder than the frozen river.

I shivered as the grand duchess's gaze swept across the crowd, and she caught my eye with a small, regal smile. I wished with all my heart that I could swear total allegiance to the Light Court and rid myself of my debt to Miechen. But my family would still have ties to her court, and I could not leave them unprotected. Bitterly I wondered how different my life would have been if my parents had been aligned with the Light Court all along. It was no use wishing, however. I did not believe in fate, but somehow, I knew my life was following some dark design.

I touched Maman's shoulder. "There is an old friend I must greet." I slipped back into the crowd, not bothering to wait for a reply. She would worry, and I would get into trouble, but the Dark Court has a saying: It is easier to ask forgiveness than to ask permission.

I hurried through the crowd, pushing against the townspeople that crowded the riverbank hoping for a glance at the tsar. Some looked at me as if I were insane, trying to get farther away from the Imperial Pavilion. Others ignored me, and pressed closer.

I broke into a run when I reached Nevski Prospekt. My destination was not far away: Lazarev Cemetery. I had my respects to pay. I spent the last of my Christmas coins on a small bouquet of violets from a street vendor and entered the cemetery. Even the crunch of the snow beneath my boots did not disturb the peace I felt as soon as I passed the cemetery gates. The trees were barren, of course, but the tombs were still difficult to read. It had only been a few months since Dr. Kruglevski's funeral, but it seemed to me like a lifetime had passed since then. I made my way to his grave and brushed the snow aside to lay the flowers there. I crossed myself and said a short prayer for my old friend.

"You still feel responsible for his death, do you not, Duchess?"

I jumped up, startled. I had not seen anyone else in the cemetery. "Dr. Badmaev." I curtsied, shaken by the way the Tibetan doctor seemed to have appeared out of nowhere.

His face was kind. "It was not your fault, Your Highness. It was the doctor's fate to die on that day. Vampire or no."

"But I should never have left him alone with Princess Cantacuzene. I was the only one who knew how dangerous she really was." The only one besides Grand Duchess Miechen. And Queen Milena of Montenegro.

"Let go of the guilt, Duchess, or it will keep you its prisoner. Dr. Kruglevski would not have wanted that. What do you think he would have wanted you to do?"

I smiled sadly as I idly rearranged the flowers. "He would have expected me to attend medical school and become a brilliant doctor."

"But the tsar will not let you leave the country." The Tibetan doctor stood calmly with his hands clasped in front of him. The cold did not seem to bother him in the least.

"How do you know this?" When he showed no hint of replying, I sighed. "Of course not." Despite what George had told me back in August, the tsar did not believe in women becoming doctors.

"There are other paths of medicine, Duchess, that do not require the tsar's permission."

I looked at him skeptically. "What do you mean?"

"I am offering you the opportunity to learn the secrets of Eastern medicine. Become my pupil. I have seen your gift, and I believe you would become an excellent doctor."

I laughed bitterly. "My gift is unholy. I could not routinely return the dead to life. It would not be right."

He shook his head with a smile. "I did not mean your dark ability. I know there are many who would use your gifts for unholy purposes, but I speak of your healing ability. It is related to the other, with your gift to see cold light, but it is important on its own. There are always two sides of every coin, Duchess. Light and dark. Day and night."

"East and West?" I asked, and he nodded. "I'm sorry, but Eastern medicine consists of folk medicine and herbal remedies. I need to study the most modern research. Western medicine is more effective. One way or another, I must go to Zurich one day and become a proper doctor."

His smile was still kind. "I will not withdraw the offer, Duchess. Come and visit me when you are ready to unite both sides of your own nature." With a polite bow, Dr. Badmaev left me standing in the cemetery.

I was ashamed. I had insulted not only the man, but also his own country and beliefs. Even his own education, which I was certain had been just as intensive as Dr. Kruglevski's. But if I wanted to earn the respect of other doctors, I would need a respectable degree. One day.

I shivered and drew my cloak around me more tightly. It was time to return to my mother. I took one last glance at Dr. Kruglevski's grave before leaving him. What if I'd used my dark gift to bring him back? He would have been a monster, like Count Chermenensky. To bring someone back like that was not a kindness.

But what if I could find a way to perfect my gift? Retrieve someone from the dead and restore them to their previous life? Would it be possible? Would it be right? To defy the natural order of things would be unholy. Wouldn't it? To deny the dead their eternal rest was a blasphemy. Would God have mercy on my own soul when my life was over? I was filled with dark thoughts as I hurried back through the cemetery.

The Tibetan had caused me to question my own motives for becoming a doctor. Was it truly a desire to help people or to express some suppressed desire to tamper with death? Perhaps my heart did belong with the Dark Court after all. Because it appeared to me that I certainly did not have a soul.

I hurried back through the cemetery only to stop and stare in shock as I saw a fresh grave, with several frost-covered bouquets wilting on top.

NATALIA MAXIMILIANOVNA METCHERSKEY
BELOVED TEACHER AND FRIEND
31 JULY 1819–30 DECEMBER 1889

Beloved? I shook my head. I wondered who had ever loved this brittle and coldhearted woman. Madame Metcherskey had always been nasty to me, as well as to the rest of the girls at Smolny. Still, I felt bad about her passing. I crossed myself and said a short prayer for her before continuing on.

CHAPTER TWENTY-EIGHT

❦

Going back to Smolny was not as bad as it had been in September. It was even worse. I knew it would only be a few more months before the winter term was over, but I was determined to deal with the young ghost. I was surprised to find myself almost happy to see Alix and Aurora and the Bavarian princesses again. Elena would not stop talking about her new baby brother. Erzsebet and Augusta would not stop talking about the upcoming St. Petersburg winter season. "There will be ballets and operas, and so many balls! Our cousin has finally been presented to the empress and she will be attending all of the festivities! She's promised to write us daily and tell us everything!"

Princess Alix unpacked her small suitcase and stayed silent. When the princesses asked about her holiday, she only smiled and shrugged.

"She tries to be so mysterious, when there is nothing to be

mysterious about," Elena whispered to me later, as we walked to the dining hall for dinner. "She is so dull!"

"Then why does she bother you so much?" I asked.

Elena sighed, frustrated. "I suppose part of it is the way the tsarevitch looked at her when they danced at the Smolny Ball."

I found myself feeling sorry for the Montenegrin princess. I squeezed her hand. "He's not for you, Elena."

She pushed my hand away. "What do you know of it? He has always belonged to me!" Tears formed in her eyes.

"Elena—"

With a cry, she stormed past me, back to our room. I watched her leave with worry. I was starting to believe she really loved Nicholas Alexandrovich.

I sighed. And what if Alix had done more than just catch the tsarevitch's eye? She was the granddaughter of Queen Victoria, but not someone his parents would approve of for such an important alliance. Elena was the daughter of a king. Even if he was a poor king. He was still a very powerful man. And a dangerous one at that.

"Are you coming to dinner?" Augusta asked as she met me in the hall. "There is a new cook, we heard. He used to work for the Yussopov family."

I smiled. Maman and Papa both had commented several times before on the splendid dinners they'd had at the Yussopov Palace. Princess Zenaida Yussopova was the richest woman in St. Petersburg, with more wealth than the imperial family. I was sure the cook was used to a kitchen pantry stocked with the freshest and rarest foods. What culinary magic he would be able to perform with our simple Smolny kitchen, I couldn't wait to discover.

As I passed the library, I saw something moving from the corner of my eye. Something dark and large and fast. I stopped and peeked inside. Of course there was nothing. No one was in the tiny reading room, alive or dead. My heart beat wildly, but I took a deep breath and hurried on to the dining hall. I needed a good supper and then a good night's sleep.

CHAPTER TWENTY-NINE

〜◦∾

I slept very well my first night back at Smolny, after a wonderful dinner of potato and cabbage soup. No tossing or turning, and no strange or frightening dreams. I awoke the next morning feeling better than I had in months. Everyone seemed to be in brighter spirits, even the Montenegrin princess. Elena smiled at me and Aurora both as she hopped out of bed and got dressed. And Aurora smiled back.

Even with our brief memorial service honoring Madame Metcherskey, the somber mood at Smolny seemed to have changed. Madame Tomilov and Madame Orbellani were smiling at everyone over breakfast as well. There was a lightness to everyone's mood. Sister Anna decided to sing our morning grace before breakfast. Her voice was a very sweet, pure alto.

We ate warm, fluffy biscuits with raspberry and strawberry jam. A special treat, thanks to our new cook. Outside, it was a gloomy winter day, but inside the Smolny Institute, one would have thought it was sunny spring.

Even the oldest students skipped to their classes. And I skipped right past the library, wondering what had happened to our ghost. Had Madame Tomilov done something to get rid of her over the holidays? Was that the reason for the dramatic change in mood? I let the Bavarian princesses go on ahead and turned back to investigate.

"You won't find her in there right now," Alix said, as she walked down the hall in her calm, dignified manner.

"What is going on?" I asked. "There is something not quite right this morning."

"What could possibly be wrong?" Alix's mouth twitched. She was trying very hard to hold back a smile.

"Are you feeling all right?" I asked her.

She pulled a leftover biscuit out of her pinafore pocket and stuffed it into her mouth. She licked the jam off of her fingers. "I'm feeling wonderful, Katerina!" She giggled as she skipped off to class. I watched as Elena linked arms with her and off they went together, like best friends.

I sighed. There was definitely something wrong at Smolny. Why did I think the biscuits were to be blamed?

Of course it wasn't my place to look into this, but I had to. Instead of going to class, where I knew I wouldn't be able to learn anything anyway, what with all the skipping and singing, I slipped downstairs into the kitchen, where the staff was washing the pots and pans from breakfast.

They were singing in the kitchen as well. Joyful French love songs. *Mon Dieu!* It was too early for such impropriety.

I found the cook, a youngish-looking man, peeling apples by the window. I couldn't help gasping as he looked up at me and smiled. His eyes were so blue, it hurt to look at them. I could do nothing but smile. I couldn't stop myself.

"*Oui*, Mademoiselle?" he asked. He tossed the apple into a large bowl with the others and wiped his hands on his apron. "Shouldn't you be in class?"

I shook my head. "No. I mean, yes . . . I should, but I needed to ask you . . ." What had I wanted to ask him exactly? It seemed no amount of glamour could hide what he was from me. He was beautiful. Too beautiful to be human. Too beautiful to be harmless. "Why did you come to Smolny?" I asked. "What have you done to us?"

His clear blue eyes blinked. Then he grinned, showing the faintest flash of his sharp, tiny teeth. "I serve at the will of Her Imperial Majesty. She has been informed that there is an unfortunate lost soul that has been trapped here within her spell. I am here to make sure that it does not harm anyone."

"Do you know who she is? Can you get rid of her?"

"Sadly, no. I'm afraid even Her Imperial Majesty does not know who this lost soul is. And no, I cannot do anything to expel it. Only a necromancer such as yourself could do that." He searched through the cupboards for something.

My jaw dropped. In a most unladylike manner. "But I'm powerless under the empress's spell here. How can I do anything?"

He began to roll out a piecrust with his marble rolling pin. "It is true. There is nothing you can do, while the empress's spell remains. That is why I am here. To make sure everyone forgets about the ghost."

"How does your magic work, then?" I asked. "Is it stronger than the empress's spell?"

"Of course not. My fae glamour inserts itself within the

fabric of the empress's fae spell. The glamour is only an illusion. Nothing more. And all the more pity for you, since you see through it. The lost soul will still be able to affect you with its malicious tantrums." He was making apple turnovers. It smelled heavenly when he sprinkled the cinnamon and sugar over the apple pieces. It brought a smile to the corners of my lips.

"Here," he said with a dramatic sigh. He reached over into the picnic basket on the kitchen table and pulled out two blueberry muffins. They were still warm. "These should keep you protected until lunchtime. But stay away from the library."

"*Merci*, Monsieur . . ." I smiled helplessly, realizing I did not know his name. It would be helpful if I did.

He grinned his wicked grin again. "Oh no, you're not getting that out of me. You may call me Sucre. That is the name Madame Tomilov knows me by."

"*Merci*, Monsieur Sucre." I curtsied politely, afraid to eat the tempting muffins. They smelled divine. Their sweet scent rose up out of my hands, like a whisper. I knew it was only an illusion. The glamour, the fae called it. Would it hurt me to not see reality for a little while? It would be so nice to not worry about the lost soul, as Sucre called her. "Have you seen her? The ghost?"

The cook scowled and spat on the floor, muttering something in a language I'd never heard before. Definitely not French. And not Russian. "No, and I hope that I do not." He opened the large oven door and placed the tray of turnovers inside. "Now, it is time for you to go, Mademoiselle. I cannot let you see all of my tricks."

"But—"

His eyes flashed. The blue was unbearable. "Now, Mademoiselle." His voice was soft, but deadly.

I curtsied again. "Of course. Thank you once again," I said, waving the muffins at him as I turned to go.

"And tell your Bavarian friend she should not be wandering into the kitchen late at night. You would not want her to eat something that disagreed with her."

My skin turned cold. Would he really dare to harm one of us? "Of course not, Monsieur." I gritted my teeth and left, not bothering to glance back at him. I hurried outside into the frozen courtyard and tore the blueberry muffins into tiny pieces, scattering them into the wind. I'd let the rest of the students skip and sing along with the beglamoured instructors and Sister Anna. I wanted to be able to see the evil things that were stalking us at Smolny.

CHAPTER THIRTY

ᘐᓍᕽ

The apple turnovers were a special treat for dessert that night after huge bowls of belly-warming cabbage stew. Sister Anna brought out her ukulele and even persuaded Madame Tomilov to sing with her. Madame Orbellani had a bright blush in her cheeks as she danced a polonaise around the dining room with Elena. I pushed my turnover toward Augusta's plate. She gobbled it happily.

I could not understand why the empress wanted everyone so giddy. Of course she wouldn't want everyone sleep-deprived and pale, but this much happiness was abnormal. And definitely not healthy. Monsieur Sucre. I frowned. I began to wonder if it was indeed the empress who had sent the fae cook, or someone with mischief in mind. Would Miechen have even told the empress about the ghost? Or did Miechen send the cook herself?

"Dance with me, Katerina Alexandrovna!" Elena said, trying to pull me away from the table. She was laughing and out of breath.

Sister Anna was now playing an old folk ballad based on the tale of St. George and the dragon. In her song, St. George actually turned into a dragon to fight the evil one. It was an interesting version of the story. I smiled and shook my head at Elena. "Dance with Erzsebet. I have studying to do."

Augusta was laughing. "Can you imagine turning into a dragon?"

I shrugged, but Alix looked fascinated with the idea. "Yes," she whispered. "Wouldn't that be wonderful?"

Augusta laughed again. "I would be the dragon princess and you would be the dragon queen." She took Alix's hands and they swung around the table, just like Elena and Erzsebet.

I left the dining hall and passed the library on my way back to our room. I paused, remembering Sucre's warnings, but I needed to borrow the German text of *Faust* for our upcoming German exam.

I peeked into the library, seeing nothing unusual. Cautiously, I stepped into the room and approached the bookcase. The temperature in the room dropped suddenly to below freezing. I could see my breath as I gasped.

"I am not here to hurt you," I whispered, trying to remain calm. "I only want to help you. But I will need to know your name to do that."

I heard a low hiss behind me as several books flew off the shelves toward me. I threw up my arms to shield myself—a few of the books were heavy. *"Mon Dieu!"* I screamed.

The gloom and malice all came flooding back to me, and I started to regret throwing away Sucre's muffins. I could feel the ghost trying to hurt me. My chest tightened, making it difficult to breathe. Why was she so full of hatred? And why did she haunt the library?

Goethe's *Faust* was one of the books that had fallen from the shelves. I grabbed it quickly and retreated to my room, leaving the other books open on the floor. The ghost could clean up her own mess. The dark feelings had passed as soon as I crossed the threshold into the hallway, and by the time I returned to my room and sat down on my cot, I could breathe easily again. I pushed up my sleeves to look at the bruises on my arms from the books hitting me. At least they would be hidden under my long sleeves, so Madame Tomilov and Sister Anna would not see. Hopefully, Elena and Aurora would not see them either.

I was already changed into my long-sleeved nightgown and tucked under my covers, reading *Faust*, when the girls returned to our room sometime later that night.

They were giggling and out of breath. "Katiya, why did you leave the dining hall? You missed all the fun!" Elena gushed.

Aurora flopped back on her cot. "We wanted to dance all night, but Madame would not let us!"

Elena shook her head. "I think Madame *would* have let us, if Sister Anna had not reminded her we needed to go to sleep."

"Are all of you ready for our German exam tomorrow?" I asked. "Madame Orbellani *sagte dass es schwierig sein würde.*"

Aurora rolled her eyes. "Of course I'm ready. I don't care how difficult Madame Orbellani believes she's made it. I grew up with a German nanny."

"And I grew up in Germany," Alix said.

"I plan to copy off of Alix," Aurora said.

"And I plan to copy off of Aurora," Elena said, still twirling around the room.

Aurora laughed as she got ready for bed. "Then I shall mark every answer wrong on purpose."

Elena stuck her tongue out at Aurora playfully.

Alix smiled at them, looking more animated than she had in months.

I was glad the three of them had warmed up to each other, even if it was only because of some enchanted pastries. Still, I couldn't help feeling a little bit left out. Which was ridiculous. Elena and I weren't really friends. She'd tried to poison me, and had cast a charm on me. We could never have a true friendship, like the kind Dariya and I shared. I would never be able to trust any of the Montenegrins. And pastry or no pastry, I wasn't sure I trusted Alix of Hesse-Darmstadt either.

CHAPTER THIRTY-ONE

〰

On the first sunny day, Madame Tomilov allowed Sister Anna to take our class out for a walk in the courtyard. The sister had argued that we needed fresh air and exercise to keep us strong and healthy during the winter months, and the headmistress had agreed. She sent along a picnic basket full of Sucre's apple and cinnamon muffins.

Elena seemed to be acting more like her normal wicked and conniving self, however. She grabbed my arm and we hung back behind the others, allowing Aurora and the rest of the girls to hurry ahead.

"What is it?" I whispered. "They'll never let us out again if you do something horrible."

"I just wanted to speak with you, Katerina Alexandrovna. Without Alix listening. I found something mysterious under her bed last night."

"What were you up to?"

190

Elena shrugged. "I needed to put something there. I did not expect to see witchcraft already in place."

"Witchcraft?"

"The box she keeps tucked under her bed. It has a red ribbon coiled up inside."

"And what makes you think that it is witchcraft? You had no right to search the princess's things, Elena."

"There was a protective symbol scratched inside the box's lid. A German hex symbol."

"How do you know?" But I already could guess. I shook my head. "Never mind. Your sisters."

Elena smiled. "They are extremely well educated, Katerina. Not only did they finish at the tops of their classes here at Smolny, they also were tutored during the summers at home in Greek and Persian. We have quite a large occult library at home in Cetinje."

Briefly, I regretted missing out on this library when I was in Montenegro last spring. "Perhaps it is something a superstitious servant gave her."

"Anyway, I wonder what the ribbon is for."

I looked at Elena. "And I wonder what you were planning on putting under her bed."

Elena took my arm in hers as she looked up at the sky and smiled. "Oh, just a little something to keep her from looking her best."

I shook my head again and sighed. I realized nothing magical would work under the empress's spell, so Alix was safe for the moment from Elena's creepy trinkets. But whatever magic was in that box would not be able to work either. What was the German princess hiding?

I wished that Alix and I had become closer friends during the school year, but she kept mostly to herself. She definitely had her own strange secrets.

"What is that?" Elena asked, stopping just before we reached the archway leading to the outer courtyard. In the snow, under a barren hedge, there was a pile of dark cloth. Just beyond the empress's enchanted barrier.

Aurora and the Bavarian princesses were walking back to join us. They spotted the cloth at the same time. Aurora reached out and picked it up, shaking the snow off.

Her hands passed easily through the empress's wards. It was good to know I had one roommate with no supernatural abilities.

"It looks like a woman's shawl," I said. "Someone must be very cold."

Aurora held it up. The black wool was fringed and dotted with tiny pearls. "It's beautiful. I'm keeping it."

"It's dirty," I said. "Not only has it been lying here in the snow, it also looks valuable. Someone will be looking for it."

Aurora wrapped herself up in it and spun around. "Ugh, it smells horrible!" She unwrapped it and threw it toward me, but it fell to the ground.

I sighed and picked it back up, folding it carefully. "We should give it to Sister Anna. Maybe she can clean it up and find its owner."

The shawl did have a peculiar smell to it. An earthy smell of decay. My heart pounded in my ears and I felt dizzy. It smelled of a tomb.

"Katerina?" Elena was staring at me.

I took a deep breath. There was a logical explanation. I was certainly mistaken. The shawl had probably been lying under that shrub all winter. It probably just smelled because it had been outside in the damp for so long, not because a dead person had been wearing it.

"Katerina Alexandrovna! What is wrong with you? You look pale as a ghost!"

I looked at Elena and tried to shrug nonchalantly. "I just felt a chill all of a sudden. Let's hurry and catch up with the others."

"Should we take the shawl or not?" Elena looked doubtful.

I sighed and hesitated. "It would be the right thing to do."

"Well, come on, then. I'm starting to lose feeling in my hands out here."

"Perhaps the cook will make hot cocoa for us when we return," Augusta said hopefully.

Elena grinned. "He's very handsome, for a cook, is he not? Aurora says he can't be more than twenty, but I think he's much older."

I held my tongue. It was the glamour that made him appear so young. He looked to me like a man in his late thirties or early forties, but as a member of the fae, he could have been over a hundred years old. "Leave him alone, Elena." I started walking, leaving her behind.

Her laughter followed me as I hurried to catch up with the others, the shawl bundled up in my arms.

Sister Anna, who had not even noticed our absence, took the shawl disdainfully. "One would certainly hope the woman who lost her shawl was not in the habit of losing her clothing in the woods frequently."

Elena giggled and whispered to me, "Perhaps we should tell her we found a pair of drawers in the woods as well."

I rolled my eyes but grinned. Poor Sister Anna.

Alix sat in the dining hall by herself that evening, apparently deep in thought. I worried about her, even without Elena being able to cast any charms on her. I left Elena chatting with Erzsebet and approached Alix.

She looked up but said nothing.

"Were the winters at Hesse-Darmstadt as cold as the winters here in St. Petersburg?"

She shrugged and looked intently into her cup of cocoa.

"I guess it is difficult to adjust to living away from home for the first time. Do you hear often from your family?"

Alix finally looked up at me. "What do you want, Katerina Alexandrovna? I'd like to be left in peace."

"Why must you be so mysterious?" I asked, growing impatient with her. "You know about the ghost. Don't you wish to help get rid of her? And protect the students?"

"She is not harming anyone," the princess said stubbornly.

"But she has before, and I'm certain it won't be long before someone else gets hurt. Please help me, Alix. You know something that you're not telling me."

"Why? Why can't you just leave me alone?"

She didn't cry, but looked as if she might. Without another word, she stood up and left.

Disappointed and just a little bit puzzled, I rejoined Elena and Erzsebet. I had learned nothing about Princess Alix of Hesse-Darmstadt. She was almost as much of a mystery as the Smolny ghost.

CHAPTER THIRTY-TWO

It was the height of the St. Petersburg winter season, and most of the girls bemoaned the balls and ballets we were missing. Pepita's staging of the ballet *The Sleeping Beauty* had debuted at the Mariinsky Theater. It was said even the tsar liked it, although his comments were not effusive enough to please its composer, Tchaikovsky. There was a much-talked-about ball, given by Grand Duchess Ella, where everyone wore emeralds. Elena sulked and obsessed over whom the tsarevitch had danced with. Alix sulked too, in her own dark corner of our room.

It was also the full moon, and I contemplated how much of an effect on my roommates that had.

I sat on my cot and sulked myself, wondering what George Alexandrovich was up to in Paris. I wondered exactly what dark magic he was learning.

"The Black Lily has great plans for him."

195

I sighed and rubbed my temples. *Danilo, do not tease me if you are not going to tell me everything you know.*

His laugh filled my head. *"They are waiting for an auspicious time to hold their great ritual. And then George will be initiated into their Inner Circle."*

Their Inner Circle? Are they organized in a similar fashion as the Order of St. John?

"Very similar. As are most occult orders these days."

Danilo, you wouldn't know who the current Koldun is for the Order of St. John, would you?

He laughed again. *"Your precious George would not tell you?"*

I was a little mad at myself for not thinking to ask George when I saw him.

"I do not know who the Koldun is, Duchess. That is one of their most closely guarded secrets."

I sighed. The crown prince was no help at all. It did concern me, though, that he knew George would one day become the next Koldun, and what would Danilo do with that information? What could he do?

Alix and Elena were both deeply absorbed in either their own thoughts or their geography books. I couldn't tell which. I didn't dare disturb them to say I was going to the library.

"Watch out for the ghost, Duchess." Danilo was still listening to my thoughts.

Thank you kindly for your concern, but I must learn who she is.

"Why? There is nothing you can do about the ghost while you are safe behind the empress's spell."

There has to be something, Your Highness. I can't let her hurt anyone else.

There was no answer, which surprised me. Only silence in my head. Where had the crown prince gone?

It was nice having my thoughts to myself again as I hurried to the library. It seemed as if Danilo had been in my head more and more often over the past few weeks. I was getting tired of his interruptions at the most inopportune times.

A frightened girl from the Blue Form came running out of the library. "There's something horrible in there!" she cried, grabbing my arms. I hugged her to me, trying to calm her down.

"What did you see?"

"Nothing, but something is still in there! I'm not crazy! I heard it laugh!"

I pulled away from her to look at her closely. "Did anything hurt you?"

She shook her head. "Please don't tell the headmistress! I don't want her to think I'm crazy!"

"You are not crazy. Run down to the kitchen and see if the cook has something warm and sweet for you to munch on."

"Do you think he'd let me?"

"Tell him that Katerina Alexandrovna sent you," I said, smiling kindly.

She started downstairs, but turned back. "You're not going in there, are you?"

"Just to get a book. I'll be right back out."

She shuddered and hurried down the stairs toward the kitchen. I hoped Sucre would be helpful and make her feel better.

The library was freezing. The ghost was there. I took a step into the room. "I'm not here to hurt you. I just want to find out who you are. Were you a student at Smolny?"

The bookcase began to shake. I took a tiny step back, closer to the door, and the shaking stopped. Was I making her nervous?

"I wish there was a way we could communicate," I said. "You could tell me what your name is, and how old you were when you—"

A heavy force came out of nowhere and knocked me on the side of the head. I fell to the floor in a daze.

The room began to spin slightly.

"Katerina? What have you done now, my beloved?" Danilo's voice was sarcastic.

I felt like someone was kicking me in the ribs. I curled up on the floor, holding very still, and trying very hard not to cry out. I'd never felt pain like this before. I had to get out of the room. Trying to reason with a ghost was one of the stupidest things I'd ever done.

Over and over, the cold force slammed into me, knocking the wind out of me. An angry young girl's voice hissed around my head. *"I don't want to talk about it. I don't want to talk about it."*

I tried to crawl back out of the library. There was a dull roar in my ears, like a winter storm had kicked up inside the tiny room.

"I don't want to talk about it. I don't want to talk about it." Books began to tumble off the shelves.

She was throwing a temper tantrum.

"It's all right," I groaned, holding my side. "You don't have to talk about it." I pushed myself up carefully and stepped back out of the room. I could not take in a very deep breath without pain. I knew it had been foolish of me to try to deal with the ghost alone, but now I was furious. From the hallway I whispered to her, "Once I find out who you are, I'll find the means to send you away. I will not let you hurt anyone here anymore."

CHAPTER THIRTY-THREE

∿

I went to the kitchen to see if the Blue Form girl was feeling better. The kitchen staff was busy scrubbing pots and pans. I found Sucre at the kitchen table studying an almanac.

"*Bonsoir*, Monsieur Sucre."

"But it is not possible," Sucre muttered to himself. He looked up and saw me. "Ah, it is the Dark Duchess," he said, sighing. "*Comment allez-vous*, Mademoiselle?"

"I am well, Monsieur Sucre. What are you studying?"

He frowned and pushed the almanac away. "It is nothing. What brings you to the kitchen? Are you wanting something to eat?"

"No, Monsieur. I wanted to see if a young girl had come to see you. She was badly frightened by the ghost."

Sucre's mutterings were in a dialect I could not understand. His eyes seemed to glow a brighter blue than before. "Why doesn't the headmistress lock up that damned room? You children have no business disturbing that . . . that thing that lives in there."

"But she doesn't just stay in the library. She's been in my room. And here in the kitchen too."

Sucre looked as if he were about to say something, but was cut short by a loud shriek from the back of the pantry. His face grew dark as he rose from the table to investigate.

I caught a glimpse of the piece of paper tucked into the almanac he'd been reading. The handwriting was barely legible: *Wolf's Heart*. The almanac was turned to March, with the eighth day circled. I shuddered, not knowing if it was a recipe or some faerie ritual.

I followed Sucre to the pantry and peeked through the crowd, wondering if the ghost had scared someone again.

Two women sank to the floor, crying and crossing themselves.

Next to them, the kitchen girl, the one who'd been injured by the ghost the night of the Smolny Ball, lay dead.

Sucre quickly shooed everyone out of the pantry and closed the door. I could see his glamour straining to seal the door shut, as he worked his faerie magic on the kitchen staff. He pulled a loaf of brown bread out of the oven, the steam rising from its warm surface.

The scent was heavenly, but it could not make me forget what I saw. A cold, pale body. The girl's black eyes glassy and vacant like a doll's.

The others, however, were easily fooled. I watched them dig into the bread hungrily. They were soon smiling and whistling as they returned to work.

I glared at the cook. "What are you going to do about her?"

"I will move her when the others leave."

"What happened exactly? Can a ghost actually kill someone? Now will you try to get rid of her?"

"You would be wise to tell no one what you've seen here, Duchess." Sucre smiled a little, baring his tiny, sharp, pointy teeth. Sucre was too tall, too slender to be completely human. I wondered why no one else had ever noticed this. Even hidden behind a large flour- and sugar-dusted apron. His raven-black hair was long and pulled back in a queue like some wild Romantic poet's.

"But we have to warn the others—"

Sucre's eyes flashed a deep, dark sapphire blue, dark as midnight. "Not a word. I will take care of this without your assistance, Mademoiselle."

Too frightened and too angry to say anything more, I merely nodded and heard his low, soft laughter behind me as I hurried back to my room. How dare he laugh at a time like this? The faerie was heartless.

Aurora was curled up in her bed, studying her German grammar book with extreme studiousness. Elena had pressed herself up against the tiny window and was staring out into the darkness.

"What is it?" I asked, immediately feeling the prickling on the back of my neck again.

Elena shook her head slowly. "We don't know. There was a noise outside like someone crying. Alix thought it was a student."

"And she went to find out? How foolish!" I was filled with dread. Dread that the ghost could appear outside of the school. If that was possible, she was more powerful than I'd imagined.

Elena grinned and turned away from the window. "Alix

didn't say anything. We were both looking out the window, and I couldn't see anything, and then all of a sudden she left. She did the strangest thing, though. She pulled the box out from under her bed, unrolled the red ribbon, and took it with her."

I grabbed my woolen cloak. "Are you coming?"

"We don't know who or what is out there," Elena said. "It's far too dangerous." She shrugged and plopped back down on her cot, picking up her book. "Besides, I'm sure Alix will be back soon," she said with a dramatic sigh. "Unfortunately."

I rolled my eyes and left, regretting that their sugar-coated truce hadn't lasted very long. I crept down the stairs as quietly as possible, wondering if Alix had been bold enough to leave the building.

She hadn't. I found her just inside the front door. She looked at me. "There is a great evil outside, Katerina Alexandrovna," she whispered.

"In the courtyard?" I could feel the panic rising up inside. Nothing should have been able to get past the empress's spell. Had the spell failed?

Alix shook her head. "I think it's in the woods just past the courtyard. I don't think you should go out there."

"Can you see it?" My mind was racing. If it wasn't the ghost, could it be that Konstantin had found me? I wished that George could hear me. If the lich tsar was out there, Tsar Alexander needed to be warned. "What did he look like?"

"He?" Alix frowned. "I did not get a good look, but it sounded to me as if the thing was female."

"Thing? Female?" I brushed past her and opened wide the front door.

"Katerina, don't! Stay inside!" Alix whispered, her fingers digging into my arm.

CHAPTER THIRTY-FOUR

❧

"Katerina Alexandrovna!" Alix whispered. "Have you gone mad? It's too risky to go out there!"

I turned on her. "And what were *you* going to do? Why are you here, Your Highness?"

Her jaw dropped a little, and she looked as if she were about to say something, but changed her mind.

"Alix, whatever special powers you normally have, I don't think they will work right now the way you want them to."

"What do you know of special powers?" she whispered, her blue eyes suddenly large and bright in the light of the full moon.

I took a deep breath. "Your red ribbon. What is it for?"

She frowned, and I could have sworn I heard her growl. "It would be dangerous for you to know, Duchess."

My smile was grim. "I know lots of dangerous things."

We both were startled by a moan just outside of the courtyard. Princess Alix was right. It sounded female. And hungry. And sad.

I took a step out into the snow-covered yard. "Hello?" I whispered.

"Mistressss." The voice was vaguely familiar. And definitely female.

"*Mon Dieu.*" I felt the blood drain from my face, and grew sick to my stomach. This could not be happening. Not again. "Oh no," I whispered.

"*Merde,*" Alix agreed, nodding. But she followed me to edge of the courtyard, to the edge of the empress's invisible barrier. "Who is it?" the princess asked.

The figure stepped out from the shadows into the moonlight and moaned softly.

I sighed unhappily. "That is Madame Metcherskey, a former teacher here at Smolny."

Madame Metcherskey, or what used to be her, stumbled toward us, clutching her burial shroud. She turned her dull, lifeless eyes toward me and reached out with pale, blue hands. "Mistressss," she hissed. "What have you done to me?"

CHAPTER THIRTY-FIVE

⟡

"Katerina Alexandrovna!" Alix cried out hoarsely. "What have you done? This is an abomination!"

I grabbed her. "You must swear not to tell another soul about this."

She tried to back away from me, pale and shaking her head. "You are a wicked person! I would expect something like this from Elena, but not you."

"I have not done this on purpose. Please, Alix. Please believe me."

"Mistressss . . ." Madame Metcherskey stumbled toward us, but was kept out by the magic barrier. "You must release me." Her face and lips were completely colorless. My heart hurt to look at her. And I feared that the noise she was making would wake the headmistress. There was a malice in her eyes that I'd never seen when she was alive. I knew she had never liked me when she lived, and now she'd never forgive me for doing this to her.

Alix shook her head. "No, not even Elena could do something so evil. You must fix it, Katerina."

"I can't. But I have to get her somewhere safe." I took a step forward. "Madame Metcherskey, you need to go see someone who may be able to help you. He has helped me before."

Alix's eyes grew even larger. "You've done this before? Katerina Alexandrovna, your soul must belong with the damned!"

"Mistresss, release me from your bidding. I have unfinished work to complete."

Madame Metcherskey did not behave the same way Count Chermenensky had. I wasn't sure if what had happened to her was the same thing that had happened to him. How could I raise the dead without realizing how I was doing it? I still did not know much about revenants and ghouls, but I was too afraid to let her roam the streets of St. Petersburg on her own. I took a deep breath. "No, Madame. You must do as I tell you. Go to the office of the Tibetan doctor, Pyotr Badmaev, on Nevski Prospekt. He will be able to keep you safe."

Madame Metcherskey's dark eyes narrowed and she growled. It did not sound human. Alix shrank back behind me and started to cry. But I was almost certain Madame could not harm me. I took my cloak and tossed it to her. I wished I could help her cover up, but I could not touch her through the empress's barrier. The image of the frozen shawl in the garden flashed before me. It must have been hers, I thought with a shudder. How long had it been since she'd risen from her grave?

I spoke as firmly as I could, even though I was shaking with fear and shivering with cold. "Go and speak with Dr. Badmaev. Use the servant entrance. Tell him I sent you."

I hoped he would not be too angry. I hoped the doctor would be able to calm her down. Count Chermenensky had usually been docile as long as he did not feel threatened.

Madame closed her eyes, as if she were fighting with herself. "As you wish, Mistresssss," she hissed, and slowly shuffled toward the front gates.

Alix and I both held our breaths as we watched her disappear into the darkness, and then we hurried back inside. We closed the front door and leaned against the inside, sighing with relief.

Princess Alix turned to me, a chilling look in her eye. "I promise you, Katerina Alexandrovna, you will be punished for your wicked deeds. And if you are consorting with the devil, I swear on my mother's grave, I will kill you myself."

Stunned, I only stared at her as she walked quickly and silently back up the staircase to our room. I did not know what I could say to explain or defend myself to her. Necromancy was a wicked art. And I abhorred the thought of what I'd done to Madame Metcherskey. Even if it hadn't been on purpose. I had never been quite sure how I had brought Count Chermenensky back from the grave either. Did I simply have to wish them back to life? I did not know. And I couldn't let it happen again.

I rubbed my temples. I was cold and tired, but I was not sure if I could trust Alix anymore. Our room was dark when I returned. Both Elena and Aurora appeared to be sleeping in their cots. I did not think Alix was asleep, though. I sat down and huddled under my blanket, thankful at last for the warmth, but too worried to rest myself. After a long time,

Alix's breathing slowed as she fell into a deep sleep. Elena was restless, tossing and turning, and even whimpering at times while she dreamt. It was a long, black night as I watched all of them and wondered if Madame Metcherskey had made it to Dr. Badmaev's safely.

CHAPTER THIRTY-SIX

❧

"Katerina! Katerina Alexandrovna!" Elena was shaking me awake.

I had fallen asleep sitting up in my cot, leaning up against the wall. I tried to rub the soreness out of my neck.

"You will be late for breakfast." Elena dug through my trunk and threw my white school apron at me. "What happened with you and Alix last night?"

I glanced over at Alix's empty cot. She must have been in a hurry to leave our room that morning. I sighed, trying to lose the tightness in my chest. There had been no hint of a joke or teasing in her threat the previous night. I would have to be wary of her from now on.

"Katerina?" Elena still stood at my bed, looking at me questioningly.

"Alix heard a noise outside, but we saw nothing. It must have been an animal." Elena did not need to know about Ma-

210

dame Metcherskey. How would I be able to keep Alix from telling anyone? How could I convince her that she didn't see what she thought she saw?

I took a deep breath. "I think she must have had a nightmare. Alix kept tossing and turning, muttering about unholy things. That is why I was sitting up. I was afraid she would harm herself with her thrashing about."

"Really?" Elena looked extremely interested.

"Maybe the ghost was stirring up trouble again. Did you have strange dreams last night as well?"

Elena shook her head. "I slept peacefully." She finished putting her hair up and tied on her apron.

"Then I don't know what caused her distress." I shrugged, and hurried to finish getting dressed. Lying to Elena came so easily, it barely pricked my conscience anymore. What kind of person was I becoming?

I dashed downstairs with Elena to the dining room. Sucre was placing baskets of hot biscuits on the table. He seemed oblivious of the several students gazing up at him with starry looks in their eyes.

With the most polite nod, he handed me a biscuit. "Duchess, you seem to find yourself in more and more trouble every time I see you."

"*Merci*, Monsieur." I placed the biscuit on my plate as I sat down at the end of the table.

"First it was a ghost, and now you are plagued with the undead as well?" He shook his head, smiling viciously.

I glanced around in alarm and realized that no one else would hear the faerie speak unless he wished them to. Everyone was enjoying the enchanted breakfast in ignorant bliss. I pushed the biscuit to the side of my plate, and reached for my tea. "How did you know?"

"Duchess, your creature made enough noise to wake the true dead last night. All of the Dark Court knows there is a newly risen ghoul walking the streets of St. Petersburg."

"What about the empress and the Light Court?"

He nodded. "It is only a matter of time. Yes, your empress will know soon enough."

"It's not my fault," I said, cringing even as I said the words. "I don't know how it happened." The empress was not fond of me already. And now this? She would tell the tsar, and I would be sent to Siberia for certain this time. I looked up at the fae cook, who smelled of cinnamon and honey. "Monsieur Sucre, tell me the truth. To which court do you belong?"

The cook's eyes flashed from light blue to cobalt. "I serve whichever court serves me best," he said softly. "And at this time, it serves me best to belong to Her Imperial Majesty."

"You are not only here to protect us from the ghost, are you?" My eyes narrowed. "You were sent here for another purpose."

"Be careful, Duchess. It would be safer for you if you were not so inquisitive."

I swallowed my tea, and tried to calm my suspicions. I had other things to worry about that were more pressing. "What did you do with the poor kitchen girl?"

"I told you not to worry about that." He placed an extra biscuit on Augusta's plate, which she took happily. "But yes, she was killed by the ghost. And yes, I have sent her body back to the village where she came from. Her family will think she died from influenza."

I sighed, wishing we'd been able to stop the ghost before

something like this had happened. "Why was she so angry? And why would she have gone after Olga?"

"Shouldn't you be more concerned with your own creature?" Sucre asked.

"Are you going to tell the empress about Madame Metcherskey?"

"Of course not, Duchess. She will find out long before I have a chance to speak with her."

I wanted to cry. "I don't suppose you have any idea what I should do with her."

"Sending her to the Tibetan was probably not a wise choice. She will draw much attention to him."

The thought frightened me. "Will he be in danger?"

"It's too late to worry about that. And now there is a student here that knows what you are. What will you do about her?"

I almost choked on my tea. I glared at Monsieur Sucre. "Is there any secret at Smolny you do not know?"

He chuckled as he turned to head back into the kitchen. "I would not want to be in your shoes right now, Duchess."

I glanced down our long dining table. As I had suspected, no one had noticed my conversation with Sucre. Not even the headmistress, who seemed to be extremely fascinated with whatever Sister Anna was saying to her. But I spotted Alix, staring straight at me.

She had seen me speak with Sucre. She could see through his glamour just as well as I could. The Hessian princess had her eyes fixed on me with a mixture of revulsion and sadness. There was nothing I could do but smile sweetly back. As I finished my breakfast, I prayed she had not been serious when she had threatened to kill me.

CHAPTER THIRTY-SEVEN

～◎～

That night I had a terrible dream, not about the ghost, or Madame Metcherskey, or Princess Alix, but about George Alexandrovich. He was surrounded by a circle of crimson-robed men who were chanting something in low, deep tones. I couldn't make out what they were saying. George held a black candle in his hands, and was staring intently into its flame. His sapphire-blue eyes reflected the candlelight. The men's chanting grew louder before it suddenly stopped. Then George blew the candle out, leaving everyone in total darkness.

I could smell the burning wick and the smoky air burned the back of my throat. I heard his soft voice. "Isn't this what you wanted, Katiya?"

I woke up with a start and was startled to find tears rolling down my cheeks. I glanced across the room in the dim moonlight, and could make out Elena and Alix sleeping soundly in their own cots. I took a deep breath. It was just a ridiculous dream, I told myself, wiping the tears from my face. It didn't mean anything.

I tried to go back to sleep but was haunted by George's face illuminated by the black candle. He had looked thinner, his cheeks sunken and pale. Like a corpse. Why would he think I wanted him to become a black mage? I closed my eyes. Did he believe I wished that he belonged to the Dark Court as I did?

You are being ridiculous, Katerina Alexandrovna, I told myself. The grand duke was most likely pretending to be a dark wizard in order to spy on them for his father. The tsar had sent him to Paris to discover a way to prevent the return of Konstantin. George was strong. He would not be tempted by the Order of the Black Lily.

The walls in our dark room seemed to close in on me, and I had difficulty breathing. It was too stuffy, and I felt like I had to escape. It was the darkness itself pressing in. I scrambled out of bed and fumbled for my robe and slippers. I didn't know where I was going, but I had to get out of there. I held my breath as Aurora shifted in her sleep, but she did not awaken. Elena and Alix snored softly. Carefully, I tiptoed out of our room and down the hallway.

I did not even think about where I was going until I ended up at the door to the library. I took a deep breath and pushed the heavy door open. It didn't make a sound.

It was colder in the library than it had been in the hallway. I couldn't help shivering. But I did not see or hear the ghost. Whether she was there watching and waiting for me, I could not tell. "Why won't you show yourself?" I whispered, scared I would wake the headmistress or one of the students.

There was no answer. No sense that anything unnatural was present in the tiny room. Other than the chill.

"Looking for trouble, Duchess? I thought I told you to stay away from the library."

I nearly jumped out of my skin, and glared at Sucre, who was leaning in the doorway, smiling at me menacingly.

I pulled my robe closer around me. "I had a bad dream, and wanted to get a book to distract myself."

"You don't fool anyone, Duchess." Sucre stood up straighter, and folded his arms across his chest. "I am glad you were not in your room, actually. I came to tell you that you have visitors. At the front gates."

"In the middle of the night? Don't be ridiculous. And what would you have done if I'd been asleep? Surely you would not have entered a room full of sleeping girls."

Sucre smiled. "A glamour would have easily persuaded your friends that you were talking and walking in your sleep. Don't you want to know who your visitors are?"

My heart leapt for just half a heartbeat, and I immediately felt stupid for thinking of George Alexandrovich. What reason would he have to sneak into Smolny Institute when he was thousands of miles away?

"I hate to disappoint you, my love," the crown prince's lazy voice filled my head.

No. *Danilo? Why are you here?* Alarmed and suspicious now, I followed Sucre down the stairs and into the kitchen, still warm from the dying hearth fire. As he opened the outside door, however, a gust blew through, killing the flames. He stepped back, holding the door open for me.

"I feel it is necessary to protect you from your newest creature."

As I looked out into the darkness, I saw two figures standing at the edge of the courtyard, just beyond the barrier of the empress's spell. Sucre struck a match and the figures' faces were illuminated: Dr. Badmaev and Madame Metcherskey. Madame was looking even paler than before. The Tibetan doctor did not look quite his normal color either. *"Mon Dieu!"* was all I could think to say when I saw the pair. The crown prince stepped out of the shadows as well.

"Good evening, my beloved." I could see Danilo smirking even by the light of the tiny flame.

"Stop calling me that," I said to the crown prince, but I glared at Sucre. He enjoyed his little games too much. I stepped forward to greet Dr. Badmaev, but Madame Metcherskey hissed when I moved toward them. I froze.

Dr. Badmaev shook his head. "I am sorry, Duchess. She is very strong, and insists that she needs to be here. If you listen to her story, I think you will agree with her."

"Madame?" I looked at her.

"You must release me, Mistresssss. I still have tasks of my own to complete. She is in danger." Madame had been pulling on her sleeves. The edges were frayed, and looked as if they'd been chewed on. I tried very hard not to shudder.

"Who is in danger?" I asked.

Madame stood ramrod straight, her hands clasped firmly in front of her. "I was told to protect her. I am here to watch her."

"Can you tell me who she is?" I pressed, but Madame stared straight ahead, her eyes now empty and colorless. I looked at Dr. Badmaev. "Has she told you anything else?"

He shrugged. "Only that there is a Smolny student that she has been protecting for scores of years."

217

"Scores? No one has been here that long." But there was, I realized, as the back of my neck prickled with fear. "Madame? Are you protecting the ghost? Who is she?"

Madame continued to stare straight ahead and wring her hands. Slowly, her eyes focused on me. "I promised not to tell a soul. She must be kept from harm."

"What harm, Madame? She is a danger to everyone at Smolny. She has already killed someone."

"Duchess," Sucre leaned over and said in a soft voice, "I do not think even you can command her to break her vow. You must allow her to complete her mission."

"You've known about her all these years?" I asked Madame. "Why wasn't a priest consulted for an exorcism?"

Madame Metcherskey's face wrinkled into a scowl. "There were several attempts to send her soul on. Every attempt . . . failed."

"You kept her from disturbing us all this time, didn't you? She didn't start causing trouble until after you became ill and left."

"She is looking for me, Mistressss. If you had not called me back from the grave, I would have been here in spirit and would have been able to guide her to a safe place."

A stab of guilt twisted in my gut. Not only had I disturbed Madame's soul, but I had also prevented her from helping another. Everything the ghost had done to terrorize the students at Smolny, it was all my fault. "What can we do now, Madame?"

She drew herself up straighter. "We must do God's will. You must pray for our souls. Each and every one of us. I must see her."

I looked from Dr. Badmaev to Sucre in alarm. "But you can't come inside, Madame. The empress's spell will prevent you."

"I must be allowed to see her. I must talk to her, to calm her fears." She took a step toward me. Immediately there was a burst of light and she was pushed backward.

Dr. Badmaev gently helped her to stand. "Madame, we must think of another way."

"Monsieur Sucre?" I asked. "Is there a glamour you could disguise her with?" I was freezing and longed to forget all of this and crawl back into my bed.

Sucre shook his head. "No glamour would allow her to get past the empress's spell, Duchess."

I turned to look at Dr. Badmaev. It was a little awkward, after our last conversation in the cemetery. And there had been times when I'd wondered if I'd made a mistake to turn his offer down. But he smiled at me with his usual kind smile.

Madame Metcherskey was fretting and chewing on her fingernails, which were blackened from the wards. "I must see her now," she said.

"You know there is a way we can solve this, beloved," Danilo said. "Our blood bond is more powerful than the empress's spell. We can use it to help deal with your ghost problem."

"No," I said. "We can't just tear the wards apart. What would the empress say?"

Danilo laughed. "You are just afraid she won't let you marry her son. It's too late for that already, beloved."

My cheeks grew hot even in the icy night air. I hated that the crown prince was right. The empress already disliked me. Destroying her wards would not change anything between us.

"Are you certain our bond is strong enough for this?" The crown prince shrugged carelessly. I had no other choice. I worried that I was making a deal with the devil, but finally nodded. "What do you need me to do?"

"This may hurt a bit, Duchess. I need your blood."

Sucre took a kitchen knife I had not realized he was holding and grabbed my hand before I realized what he meant to do.

"Ouch!" Sucre had stabbed my palm, and a few drops of blood dripped onto the snow. He and Danilo had planned this all along.

"Now give me your hand." The crown prince held his hand out, just touching the edge of the barrier. There was nothing to see, but we could sense the power of the empress's spell between us. No one should have been able to pass through.

I lifted my hand toward him, and Danilo took it. There was a sharp tingling, not just from the injury, but also from the empress's spell as my hand passed through it.

Danilo took my hand and held my palm up to his mouth. I don't think I had truly realized until that moment how strong our blood bond was. The spell fabric wobbled and surged as Danilo drank my blood. He closed his eyes, enjoying every second of it. He drank as if he'd been dying of thirst.

I gasped at the pull I felt toward him. There was no other way, I kept telling myself. I had to get Madame Metcherskey inside to the ghost. Before anyone else was hurt.

The tingling subsided and Danilo let go of my hand with a satisfied sigh. He took a step toward me. The barrier was gone. We had torn down the empress's magic.

Moving away from the crown prince, I reached out and took my dead instructor's arm. "Come with me, Madame."

"I know the way, Mistressss." She jerked her cold arm out of my grip and pushed past me.

"I will take my leave now," Dr. Badmaev said, backing up. "Good night, Duchess. And good luck to you." He touched his hat and nodded to Sucre. "Monsieur."

"*Bonne nuit*," Sucre said, as if he were saying goodbye to a guest at a dinner party.

We hurried after Madame toward the library. She had no need for light, as she seemed to know instinctively where she was going. I shuddered, afraid of what the ghost's reaction would be. Would she truly be soothed by the presence of Madame?

Madame had already stepped into the library when we reached the doorway. She stood very still in the center of the room, with her eyes closed.

I took a step over the threshold and felt the cold hatred of the ghost immediately.

Madame's eyes flew open and she turned to me. "Get out of here, Mistressss."

"Are you all right?" I couldn't help asking. "Does she recognize you?"

"Everything will be fine. But you must leave. Now."

Before I could take a step back, I was pulled into the hallway by the crown prince. "This might be interesting, Duchess."

Madame raised her arms up. "I have kept you safe, and I have kept your secret. You must listen to me now. You must stop frightening the students."

There was a loud moan that grew into a wail. The bookcase began to shake and I feared that the others would wake up. Books began to topple off the shelves onto the floor. The wail grew louder and louder still. I had to cover my ears.

Madame did not move. She stood in the center of the room, holding her arms out as if to welcome a child. "You must listen to me now. You must trust me."

The wailing went on and on, and I could not figure out why the entire school had not come running to the library. I looked from Sucre to the crown prince. Danilo shook his head. "Madame, you must get her to stop!"

I took a step back into the library, not sure how I was going to help, but wanting desperately to do something to make the wailing and the shaking end.

Madame turned to look at me again with a hiss. "You should not have done that, Mistressss."

And then all hell broke loose.

CHAPTER THIRTY-EIGHT

The bookcases themselves began to fall over. Madame did not move, but she started to sing in a low, shaky voice. I stepped closer to listen, but could not make out the words. It sounded like an old Russian lullaby.

I heard Sucre's warning in a low voice behind me. "Duchess, get down!"

I turned in time to see a white, furry mass hurtling in my direction. I screamed and dropped to the floor. It was an enormous wolf, and it dove straight for Madame Metcherskey.

"Stop!" I screamed. I didn't care anymore if I woke every last person in the institute. I screamed until I was hoarse.

Madame never stopped singing. Not until the wolf had ripped her throat out.

The wolf held fast to Madame, growling low. Madame did not fight or struggle at all.

"Get a stick or something! Can't you stop it?" I cried,

scrambling backward out of the room on my hands and knees. "Kill it! Hurry!"

Sucre shook his head. "It's too late to save her, Duchess." He held out his hand to me but I pushed it away.

I heard a sickening crunch as the wolf's jaws clamped down on Madame's neck. My stomach heaved. Danilo pulled me up and curved me toward him so I wouldn't see.

"I wish I could throw a glamour over all of this for you," Sucre said, "but it's taking everything I have to keep the noise from reaching the other rooms."

I shook my head, not even caring that I was sobbing into the crown prince's shoulder. "It's all my fault. I brought Madame back with my horrible curse. She deserved so much better than this."

The bookcase stopped shaking, and the ghost stopped wailing too. I did not know if the wolf had scared off the ghost or not. But the wolf's terrible business was finished. It let go of Madame's neck, her spine completely severed. There was no blood since she had already been dead, but there was a terrible stench. I could not hold my stomach contents in anymore. I pushed away from the crown prince and retched in the corner.

The wolf rocked back on its haunches, preparing to leap. It stared at me with its yellow eyes and I felt a shiver run down my spine. It was as if the wolf knew me.

"Get out of the way!" Sucre said, as the wolf leapt over us and ran down the hallway. With a loud crash, it broke through the large window at the stairwell landing. It was a long drop to the snow-covered ground below.

We ran to the end of the hallway and looked out. "Careful

of the glass, Duchess," Sucre warned. The wolf was nowhere to be seen. It had landed on all four paws below us, then run off into the woods.

I looked around and back down the hall, toward the library. "What a mess!"

"No one will see it. I will make sure of it." Sucre looked me up and down. "You have caused enough trouble for the night. Clean yourself up and get some rest."

"But—"

"Now, Duchess. The crown prince and I will take care of this."

Danilo looked at the library with disgust. "I'm not sure what you wish me to do, Monsieur."

I nodded, trying hard to hold back tears, so they would not see. It was no use. Sucre spotted a teardrop and touched a finger to my cheek. "Ah, the taste of sorrow and regret," he said, licking his finger. "Bittersweet."

I shuddered and hurried back to my room. I did not care if the headmistress found them or not.

It was close to dawn, and our room was dim and gray. Elena and Aurora were still snoring, but Alix's bed was empty. My heart skipped a beat, and I ran back down the hall to tell Sucre. She could be killed by the wolf if it spotted her.

"Monsieur! Alix is missing!"

"*Oui?*" He looked thoughtful. "Return to bed at once, Duchess. I will go and look for her."

"But—"

"I am here under the empress's orders to keep all the students at Smolny safe. You will be safe if you stay in your room. Your crown prince has already taken the remains to dispose of them. Everything will be back to normal in a few hours."

I wanted to laugh. What was normal anymore? A giant wolf had sneaked into Smolny and attacked my undead teacher. An undead teacher who had been trying to calm an angry adolescent ghost out of terrorizing the students. I shook my head and headed back to my room. I was too tired to argue any more with Sucre. I decided to trust him to bring Alix back safe.

CHAPTER THIRTY-NINE

❧

I woke up to see Elena and Aurora whispering at the doorway, peeking out into the hall.

"What is going on?" I said, sitting up immediately.

Elena turned around to look at me. "It's about time you woke up. It is almost noon!"

"*Mon Dieu!*" I jumped out of bed and quickly dressed. "Why did you not wake me? I've missed my morning classes!"

"Relax, Katerina Alexandrovna," Aurora said, rolling her eyes. "Classes have been cancelled today."

"What?" I dropped the shoe I was holding. My hand was shaking. Had the glamour not worked? Did the headmistress find out about Madame Metcherskey?

Elena turned around from her vigil in the hallway. "Monsieur Sucre is hunting a wolf on the grounds."

"And Alix is missing," Aurora said. "They think the wolf might have gotten her."

I saw Elena glance under Alix's bed, then at me. The room started to spin as I realized what she was thinking. Surely not.

Was Alix the wolf? She wouldn't have been able to change while the empress's spell was in place. But last night, I had broken the spell. And perhaps I'd unleashed something in the process.

"This is getting tedious," Aurora said, sighing. "I hope that they don't cancel any balls this spring if something happened to Alix."

"Balls?" I was confused.

Aurora Demidova looked at me as if I were stupid. "She's a daughter of the grand duke of Hesse. If anything happened to her, most of Europe would fall into mourning."

Elena nodded, sadly. "Like the crown prince of Austria last year."

"And that is what concerns you most?" I looked from Elena to Aurora. "A stupid ball?"

"The Winter Ball at the Yussupov Palace. My grandmother is taking me," Aurora said. "I'll die if I don't get to go."

Elena twirled around the room holding the edges of her apron up like a skirt. "I've written to Militza and asked if she would take me as well. All of the imperial family will be invited."

I finished getting dressed and pushed Aurora and Elena out of my way. I was tired of listening to them both. Alix was in danger. I had to reach Sucre and help him find her.

I passed the library on my way downstairs and peeked inside. The room had been cleaned up and straightened. It looked as if nothing had happened in there. No ghostly temper tantrum, no werewolf attack, no decapitated undead

Smolny teacher. It was still very cold in the room, however, and I could feel the ghost mourning Madame Metcherskey. Perhaps now that her soul had been released, she would be able to help the ghost as she had intended?

I took a step inside and was pushed back by a painful blast.

My heart sank. Madame Metcherskey had been unable to appease the ghost. I had hoped her spirit would be able to rest now, but would she rest if her task was still unfinished? The memory of last night's violence made me nauseous again.

The Bavarian sisters were sitting in the front parlor with several of the younger girls. Erzsebet jumped up out of her seat when she saw me. "Katerina! Isn't it terrible? I'm so frightened!"

I embraced her. "Everything will be all right. Monsieur Sucre and the Smolny guards will find the wolf and keep us all safe."

"Alix!" Augusta cried, getting up and running to the door. I saw a flash of a woolen cloak as someone walked quickly past the parlor.

I followed Augusta into the hall. She ran after Alix and asked, "Are you all right? We've been so worried about you!"

"I'm fine, but I need to lie down." Alix did not stop. She was in a hurry to get to our room. I hurried after her. Augusta shrugged and returned to the parlor with her classmates.

"Elena and Aurora are in there," I told Alix. "It might be more restful if you go to see Sister Anna and lie down in her study."

Alix turned to me with a glare. "Why should you care, Katerina Alexandrovna?"

I wasn't sure how much I could say. "Where have you been,

Alix? Did you know there was a wolf on the loose at Smolny? It came inside the school and . . ."

No one else knew it had attacked Madame Metcherskey. I did not know what Sucre's glamour had hidden and what everyone had seen.

"And what?" Alix looked me in the eye. "Did it hurt anyone? Did it attack any innocents?"

"Innocents?"

"There are some who believe a wolf will only attack what is pure evil. And if you say this wolf was inside Smolny, there must have been a very good reason for it. It must have been defending the students from something very evil. I would be very careful on the school grounds if I were you, Katerina Alexandrovna." She turned back around and headed to our room.

I ignored her threat. "Alix, you've been hurt. Please let me take you to see Sister Anna."

She shook her head. "I am going to bed. I will be fine."

"If you're certain," I said. And then I spotted something crumpled in her right fist. A scrap of red ribbon.

CHAPTER FORTY

❧

My heart pounded in my throat as I stared at Alix limping off to our room. I suddenly remembered she'd been injured earlier in the school year. No doubt she had tried to pass through the empress's wards. Which meant that she was not normal.

"Alix, wait." I hurried to catch up to her. "Tell me about the ribbon." I grabbed her right hand and held it up. I didn't want to believe it.

Her face was grim as her eyes bored into mine. She was trying to decide something.

I squeezed her hand. "I promise I won't tell anyone. As long as you're not in any danger."

She laughed bitterly and pulled my hand off of hers. "Katerina Alexandrovna, you have put everyone here at Smolny in danger. I am protecting the others from your evil deeds. If you do not repent, I will have to destroy you, just like I destroyed your minion."

I felt a cold, nauseous feeling in my stomach. "What are you talking about?" I whispered.

A pair of young girls from the Blue Form walked down the hall toward us, whispering and giggling. Alix looked at them and frowned. "Meet me in the library at midnight, if you wish to make atonement for your sins," she whispered. "Otherwise, I will hunt you down."

I could do nothing but stare at her stupidly as she brushed past the younger girls. She was serious about her threat to kill me. Like she had killed Madame Metcherskey. I did not want to believe that Alix had been the wolf that I saw attack Madame, but was it possible? If so, Sucre had to stop hunting the wolf. I had to tell him, but first I needed to know the whole truth. And I needed to explain to Alix about my curse. I knew we'd never exactly been friends, but I didn't want her to think of me as a monster. Honestly, though, I wondered if it was true.

How ironic, if she turned out to be a monster too.

I could not find Monsieur Sucre, but I left a note on the counter in the kitchen. I kept it as vague as possible in case any of the other kitchen servants picked it up.

> *Monsieur Sucre,*
> *You may call off your hunt. It is not what you*
> *think. She will not hurt anyone else at Smolny.*
>
> *—K*

❦

I avoided Elena the rest of that day. What if she found out Alix's secret? She was jealous of the tsarevitch's affection for

Alix. Could she do something to hurt Alix? And how much did Alix know about the Montenegrins? Was Elena in danger of Alix's holy wrath as well? I needed to talk with someone, but I didn't know whom to trust.

I sat next to the Bavarian sisters at dinner, listening to them gossip about Princess Yussupova's ball. "Our aunt Therese has come to St. Petersburg for the season and will attend the ball! She says in her letter that it will be more dazzling than the empress's ball last year at the Winter Palace!" Erzsebet said. "Oh, Katerina, don't you wish we could go?"

I smiled briefly and nodded, and finished my stuffed cabbage.

"She was just saying our aunt's dress is being made by a Parisian designer and it's red and it has more than one hundred tiny pearls sewn into the neckline!"

"Sounds lovely," I said, trying to participate in the dinner conversation. "Who is her escort?"

Both of the Bavarian princesses looked at each other and shrugged. Erzsebet leaned closer to me. "She did not tell us his name, but I believe it is one of the tsar's imperial guard. She is the guest of the Demidovs, so it may be one of the Demidov princes."

I cringed, remembering the death of my brother's friend Demidov last year. He had died at the hands of Princess Cantacuzene and her Dekebristi.

"Aurora is so jealous!" Augusta said with a giggle. "She is trying to get her grandmother to take her to the ball, but her grandmother says that her education is more important!"

I glanced up at the front of the room, where Madame Tomilov and the other faculty were finishing their dinners. Sucre was standing there, speaking with the headmistress.

They both looked over at me. I felt a queasy feeling in my stomach. It wasn't caused by the cabbage.

Madame Tomilov stood up and followed Sucre into the kitchen. I asked Erzsebet and Augusta to excuse me and put my dinner plate up.

I was making my way across the dining room, toward the kitchen doors, when Elena spotted me. "Katerina Alexandrovna! Where have you been?"

Then I saw Sucre leave the kitchen with a hunting rifle.

Had I betrayed Alix?

"I have to find Alix." If I waited until midnight to speak to her, it would be too late.

I hurried back to our room, but she was not there.

Aurora was curled up in her bed, studying her German. She didn't even bother to look up. "Would you mind closing that door? There's a horrible draft in the hallway."

"Have you seen Alix?"

She shook her head. "Not since yesterday, but she must have been here this afternoon. Some of her things are gone. Katerina Alexandrovna, will you please close that door?" She shivered.

I slammed the door behind me as I left. I did not know if Alix had run away or if someone had been rustling through her things. I knew Elena was dying of curiosity about the box Alix kept under her bed, but I did not think she would stoop to petty thievery.

I hoped Alix was keeping herself hidden. I decided to look for Sucre next. On my way back downstairs, I passed the library. The frightening cold seeped out from the room, touching me out in the hallway. I wanted to hurry past, thinking of the warmth in the kitchen, but I heard a sob inside, and stopped.

I peeked in the library and saw Augusta crying in the far corner. "*Mon Dieu*, what's wrong?" I stepped across the threshold and hurried over to her. "Augusta?"

"I can't stop the tears. It all seems so pointless."

I wrapped my arms around her. "What is so pointless?"

"Life. My life is pointless. I would be better off dead." She sniffed against my shoulder. "Everyone else would be better off if I were dead too."

I shook Augusta by the shoulders. "What are you talking about? You are being ridiculous!"

She shook her head. "I think I've known it all along, but it all became clear to me just now."

"Just now?" I looked around us, bewildered by her sudden emotions. "Since you came to the library? We've got to get you out of here." I stood up and tried to pull her up with me.

Augusta was not being helpful. She tucked her arms around her knees and rocked back and forth. "I'm so cold . . . so cold. . . ."

"Where is your sister? She could not bear it if something happened to you, Augusta. And what about your mother? Your father? Your two little brothers?"

She was crying but would not move. I grabbed her by the arms and began to drag her across the floor.

"Just let me be!" she sobbed.

"What is happening?" Elena stood in the doorway, eyes wide at the spectacle Augusta was making of herself.

"Don't just stand there," I hissed. "Help me get her out of this room!" I could feel an enormous gloom settling on my shoulders. As if life itself was too heavy a burden to carry. The ghost's despair was beginning to affect me as well. Was this how she had killed the kitchen servant? "We have to hurry."

Elena sighed heavily and grabbed one of Augusta's arms, while I took the other. Together we dragged her out of the room and into the hallway. She was still sobbing.

I dropped down to hug her. "You'll feel better now. It was only the ghost making you feel so miserable."

Elena stared at us and looked back into the library. "I thought the ghost was gone. I thought after the Christmas holiday, things seemed more like normal."

I shook my head. There was not enough time to explain everything. I got back up on my feet. "Do you know where Erzsebet is? I think she should take Augusta back to their room."

Elena glared at me. "Come on, Augusta. Let's see if we can get some hot cocoa before we go to bed."

"Let me get it for you," I offered. I needed to get to the kitchen anyway to find Sucre.

"*Merci*, Katerina," Augusta said. "You are the best friend."

Elena's look was venomous.

"Thank Elena too," I said quickly. "I would not have been able to pull you out if she hadn't been here to help."

Augusta threw her arms around Elena's neck. "*Merci!*"

Elena's face softened a little as she hugged the Bavarian princess back. "You'll bring me some cocoa too, won't you, Katerina?" she asked over Augusta's shoulder.

"Of course." I turned and hurried toward the kitchen.

The dining hall was empty and dark, with only two gaslights along the wall still lit. As I walked closer, I heard two deep voices speaking French within the kitchen. One was

Sucre. The other sounded familiar but I could not quite place it. Slowly and silently, I pushed the swinging door open, just an inch. I covered my mouth to hold in my shock. The fae cook was talking to Papus, the French wizard.

"Did you find the beast?" Papus was asking.

"Not yet, but I know who she is now," Sucre answered. "I suspected her all along, but now I have proof."

Papus shook his head. "And it is truly a student? The grand duke may not care, but I have a problem with killing a child."

"You need a werewolf's heart for the ritual, do you not? What does it matter about the body it comes from?" Sucre spit on the ground. "All werewolves are killers. I am sworn to hunt every last one down."

Papus sighed and nodded wisely. *"C'est vrai."*

"You will have your wolf's heart before the night is over."

"Magnificent. The grand duke will be pleased."

I felt my blood run cold in my veins. No. It wasn't possible. I blinked back tears and slowly, silently, let the swinging door close. I had to find Alix and warn her. Was George a part of this horrible plot? I refused to believe it. Papus had to be talking about one of the other grand dukes.

I couldn't even begin to think about what the Frenchman's words implied. I had to protect Alix first. I should never have trusted Sucre. Dark Court or Light, one should never trust the fae.

CHAPTER FORTY-ONE

❦

I searched all over the school grounds but could not find Alix. It was close to our curfew, and I knew Madame Tomilov would be checking to make sure everyone was in their beds. I had to return upstairs.

No one else was in our room. It was eerily, unnaturally quiet. I turned around and tried to leave, but the door was stuck fast. I could not escape.

Over the sound of a thousand fluttering bird wings, I heard the strands of Iphigenia's aria in my head, soft and mournful. I was overwhelmed with a sudden feeling of unbearable sadness. My legs were suddenly weak, and I slid to the floor. It hurt my heart and made my breath catch. "Why?" was all I could think to ask. "What made you want to die?" Because at that moment, dying was all I could think of as well.

There was no answer. Just the drumming of a heartbeat, slowing down. And slowing down. But it did not stop completely. It was maddening. I had the insane urge to stop it. Stop it. Stop the beating. Make it stop.

Filled with a bitterness that was tinged with regret, I thought of my parents and my brother. They did not need me to ruin their lives. There was no way I could protect them. None of the girls at Smolny had any need of me. Some of them were starting to fear me. I did not want to be considered a monster. I felt sick to my stomach. Like I'd swallowed something black and poisonous, and it was spreading slowly throughout my body, slowing me down. It spread from my chest to my belly, then down my arms and legs.

Stop the beating. I hugged my arms around my knees, rocking slowly, keeping in time with the heartbeat. The tiny candle flame on the bed stand was dying, and the shadows in our room were deepening. It was exhausting, listening to that torturous heartbeat, and I thought how easy it would be to fall asleep, how nice it would be not to have to wake up again.

"Come with me . . . ," a young girl's voice whispered above the muted heartbeat. "Katerina Alexandrovna . . . ," she coaxed. "It's beautiful here."

I heard her sigh. "So beautiful . . ."

I sighed too. I wanted to be someplace beautiful. My life was ugly. Full of pain and sickness and so much ugliness. I had to leave. I had to escape. A pale girl was slowly taking shape, and showing me the path. Her hair was so blond it was nearly white.

"Who are you?" I asked. "Please tell me your name."

Her thin, colorless lips curved slightly. "Sophia Konstantinova."

"Sophia, how lovely," I mused aloud. The heartbeat was

still beating slowly, vibrating in my chest. I wanted to rip my skin open, set the beating heart free. It felt like a caged animal in my chest, struggling to get out.

I closed my eyes and took a deep breath. My own heartbeat had slowed to match the slow cadence of the one I now realized was coming from the pale girl. How could she have a heartbeat if she was a ghost? My head swam in confusion. She was dead, wasn't she?

Her gray eyes were almost colorless and she stared at me, holding something behind her back. "It will be beautiful, Katerina. I promise."

Slowly she pulled her hand out to show me a faintly glowing rope. She had carefully looped it into a noose.

I shook my head. This was not what I wanted, was it? It was so hard for me to think. To remember.

"This will be easy," she murmured, and stepped closer. Without asking, she lifted my hair off my neck and held the noose over my head. "You have to stand up, Katerina. Only for a little bit. It will be over quickly. You'll see."

I didn't want to hurt anymore. I didn't want to think about anyone I loved anymore. The pain was too much. What was the point in caring for someone when it only brought them pain? I let a sob escape. I was ready to lay all of my burdens down. Every last one.

Sophia smiled, and this time her lips parted just enough for me to see the horrid black fangs.

I was back on my feet in an instant. My heart sped up, beating its own rhythm. I took a step backward. "Why did you kill Olga? The girl in the kitchen?"

"She took my doll! The one Natalia kept safe for me in her room. That peasant girl stole it when Natalia left."

240

"Who is Natalia?" I asked. There was nowhere for me to hide from her.

"She was my friend! And you took her from me! You and that horrible beast."

Natalia Metcherskey, I remembered from her headstone at the cemetery. Had Madame Metcherskey been Sophia's friend when they were both little? I could not imagine Madame as a young student here, dressed in the brown and blue Smolny uniforms. Had she seen what had happened to Sophia? What a terrible thing for a little girl to witness. And then to grow up with your best friend a ghost. Perhaps Sophia had not been so violent in the beginning. Perhaps she had slowly lost her sanity as the years passed and her friend Natalia grew up. I almost felt sorry for the ghost.

"Why do you want me dead, Sophia?" I asked, glancing around for a way to escape.

Sophia's laughter sent chills down my spine. "Silly girl," she said. "I want everyone dead." She flew at me, her arms stretched out and ending in icy claws.

I backed away from her and her rope, rolling across the floor and bruising my shoulder. I still could not see her cold light, so there was nothing I could reach for, or grab on to her with. I could feel her cold presence, though, and her touch was like a spike of ice straight to my bones.

"You are the necromancer my father wants," Sophia said as she danced around me. "I want you to stay and play with me here. Forever."

I felt sick. "And who is your father, Sophia? When were you born?"

"I am daughter of Konstantin Pavlovich, tsar of all the Russias."

241

I should have expected this all along. Somehow, I should have known the ghost was connected to the lich tsar. "And who was your mother?" It wasn't Princess Cantacuzene. And Konstantin's first wife, a Coburg princess, had returned to her home country without ever bearing him any children. Sophia had never been recognized as Konstantin's legitimate child.

She stomped her foot. "My mother would have been queen of Byzantium and empress of all the Russias. I would have been a grand duchess."

"But you weren't. Konstantin hid you away at Smolny long ago, Sophia Konstantinova." Slowly, I backed away from her, edging along the wall. She still blocked my path to the door-way. I wasn't even sure if the door led back into the Smolny hallway anymore. I was not even sure where I was. Limbo? Hell? "Tell me your mother's name. Had she been a Smolny student too?"

Sophia's eyes blazed white-hot. The rope she held seemed to stretch out in her hands and actually reach out for me. I had nothing to defend myself with. No reason for her not to rush forward and attack me.

"Surely the princess Cantacuzene was not your mother. How did you get along with her? Did she and your father visit you often?"

The walls began to shake with Sophia's fury. I had struck a nerve with her. Feeling a bit bolder, I pressed on. "She must have resented you a little. And I'm sure you resented her for stealing your father away to Poland."

"She was a blood-sucking demon," Sophia hissed, never taking her fiery eyes from me. "She wanted me to become just like her. She wanted my very soul."

I'd managed to get halfway around the room. The door was very close to me now, but she still blocked my path. I tried to keep her talking. "But you didn't let her, did you?"

She laughed, and I could see no trace of sanity left in the poor girl's mind. "Of course not! I stayed here and hid. Now she'll never be able to get me."

"That's true," I said in an attempt to sound soothing. My mother always did it so well. "You're safe now, Sophia." I wondered if I should dare get close enough to try to pat her hand, or something equally comforting.

She spun around and stared at me suspiciously. I guessed I hadn't sounded soothing enough. "You'll be safe too, Katerina. I can make it so Konstantin and Johanna will never hurt you."

I shook my head. "You don't understand, Sophia. He can still hurt other people if I die." I swallowed back the heavy lump in my throat. "People I care about." I took another sideways step toward the door. "Please let me go, Sophia. Nothing will happen to you."

"No! I can't let you leave!" The rope stretched out toward me again, this time snaking around my arms. It was so cold, it stung my skin. I cried out in pain and surprise.

Cold light. There was a faint, bluish glow if I looked carefully. Not only could I see it again, but I could definitely feel it as well. I tried not to panic. The rope coiled tighter up my arm and slid around my neck. I had to try even harder not to panic. It wasn't working. "Sophia, please." I closed my eyes, trying to will the cold light to rise up in me and push back the binding of the rope. It fought back even harder. The noose tightened.

Slowly she shook her head. "This is the way it has to be,

Katerina. You must understand. Johanna will not give you up. Neither will Konstantin."

I closed my eyes to try to shut out the stinging cold of the rope. It was unbearable. "But Johanna is dead. She cannot hurt anyone anymore."

"I don't believe you. She said she would come back for me. They both said they would come back for me."

"Konstantin has been defeated by the bogatyr. He will not be returning." I gasped as the rope loosened just a little. "Sophia, I want to help you. There must be a way to release you from this limbo at Smolny, so you can be at peace."

She giggled. "But I am at peace, Katerina. I want everyone here at Smolny to be just like me."

I sighed. I was tired of pleading with and coaxing her. "I cannot let that happen, Sophia. You are going to let me go, and I am going to make sure you never hurt anyone else here or anywhere else again."

She grinned, her black, razor-sharp teeth flashing ominously. "I don't know what I'm going to do with you, Katerina. You make me so sad. I wanted you to stay with me, I wanted to protect you from Konstantin and Johanna, but I might let them have you after all. I'll trade your soul for mine."

The rope uncoiled from around my neck and wrapped itself around my arms, pinning them close to my body with its stinging chill. I tried to take a deep breath, thankful I wasn't being strangled anymore, but the rope had my chest bound tight. I could barely breathe.

Sophia laughed again. "I'll keep you just like that until my father comes looking for me. Then I will give him the best present a daughter could ever give."

I closed my eyes, trying to block out the freezing pain. I tried to fight down the rising fear I felt in my belly. It would serve me no purpose. So I fought the fear with my own cold light. It uncoiled around me, feeding on the blackest, ugliest emotions I could give it. Darkness to fight light. It felt unnatural, and utterly wrong, but it seemed to be working.

"Nooo! What are you doing?" Sophia wailed. "You'll ruin everything!"

I opened my eyes and stared at the ghost. "*Sheult Anubis.*" Her own cold light became wrapped in my shadows, until there was nothing left of her to see. I felt nothing but cold. No emotion, no feelings toward her now at all. I did not feel sorry for hurting her, and yet I had no desire to harm or punish her either. There was nothing but a gaping void inside. And the freezing cold.

"Maman! Maman!" Her cries echoed in my ears. I had no way of knowing if she was crying for her mother's help, or if she had seen her poor mother in whatever afterlife place I was sending her to.

Sophia had disappeared beneath the shadows, and I could not hear her screams anymore. I shivered as the room fell completely silent. I did not know where the shadow had taken her, but I vowed I would find out before I ever did that to another soul, living or dead, again.

It had been completely irresponsible. What if I'd banished the ghost to a more desolate place than here? What if I'd condemned her to hell itself? Revolted by my own behavior, I was suddenly overcome and retched in the corner of the room.

If I had sent her someplace that awful, then I would no doubt be joining her for my own wickedness at the end of my days. I wiped my mouth on my sleeve, and used the wall to keep me steady as I made my way to the doorway.

The bluish glow was gone. The cold was fading, and I felt my limbs slowly warming back up. My blood was circulating again. I could feel my heart, pounding strong and fast, in my chest. "Hello?" I cried feebly. I had no idea what time it was, why no one was upstairs getting ready for bed.

I made it to the hallway before collapsing on the floor in front of all my teachers and classmates. One of the last things I heard was Elena's voice. "Madame Tomilov! Send for Sister Anna!"

CHAPTER FORTY-TWO

〜❧〜

"No! I'm fine!" I said, struggling to sit up. Someone had carried me to my cot. I looked around, disoriented and sore. "What time is it?" I asked.

"You've been out all day," Aurora said. "And Alix is still missing. Madame Tomilov will have to notify the princess's sister soon."

I had to find Alix before Sucre did. Why hadn't I realized his treachery earlier? If anything happened to Alix I would never forgive myself.

Aurora and Elena both watched me get up and stumble across the room. They were looking at me as if I'd grown two heads.

"What is wrong with you?" Elena asked. "You look as if you've seen a ghost."

I wanted to laugh hysterically. But there was no time. "Please, both of you. Please help me find Alix. I'm afraid she's in danger."

I wanted to shake some sense into both of them, but it was hopeless. How could I tell them that our roommate was really a wolf? And how could I convince them we needed to save the wolf from being killed by the cook who was really a dark faerie? "Never mind," I said finally. Instead of saying anything, I went to Alix's bed and bent down to reach underneath.

"What are you doing?" Elena shrieked. "You told me not to—"

I ignored her and pulled the wooden box out from under Alix's bed. Even Aurora got up to see what was inside. I held my breath, hoping for the best.

But the ribbon was gone.

"*Zut alors,*" I hissed under my breath. I threw the box onto Alix's bed. The missing ribbon meant that she could be in wolf form right now, and was hopefully stronger than she'd be as a human. Although Sucre probably needed her alive for the wizards' ritual.

I went to the window and pressed my forehead and hands against the cool glass. Daylight was fading. Looking down into the courtyard, I saw something that made my heart stop. Sucre and Papus were pushing someone into a black carriage. Alix. She was holding her hands together in front of her as if they were bound. She looked up toward the institute and her gaze rested on our window. She glared up at me as she disappeared into the carriage.

Alix thought I had betrayed her. And she had no reason not to. If anything happened to her it would be my fault. I fought back angry tears as I watched the carriage roll out through the front gates.

I had to find out where and when they planned for this ritual to take place. "I need to leave Smolny," I said.

"Tonight?" Elena asked. "Did you want to go to the Yus-supov Ball?"

"Don't be ridiculous," I snapped. "We need to rescue Alix."

"You will need my help if you wish to save your friend, although I cannot fathom why you would call that one a friend." The crown prince was always there, at the edge of my thoughts, listening in.

"We don't need your help," I snapped. Elena looked at me as if I were insane.

"But it will make your rescue easier. You don't have a carriage, do you? Mine is just outside the school, waiting."

Why would you want to help me? I remembered not to think aloud this time.

"Perhaps because I want your gratitude?"

I will be extremely grateful, Danilo. But you know I will never marry you.

The crown prince merely laughed. *"We shall see about that. Meet me at the front gates of Smolny."*

The Montenegrin princess was still staring at me, her arms folded across her chest. "I don't know what you're planning, but I'm coming with you," she said.

"The two of you will be in trouble for sneaking off the school grounds." Aurora said. "I, for one, am staying put."

"Katerina, you will need help saving poor Alix's neck." Elena grabbed her cloak and pulled it around her shoulders. "Come on."

I sighed as I picked up Alix's coat. I had never gotten mine back from Madame Metcherskey.

"Are you coming?" Danilo sounded anxious. *"The members of the Order of St. Lazarus are standing guard at the front gates. Give me some time to distract them."*

I reached the front door with Elena behind me. I hesitated and turned to her. "Are you sure?"

She grinned. "No one can pick on the Hessian princess but me."

I rolled my eyes and we slipped out of the front door, closing it silently behind us. The moon was full again, and the snow-covered grounds were lit up brilliantly. We decided to slowly walk under the shadow of the trees for cover.

There was a huge fireball in the sky outside the gates. We heard the moaning and shuffling of the undead soldiers. They were frightened by the fire. I did not want to hurt any of the undead creatures. But I did not want them to stop me from leaving.

Once the smoke had cleared and the guards had run off, we could see Danilo standing just outside the huge iron gates.

Elena was delighted to see her brother. "What a pleasant surprise! Katerina is always talking about you!"

"He knows that is a lie," I said as I followed her through the open gates. There was nothing left of the empress's spell any-more. I did not want to think about what she would do when she discovered what I'd done. "We have to find Alix. Before Sucre harms her."

Elena pouted. "But with her out of the way, the tsarevitch would pay more attention to me. I expect he is dancing at the ball right now. And what a pity Alix isn't there."

I stopped and stared at her. She was smiling wickedly. "Elena, they want to sacrifice her for their ritual. They want to cut her heart out."

Elena's eyes grew large and her smile faded. "The darkest of dark magics. I wouldn't wish that on my worst enemy." She sighed. "And Alix of Hesse is my worst enemy. We have to rescue her, of course."

Danilo put his arm around me, his hand at the small of my back. "Ladies, we must hurry. The ritual is taking place at midnight at Vorontsov Chapel."

At the Order's headquarters. I took a deep breath, knowing that George Alexandrovich would be there. But I could not think about him right then. The crown prince led both of us to the carriage and we took off for Vorontsov Palace. "And how do you know this, Your Highness?" I asked him.

But Danilo merely smiled at me.

⚬

There were several carriages and sleighs out on the streets of St. Petersburg that night. The Yussupov Ball was a grand celebration for the Light Court, and most of the aristocracy was en route to Princess Yussupova's palace on the Moika Canal.

"Why did the wizards have to pick tonight to have their ritual?" Elena said, still pouting.

"It's the spring equinox," Danilo said. "The perfect balance of night and day."

I did not trust Danilo completely, or his motives for helping me. I could not figure out what he would gain from saving the Hessian princess or from stopping the Koldun's ritual.

"The Koldun is a longtime enemy of my father." It still startled me when the crown prince read my thoughts. He was staring out the window into the darkness. "He poisons the tsar against Montenegro." He had lied to me. He had known who the Koldun was all along.

"Your Highness, your father and mother poisoned Montenegro's ties to Russia with their own witchcraft. The Koldun had nothing to do with it."

Danilo turned and smiled, his teeth white and sharp, and uncomfortably close in the tiny carriage. "Duchess, I have pledged to help you rescue your friend and stop an evil ritual. You need know nothing more of my motives, except that they spring from my devotion to you." He picked up my hand and brought it to his lips.

It frightened me that I might easily fall under his spell again. Last year, I'd willingly accepted his marriage proposal. And I'd kissed him. I couldn't let that happen again.

It was still difficult to resist that mesmerizing pull I felt when the crown prince touched me. But not impossible. Elena giggled as I pulled my hand out of Danilo's grasp and scowled at both of them. I could not trust either one of the Montenegrin siblings. I had no weapons on me, I could remember no new spells from *A Necromancer's Companion*. I had no idea what I would do when I reached Vorontsov Palace. I only knew I could not let anything happen to Alix.

Danilo had the carriage let us out a ways down from the palace gates. It was close to midnight, and the ritual would soon begin. I almost slipped as I climbed down from the carriage without waiting for help. "Careful, beloved," he whispered, catching me around the waist.

"Please stop calling me that." I rolled my eyes and hurried through the trees toward the palace entrance. I had sneaked into this building before, and knew my way through its halls.

Elena and Danilo caught up with me and we crept around the back, where a black carriage was waiting. Two men stood guard. Members of the Order of St. Lazarus.

I put a hand on Danilo's arm to stop him. "They're just like the soldiers at Smolny."

His grin was vicious. "Do not worry for me, Duchess." He stepped into the shadows and I heard him whispering strange words. A mist rose up under the feet of the guards. As it rose higher, the guards were enveloped in the mist, and they fell to the ground.

I stared at the guards. The crown prince's magic had knocked both creatures down.

"It will only stop them temporarily. We must hurry." Danilo motioned for us to follow him.

Elena was so quiet and elegant as she followed her brother. I wondered what kinds of adventures the two siblings had had growing up in the Black Mountains of Montenegro. I had constantly harassed my older brother as a child. Petya never wanted me to play with him. I realized I was almost jealous of Elena and Danilo.

We reached the black carriage and Danilo glanced inside. He shook his head. "She's not there. They've already taken her to the chapel."

I sighed and leaned against the wall. I knew Alix's rescue would not be easy.

CHAPTER FORTY-THREE

❧

"This is impossible," Elena said. "You can't just walk in there, interrupt a coven of wizards, and steal their sacrificial victim."

"She can too," Danilo said, looking at me with what looked like admiration. "Katerina Alexandrovna can cloak herself in shadow."

I shivered, unhappy that Danilo knew so many of my secrets. And now Elena did as well.

The crown prince took my hand and pulled the glove nearly off. His finger touched the spot where Sucre had stabbed me the night before. "Our bond works both ways, my duchess. Just as your blood gives me extra strength, my blood gives you extra power."

I pulled my hand out of his. "No. I do not need your blood."

Elena laughed. "You must not care enough about Alix to save her, then."

I glared at her. "I need you to create a distraction while I find Alix."

Danilo nodded. "Once you've saved her, go to Militza's. I can send for my own carriage later."

I shook my head. "No, we must get Alix back to Smolny. Or take her to her sister, Grand Duchess Elizabeth Feodorovna."

"She is probably dancing the night away at the Yussupov Ball," Elena said, pouting again.

"Then we go back to Smolny. Hopefully we will be able to sneak in again without anyone knowing that we left."

Elena's laugh was short. "Of course. A piece of cake. And Monsieur Sucre?"

"Leave him to me," the crown prince said. He took my hand and pulled it to his lips. "Once more, for luck, my duchess." With a wicked grin he turned my hand palm up and I felt his tongue on the wound from the night before. The tingles shot through my body again as his power increased. I felt a strange but familiar longing. At that moment, if he'd offered his blood to me again, it would have been very difficult for me to refuse.

"Katiya?" George Alexandrovich stepped out of the portico shadows. His face was much thinner, much paler than the last time I'd seen him. Had it only been a few months ago, at Christmas? It seemed like ages.

I took a step back from Danilo, but the crown prince did not let go of my hand. George's eyes grew cold as he stared from Danilo to me.

"Where's Alix?" I asked. "I know Monsieur Sucre brought her here."

There was no emotion in George's voice. "That is not your concern, Duchess. This is a private ceremony of the Order."

Cold fury burned inside me. "It is my concern when you plan to kill my classmate and take her heart for your dark ritual. I won't let you do it."

George's laugh was bitter. "Is that what this is all about?"

I pulled away from Danilo and tried to go to George. "I've been sick with worry for you," I whispered. "Please tell me you weren't going to let them hurt Alix."

"But my dear," George said, stepping back away from me. "Tonight is the night of my initiation. Isn't this what you wanted?" He smiled a grim and vicious smile before he disappeared back inside the building.

I wanted to chase after him and demand an explanation, but the guards at our feet began to stir.

"Come on," Danilo said, grabbing me and Elena by the arms. We hurried into the chapel. George was nowhere to be seen.

"So much for our well-thought-out plan," Elena grumbled. "Any other ideas?"

"I'm still going to save Alix," I said. "You two wait here." I closed my eyes, and took a deep breath. *"Sheult Anubis."*

Nothing happened. I looked up at Elena and Danilo and started to panic.

"Try again," Danilo said patiently. "Focus on your powers."

I closed my eyes and imagined my cold light, coiled tightly within my belly. *"Sheult Anubis."* I felt the light stir, and I pulled the shadows around me, cloaking myself with the darkness.

Elena gasped. *"Mon Dieu!"*

"Very good, Katerina," Danilo said. "Now go and find your werewolf. You'll know when the time is right to get her."

I hurried into the Great Hall, where an unholy ritual was taking place. The room was smoky with incense. The censer hung from the ceiling in the middle of the room, burning frankincense and myrrh.

Robed men were standing in a circle, each one holding a black candle and chanting in an ancient language. It wasn't Latin or Greek, to my knowledge. I wondered if it was Egyptian. Their hoods prevented me from recognizing any of them, although I realized the man holding a golden staff had to be the Koldun.

There was a familiar ornament at the top of the staff: the Talisman of Isis. I felt dizzy, remembering that I was the one who had given the talisman to the Order for safekeeping after the fight with Konstantin at Peterhof.

As I advanced, I kept to the dark side aisles, away from the candlelight. But I could see Alix, gagged and bound, and kneeling on the floor in the center of the circle. As quietly as I could, I moved closer. A sharp, stinging feeling coursed through me with every step. I looked down and saw the protective ring of salt they had prepared. I had touched the wizards' protective shield. There was no way I would be able to get inside the circle to reach Alix. I could destroy the ring of salt, but then Alix would be in even greater peril.

The Koldun raised his staff and pounded it on the marble floor, silencing the others. I could hear Alix's rapid breathing, and yet she was calm. I hoped she wasn't planning on doing anything foolish herself. I was being foolish enough for all of us.

I could not tell at first which robed wizard was George. I slowly circled the room, looking from one candlelit face to another. Their shadows danced across the walls behind them. I found him at last standing opposite the Koldun. His gaze was intent upon his flame.

A large book lay open on a stand in front of the Koldun. When the chanting had stopped, he had stepped forward and begun to read from the book. It was some kind of incantation, in a language I recognized. My small knowledge of Latin, however, only allowed me to understand a few of the words: "darkness" . . . "rise up" . . . "embrace" . . . "glory."

The Koldun looked up from his book and across the room. "Initiate, step forward."

I watched the nightmare unfold in front of me, unable to do anything.

One figure entered the center, and the wizards closed the circle around him. He pulled his hood back, and stared straight ahead at the Koldun. George Alexandrovich.

The Koldun removed his own hood and I had to cover my mouth to suppress a gasp. It was Grand Duke Vladimir Alexandrovich, the tsar's brother. Miechen's husband. "Initiate, your knowledge and skills in the occult have been examined by the peers standing with you this night. Your soul shall be examined by the Holy Ones and if it is accepted, you will become one of the innermost circle of the Order of the Black Lily. Are you ready, George Alexandrovich?"

"I am." His voice boomed out across the silent room.

No. George, please don't do this. I concentrated every bit of my energy into trying to get the message to him.

The Koldun took a ring from the center of his large book and held it over his head. "Holy Ones, we invoke you. This ring will protect George Alexandrovich and keep him safe when he is within the sacred circle."

George, I love you. I couldn't stop the tears that began rolling down my cheeks.

There was no hint on his stone-cold face that he'd heard

my message. He held out his left hand for the Koldun to place the ring on his finger. The Koldun kissed George on each cheek. Then both wizards stepped back and took their original places with the others.

The Koldun looked around and smiled. "Now our coven is complete. Thirteen of the most powerful sorcerers in all of Europe. Tonight we shall combine our powers and cast the most ambitious ritual attempted since the mage Levi left the physical planes. Tonight the lich tsar Konstantin Pavlovich will be conjured and destroyed."

Destroyed? Killing Alix was going to save the tsar from Konstantin? There had to be another way. I glanced around the circle and then frowned. Even with George and the Koldun, there were only twelve robed wizards present. Did Grand Duke Vladimir miscount?

George, you can't let them do this.

He remained as still as a statue. There was no hint that he'd heard me.

Someone has to save Alix. And if you won't, I will. I tried another step toward the shield but was held back. I was afraid I would lose my shadow cloak if I tried to penetrate the magic circle a third time.

The thirteenth robed wizard slowly approached the circle. He was allowed to enter, but I still could not pass the magical barrier.

Hidden or not, I could not stand by and watch Alix be sacrificed. I took another step forward.

"I'm afraid you are too late, my beloved. The fun is just about to begin." The thirteenth wizard pushed his hood back and smiled. It was Danilo.

CHAPTER FORTY-FOUR

❧

The crown prince had been deceiving me all along. I should not have been so shocked. But George's deception hurt even more. How could he willingly give up Alix's life to defeat Konstantin?

"*He cannot risk it, beloved.*" Danilo's voice was poisonous in my head. "*Of course, there is a chance that the lich tsar could be defeated some other way, but would you risk the tsar's life on it?*"

Why did you bring me here, then? If you planned to help them kill Alix all along?

"*We needed the full coven. We needed to be sure the tsar's son was committed to his initiation.*"

But why . . . I felt so foolish. And used. Danilo had wanted George to see him kissing my hand. And it probably seemed as if I were enjoying it. I looked across the circle at George. *I am so sorry.*

"*It's a little late for that now, Duchess,*" Danilo said with a sneer.

There was a pounding and the Great Hall doors opened. Suddenly, the room was flooded with the tsar's imperial guard. It was the Preobrajensky Regiment. Members of the outermost circle of the Order.

"What are you doing?" the Koldun roared. "This is a private ceremony! You are forbidden to enter this room!"

A familiar voice barked out, "This ritual is over by the order of the tsar." It was my brother. I'd never been so happy to see Petya in my life before.

One by one, the Black Magi were being arrested, and their hoods were removed. I watched Papus and Sucre as they were handcuffed and led away. The protective circle was weakened just enough for me to slip inside.

I knew my original plan was ruined, but I still hoped to get Alix back to Smolny before the headmistress realized she was missing. I fortified my shadow cloak and brushed past two wizards toward Alix. Right in front of the Koldun, who was being arrested by my brother.

I bent down to untie the ropes around Alix's feet. "Don't be frightened," I whispered. "It's only me. I'm going to get you out of here safely."

"Do not touch me, demon."

I let the shadows fade from around me. "Alix, I am so sorry that Monsieur Sucre came after you. I won't let them harm you."

"I can take care of myself, Katerina. Take your hands off of me." She growled softly, only for my ears to hear.

She unnerved me but did not frighten me. I finished untying the knots around her ankles and reached for the rope around her hands. "Nicholas must be worried sick about you. Don't do anything that would take you away from him, Alix."

She glared at me. "It is unnatural to walk in darkness as you do."

"No more unnatural than changing into an animal and ripping someone's throat out." I grabbed Alix's hands. The knots were finally undone.

Alix jerked her hands out of mine. "If I could have changed, I could have chewed through the ropes and killed the Koldun."

"And you would have been executed for killing the tsar's brother. We've got to let the tsar's men take care of this. Come back to Smolny with me. We can sneak back in before Madame Tomilov knows any of us are gone."

Alix shook her head. "The tsar's life is in danger. What if they bring back Konstantin? We must stop the Koldun."

"It was you," I said. "Fighting with us at Peterhof. The white wolf."

"Of course," Alix whispered. "My sisters were there as well, but I kept close to protect the tsarevitch."

I glanced around the room. "The guards have stopped the ritual. The tsar should be safe."

Elena approached us in the dark shadows of the hallway where we were hiding. "I know a way out of here. Where no one will notice three silly students."

But at that moment, some of the magi began to fight back. A blinding light filled the Great Hall as Papus broke free of his captors and shouted, "Brothers! Do not surrender!"

The soldiers fell to the floor, moaning and writhing in pain.

I gasped, searching wildly for Petya. But he was not in the Great Hall. Where had he gone?

I looked around at the other wizards, all of whom had now been unmasked by the imperial guard. I did not see George or Danilo.

I was worried that Papus would kill the tsar's men with his spells. The Koldun was fighting back against the guards as well. "We've got to help the guards."

"Katerina, are you insane?" Elena asked. "We have to get out of here. We can't fight wizards."

Alix looked at me, her face grim. "I don't think that mage wanted to protect the tsar," she said, pointing at Papus. "It sounded to me like some of the members of the Order were planning to double-cross the others."

Sucre and Danilo did not have the tsar's best interests at heart, I was sure. And neither did Papus, it seemed. Had the Koldun been aware of the true goal of tonight's ritual? Had he plotted against the tsar as well?

"Where is your ribbon?" I asked. "If you can distract the Koldun, I think I know a spell that can stop him."

Alix put a hand on my wrist and squeezed it painfully. "No. You cannot use evil to fight evil, Katerina Alexandrovna," she said.

"Both of you are insane," Elena said, exasperated. She shook her head and ran off.

"Elena, wait!"

Alix glared after our roommate. "She will not help us."

"But what if she goes to warn her brother?"

"I think the grand duke can take care of him," Alix said, nodding behind me.

I ran to the doorway where Alix was looking. We could hear lots of shouting and crashing of furniture coming from beyond the Great Hall. George and Danilo were fighting. "No!" I gasped, feeling sick and dizzy at the same time.

It was a magical duel. The crown prince and the grand duke circled each other warily. Danilo held up his left hand and muttered something in Serbian. The room began to fill with smoke.

George waved his hand and the smoke cleared just as rapidly.

Alix was behind me, tugging on my sleeve. "Come on," she whispered. "The Koldun has to be stopped."

But I couldn't move. I was frozen with fear for George.

"There's nothing you can do to help him," Alix said. "They've sealed the room."

There was a magical barrier similar to the empress's Smolny spell preventing me from entering the chamber. I wasn't sure who had put the barrier up, but I had a feeling it had been George.

The tsar's son was holding his own against Danilo. He deftly countered everything the crown prince threw at him. It was beautiful watching him. Both wizards had shed their robes and were wearing only black uniforms that allowed them to move more gracefully.

A ball of blue fire shot across the room from Danilo. George ducked and the fire slammed into the wall behind him, scattering chunks of plaster with its blast.

"Katerina!" Alix was still behind me, trying to pull me away. The Koldun was still attacking the tsar's men in the Great Hall behind us.

I turned reluctantly to follow her as George went on the offensive and blasted Danilo with a bolt of lightning.

Most of the tsar's men were already incapacitated and writhing on the floor. I could not do what Alix wished. I could not stand by and not use my powers, when there were innocent people being hurt. I closed my eyes and gathered up every ounce of power I ever believed I possessed. The cold light stung as it uncoiled from deep inside me. I did not want to kill the Koldun, but I would not let him hurt another member of the imperial guard. I had to save my brother.

My cold light reached out, seeking the Koldun. The cold light was attracted by the wizard's shadowy aura. He was wounded, already dying.

Alix took her ribbon from a hidden pocket in her skirt and drew it around her neck. The transformation from girl to wolf happened so fast I could not believe my eyes. A blur of white fur blew past me and leapt at the Koldun. The two went tumbling back and slid into the wall on the far side of the room.

When the Koldun ceased casting his spell, the last of the protective wards fell apart.

CHAPTER FORTY-FIVE

꘍

There had been more than two times as many imperial guards as there were wizards, and yet the wizards seemed to be holding their own. Until the Koldun lost his concentration. The last of the magic protections ended and the Great Hall was flooded with everything the wizards had been keeping out. Their ceremony had attracted all sorts of spectral attention, and not all of it had been beneficent. Which made perfect sense. A Dark Court ritual would of course attract the darkest of spirits.

I saw and felt the bone-chilling cold light sweeping past me as it rushed toward the Koldun. Alix tumbled out of the way. I caught a glimpse of the damage she had done to the Koldun before the angry spirits surrounded him. They attacked him much like a swarm of angry bees. It was a horrible death. Even if he had been a horrible man.

I repressed a shudder as I hurried over to Alix. I reached for the ribbon around her neck, to help her change back, but she growled at me. Her fur was matted with blood. "Let me help you, Alix."

With her fangs still bared, she pushed past me and ran for the door. It occurred to me that perhaps she did not want to transform in front of everyone. I hoped she could return to Smolny safely.

There was only one thing left for me to concentrate on: George and Danilo's duel. They were still at it in the room outside the Great Hall, throwing balls of energy at each other as well as trading sword blows. I ran to the doorway, but felt someone approaching behind me.

"Katiya, what the devil are you doing here?" It was Petya. Behind him was Nicholas Alexandrovich.

"Trying to save the grand duke. Let go of me. I have to help him."

The tsarevitch shook his head and chuckled. "Georgi's doing just fine on his own, Duchess."

A fireball exploded behind the Montenegrin crown prince. He ducked and almost lost his right ear to George's sword.

"Enough of this," Danilo snarled. From his breast pocket he pulled out a revolver.

I gasped. "Danilo, no!" I pushed out of my brother's arms into the hall, flinging myself in front of George. I felt sharp pains in my head as I hurtled through the magic barrier.

"Katiya, wait!" George shouted. He mumbled something in Greek as I heard a shot.

The room filled with gun smoke. Danilo's revolver had misfired. He dropped the weapon to the ground as he searched for a way to escape in the haze.

George's arm was around my waist, pulling me closer to him, and I felt his warm lips pressed against my ear. "Go back to your brother, Katiya. I can't worry about you right now."

Mon Dieu. There were so many things I wanted to say to the arrogant grand duke, but there wasn't time. He let go of me as several men rushed into the room from all directions. I could not find Petya or the tsarevitch in the confusion.

My arms were grabbed from behind by two very strong hands. "Oh no, Duchess. You are coming with us." Sucre had found me.

"How did you get away from the guards?" I asked. I looked around, hoping Petya was unharmed and would realize that I needed his help.

Sucre just laughed. "Do not worry your little head about such things. We have business to finish."

"You are insane. Let me go."

I struggled, but his fingers dug more deeply into my arms. "Without the Koldun, we are not obligated to protect the tsar any longer," he said. "Konstantin will be raised with your help, little necromancer. And not so we may put an end to him."

The Koldun hadn't been part of the true plot, then. He'd really believed he was helping to destroy the lich tsar. I didn't know if I'd ever be able to tell Alix the truth.

Sucre pulled me into a smaller chamber off of the Great Hall. Here sat the golden throne I had seen in the Crimea. The sight of the throne filled me with dread. "No . . ." I tried to pull back from the wizard but he wouldn't let go.

"Oh yes, Duchess," Sucre said. His grin was wicked. "You are going to help us find the lich tsar. And then you're going to help him return to us."

"I won't help you." I looked all around the room, looking for doors, weapons, anything. I needed to get back to help George. Even if he didn't need, or want, my help.

I heard the door behind us close and the bolt slide into place. Danilo appeared. He was in on the plot as well. He smiled as he walked around me. "I will finish dealing with your grand duke later. After you have helped us raise the lich tsar."

"We knew you wouldn't help willingly, Duchess," Sucre said. "But we know you wouldn't want anything to happen to your Smolny friend, now, would you?"

The crown prince pushed the throne around and I saw Alix, back in her human shape and wearing a dirty Smolny uniform. She was gagged and tied to the throne. Her eye was blackened where one of the wizards had hit her. Sucre smiled a nasty smile as he showed me Alix's ribbon and tucked it away in his coat pocket. My heart sank.

"You don't want anything else to happen to the Hessian princess, do you?" Sucre asked. "I will cut the bitch's throat in a heartbeat if you do not help us."

"Why?" I asked Danilo. "Why would you want to bring Konstantin back?"

The crown prince's face was like a mask. "Thanks to the cursed talisman we used for my ascension, I am now bound to Konstantin. If I give him what he wants, I will be free."

"He wants to kill the tsar, Danilo. You can't let that happen."

The crown prince almost looked apologetic. "If I do not, he will end up killing me. Or worse, possessing me."

The thought of being bound by blood to the lich tsar in

the crown prince's body made me physically ill. "Surely there is another way."

"We've run out of options, Duchess," Sucre said. "Help us raise the lich tsar, or the German princess will die."

I could not allow them to sacrifice Alix. "What do you wish me to do?" I whispered.

The princess's eyes grew wide and she struggled against her ropes. Sucre struck her with a violent blow to her cheek. She grew very still, but I could see the tears welling up in her eyes as she fought against the pain.

My fists were shaking. I could feel fury rising inside of me. I wanted to let the cold light loose and do something horrible to these men. They had no right to hurt us. "Let her go, and I will help you."

Danilo laughed. "You must be joking, Katerina."

"I am not." I fought to stop trembling. I fought to keep my fears down and looked him coolly in the eye. He wanted a cold-blooded necromancer, and that was what I would be. "Let Alix go, or I won't cooperate."

Sucre swore in French, and nodded to the crown prince. "We don't need her anymore with the Koldun dead. Let her loose."

Danilo had the sense to look frightened. "But she's a *wolf*."

"Not without the ribbon, she's not. Let her go. We need the necromancer more."

Alix glared at me. She was still in too much of a daze from the blow to her head to hurt either Danilo or Sucre. Staggering, she stood up from the throne and somehow managed to lunge for me. I held my arms out to catch her. "Katerina Alexandrovna," she hissed. "I would rather die than see you do this."

"See to the grand duke. And please find my brother."

I could have sworn I heard her growl as she ran past me into the Great Hall. I did not look back at her. Instead, I held Sucre's gaze, and summoned all the cold-light power I could. It had helped to kill the Koldun. Would it work again?

"Tsk, tsk," Sucre said, shaking his head at me. "I wouldn't do that if I were you, Duchess. The Koldun was killed not by you but by the dark spirits he unleashed. Don't waste your precious powers trying to fight me." He took a step closer and grabbed my hands, bruising them with his force. "It won't work."

The fae cook could read my mind. I closed my eyes. "Tell me what you want me to do, so I can leave."

Sucre laughed. "Of course. If you would be so kind, Monsieur," he said, holding out his hand. Papus appeared from the shadowy corner of the room. He pulled a faded scroll from the inside pocket of his vest and handed it to Sucre. It was the scroll he had retrieved from the cave in Massandra. He'd betrayed George and the Order all along.

Papus quickly drew a magic circle around the three of us, with the throne in the center.

I was now effectively cut off from anyone's help. There was no way the grand duke could hear my thoughts across the magic barrier.

"What do you hope to gain by raising the lich tsar? He will destroy us all."

Danilo shook his head and smiled, showing his sharp teeth. "He will be completely under my control. I have the talisman." He pulled a necklace from under his shirt and showed me the Talisman of Isis.

"You took it from the Koldun's staff?" I gasped.

271

"If I hadn't, the spirits would have taken it themselves. And what kind of anarchy would that have created?"

I shook my head. "You are insane."

"You do wound me, Duchess." Gripping me roughly by the shoulders, he swung me around so that I was standing opposite him and Sucre. We made a triangle around the throne.

"If only that were true," I muttered. His eyebrow rose slightly, but he did not reply.

Sucre unrolled the parchment scroll and began to read the ancient Greek text. When he paused, Danilo and I were to repeat his words. I could make out only some of the phrases he was chanting. *"Open the gate"* . . . *"return to the light"* . . .

The two wizards focused their attentions on the throne, as if that was where they expected the lich tsar to appear. Of course. The throne was some sort of gateway to the cold-light realm, the Graylands, where Konstantin was imprisoned. I could not allow him to return to our world. Sucre and Danilo were fools if they thought they were strong enough to control him.

I felt the temperature drop drastically in the chamber. I could see Sucre's breath as he chanted. I could feel the cold light pulling, tugging me toward the throne. Was this supposed to be happening?

The light was beginning to swirl over the seat of the throne. Very soon, the lich tsar would appear in that seat. My heart pounded with fear.

I couldn't do this. Konstantin could not be allowed to leave the Graylands. I saw the carvings along the curve of the back of the throne and realized what I had to do.

I stopped chanting the words that Sucre was reading. Instead, I began to focus on the carved words. "The path to the light travels straight through the darkness," I muttered. "The path to the light travels straight through the darkness," I repeated, louder still.

I felt another pull within my belly. The cold light inside me wanted to go, was eager even. I knew I'd probably never be able to return. But with me trapped in the Graylands Konstantin would be trapped as well. I swallowed the fear that was in my throat and read the inscription a third time. The throne seemed to hum with its immense power.

Before Danilo and Sucre could realize what I had planned, I rushed forward and threw myself into the seat. The room began to spin, and I felt the sickening cold and clammy feeling I'd experienced in the caves of Massandra. I was gone before the wizards knew what I had done.

CHAPTER FORTY-SIX

❧

The throne came with me. I knew I was doomed to die, but I still smiled. They would not be able to raise the lich tsar without a necromancer. I pulled the shadows around me, hoping I would stay hidden from Konstantin for at least a little while.

I needed to find him, however, just to make sure the wizards could not invoke him on their own. As much as I hated the idea, I had to find the lich tsar in the Graylands.

I had no sense of direction. The realm was dark and full of swirling mist, and I had no way of knowing where the lich tsar was. How had I found him last time?

Within the mist were whispering shadows and strands of silver cold light. I tried not to attract their attention. But several shadows loomed taller as they drew closer to me. I held my breath. The shadows drifted past in a hurry, attracted to something behind me.

I heard moaning. It stopped my blood cold. Who was here in the Graylands with me? I whispered, *Sheult Anubis,* more to give myself courage than anything else, and made my way toward the sound.

The mist was colder here. The moans grew louder. I didn't realize how close I'd gotten, but suddenly a cold hand gripped my ankle.

I shrieked.

The mist muffled my scream.

The cold hand loosened. "Forgive me. . . ." The person was prostrate on the floor.

"Sir?" I leaned down and gasped. It was the Koldun. Grand Duke Vladimir Alexandrovich. "You betrayed your own brother, and tried to bring back the lich tsar."

He was too weak to sit up. "Duchess. I fear I owe you a grave apology. I was very wrong to attempt the ritual of the wolf's heart. The papyrus describing the ritual was a forgery. I have made a terrible mess of things."

My eyes went wide. "Papus and Sucre created a false ritual?"

"I thought we were saving the tsar and destroying Konstantin once and for all. The French wizards had other plans the whole time."

I picked up his hand and held it. "How did you get here?"

"The spirits brought me." He laughed grimly. "My wife and I have manipulated the Dark Court for years. It is long past time the spirits took their revenge."

"But you've been serving as Koldun all this time. Does your brother trust you?"

"Both Light and Dark Courts serve the tsar, Katerina," the Koldun said. "Despite my wife's ambitions."

"Of course, there is always the slightest chance something could happen to the tsar and his family," I said, thinking of the train accident at Kharkov. "And you would inherit the throne."

"Anything is possible," the grand duke said. "But now I think my wife's fondest wish will never come true. This is the ending that I deserve."

"No one deserves to stay here, Your Imperial Highness. Not even you."

The Koldun's eyes were sad. "There is nothing you can do, Katerina Alexandrovna. I am dead. I will remain here until it is time to meet my final judgment."

"Did the grand duchess know what you were attempting to do this evening?"

"Of course not. *L'Ordre du Lis Noir* is the inner secret circle of the Order of St. John. The actions of the innermost circle are known only to the Coven of Thirteen."

"Your Imperial Highness, you should know that the Montenegrin crown prince was also part of Sucre's plot. He stole the Talisman of Isis from your staff and was trying to raise Konstantin from the dead."

The Koldun turned even paler than he already was. "But they did not succeed?"

I shook my head. "They still need a necromancer. I chose to come here rather than help them bring the lich tsar there. I guess you will have to get used to my company."

The Koldun did not laugh. "But you do not belong here, my dear. This is the land of the dead."

"And where else should a necromancer live?" I tried to sound light and frivolous, as if I did not care that I'd thrown my life away.

"St. Petersburg. In the land of the living. Especially a pretty young thing like you." His laugh dissolved into a coughing fit.

If he'd meant to make me blush he'd succeeded. "Are you injured, Your Imperial Highness?" I had not noticed any bleeding or signs of trauma. How exactly had the spirits sent him here?

His coughing settled down. "I am dying from the inside out, Duchess. Look at my cold light."

I looked at him closely, and saw he was correct. The cold light was dimming around his heart; it streamed outward, pouring out of his body, where it became brighter. There was nothing I could do. I felt more helpless than I had at Christmas when I saw the dying soldier in the hospital. I closed my eyes to blink back the tears. "Does it hurt?"

The Koldun's smile did not reach his eyes.

I couldn't stop the tears then. I couldn't stand knowing that he was suffering and I was unable to help him.

"Please don't cry, my dear. I have lived a good life."

"Think of your wife. And your children." His sons, whom I'd danced with every Christmas at the Children's Ball: Kyril, Boris, and Andrei. His little daughter, Helena. They needed their father.

"There is nothing you can do, Duchess. You are very gifted, especially for one so young. But to bring a person back from this realm, and not as a ghoul, would take a very powerful magic. I do not dare to hope you could pull such a thing off."

"Would it hurt to try?" But I already knew the risks. I could irrevocably damage his soul. And mine as well. "Do you know what I would have to do?"

He closed his eyes, looking more and more weary. "I would not even know where to look to find such a ritual. It is blasphemous. The most unholy of unspeakable acts." He coughed again. "Do not attempt it for my sake. It will damn you more swiftly than anything else."

"And was there nothing the Dark Court queen could do to protect you?" I asked. "Didn't she have spells woven around you as the empress of the Light Court does for the Tsar?"

The Koldun shrugged with a faint, helpless smile.

Then he coughed again, sounding even more pitiful. I looked around me at the darkness, trying to decide what to do. I wondered what would happen if I dragged him to the throne and sent him back that way. I couldn't go with him, because the wizards might still be waiting for me. For all I knew, they had been counting on me coming here and sending the Koldun back all along. I felt horribly and wretchedly used. By everyone.

I was too busy feeling sorry for myself to hear the lich tsar's daughter sneak up on me.

CHAPTER FORTY-SEVEN

Suddenly I was hit with a force that knocked the breath out of me. "Necromancer! What have you done to me?"

I tried to stand back up, and wished the darkness would stop spinning. "Sophia Konstantinova? Is that you?" I ducked as soon as I saw her rushing toward me again.

"You took me away from my home! Now Johanna will find me!"

"No!" I winced as I felt another sharp blow to my back. I tried to curl up into a ball. "Sophia, Johanna cannot find you here. And Smolny was not your home."

"Of course it was! Where else did I have people that cared about me? You even took Madame Metcherskey away from me!"

Ouch. "I'm so sorry, Sophia."

"Take me back to Smolny!"

"No." I curled up even tighter. She had to quit hitting me sooner or later.

"Take me back!"

Ouch. "I cannot."

She stopped hitting me. "Then I will tell my father you are here!"

"Do you know where he is?" I raised my head cautiously. She was already moving away from me. Much too quickly.

She giggled. "Of course! Come and see him! He is dying to see you."

I glanced back at the Koldun, who was resting quietly with only the occasional moan. "Perhaps I should stay with the grand duke. He is not feeling well, Sophia."

Sophia Konstantinova giggled again, farther away this time. "Of course he's not feeling well. He's dying."

I looked down at Grand Duke Vladimir. He was much paler than before, and his breathing had changed. He was barely breathing at all. He looked up at me, cold sweat breaking out on his skin. "I will have to send you back soon," I told him. "Or it will be too late."

His eyes darkened and he grabbed my wrist. "I don't want to be a ghoul, Duchess."

"Think of your wife. And your children."

"I am thinking of them! I cannot return to them in this state."

I looked down at the Koldun, my thoughts torn. Grand Duchess Miechen would never forgive me for not doing everything I could to save her husband. But would she want the grand duke back if it meant he would be a walking corpse? It would be a shame for the children to lose their father. But they did not need to see him like this.

"NECROMANCER!" The swirling gray mists of the cold light parted. I knew Konstantin was drawing near.

Had Sophia discovered a way to release him from his bonds?

The ground below my feet vibrated. The Koldun moaned as his body shifted. "Guard . . . the . . . throne . . . ," the dying man whispered. "Do not let him sit down. . . ."

I should have destroyed the throne when I first came across it in the Massandra caves. And if I could have done so now, I would have. "Your Imperial Highness, do you know a spell that could destroy the throne?"

His eyes opened immediately. "Impossible! You must leave now and the throne will disappear from this place."

"But the wizards will be waiting for me."

"Would you rather face the Black Magi or the lich tsar and his daughter?"

The Koldun had a very logical point.

I held my hand out to him. "Your family needs you, Your Imperial Highness. The Graylands are not for you. You cannot become a ghoul if you do not die. Come back with me and we will take you to my father's hospital. Dr. Ostrev is a brilliant physician. And we will consult the Tibetan doctor, Badmaev, as well. He seems to have an uncanny knowledge of supernatural ailments."

Recognition flashed in the grand duke's eyes. "Dr. Badmaev took excellent care of Miechen when she lost the twins."

The roar of the lich tsar grew louder, along with the shrill laughter of a young girl. The air was becoming unbearably cold.

"Come with me," I said. Slowly, I helped him to stand. We had to get to the throne of Byzantium before the lich tsar reached us.

But Sophia reached us first. She grabbed my arms, tearing at my sleeves. "Katerina Alexandrovna! You must not leave me!"

I fought her off and helped the Koldun to the throne, where he slumped into its seat. "Hurry," he said, his voice weak. "But do not let her come with us."

I turned around. "Sophia, you must stay here, this is where you belong now. With your father."

"And you must stay with me!" She was very strong. As hard as I tried to stay near the throne, she pulled me away.

"No. I do not belong here. Let me go."

"Katerina Alexandrovna!" The Koldun cried out and fainted. I had to hurry if I was going to save his life.

Sophia would not loosen her hold on me. Her icy fingers dug into my shoulders, and I shoved against her as hard as I could. "Konstantin Pavlovich is coming, Duchess," she said. "He will come and make you stay with me. You must do as he says. He is the tsar."

"He is not my tsar. Nor will he ever be." I finally had enough leverage to push her away. She stumbled back, and I ran for the throne.

"The path to the light travels straight through the darkness," I shouted, and grabbed hold of the Koldun's cold hand as the shadows began to swirl around the throne. There was barely room for me to sit down, and I was improperly close to the Koldun, but at that moment, propriety was not my concern.

Sophia's screams lingered in my head as the throne took us away from the Graylands. I breathed a sigh of relief as the mists cleared and I once again found myself in the Great Hall of Vorontsov Palace. The room was full of the tsar's imperial guard.

CHAPTER FORTY-EIGHT

❧

I jumped up, checking the Koldun's wrist for a pulse. There was still one present, barely. "Someone help us please!" I cried. "We need a doctor immediately!"

"Katiya? *Mon Dieu*, we thought we'd lost you!" It was my brother, pushing through the crowd of soldiers.

Close behind him was George Alexandrovich. He stopped when he saw the Koldun. "Duchess, what have you done?"

I couldn't meet his eyes. "The Koldun needs a doctor, right away. Can you send for the Tibetan?"

He left without another word. Petya called for his men to find a cot for the Koldun. They helped make Grand Duke Vladimir Alexandrovich comfortable as we waited for Dr. Badmaev. "Good God, Katiya," my brother said. "Why would you do such a dangerous thing?"

"What else should I have done? Where are the crown prince and Sucre?"

"They have been arrested and taken to the Fortress of St. Peter and St. Paul, along with Papus. The tsar will see them in the morning. Do not worry. They are held at the fortress by strong magic. They cannot hurt anyone anymore." Petya embraced me tightly. It was as if he did not want to let me go. "I never thought I would see you again, brat," he whispered.

I smiled and sniffed back a few tears. "You couldn't be so lucky."

"Katerina Alexandrovna?" Princess Alix pushed her way through the imperial guards and would have pushed Petya away if he hadn't smartly stepped aside. She threw her arms around me. She whispered in my ear, "Thank you, for everything you did tonight. I will never forget that you risked your own life for mine."

The tsarevitch was standing behind her, and bowed smartly. "Nor will I, Duchess," he said softly. Alix stepped back and allowed him to take her arm. "I am escorting the princess of Hesse back to Smolny. Will you be joining us?"

I shook my head. "I want to look after the Koldun until Dr. Badmaev arrives. But thank you kindly, Your Imperial Highness."

"I will talk with you tomorrow, then," Alix said, squeezing my hand once more. "God bless you, Katerina Alexandrovna."

"Thank you," I said, not knowing what else I could say. I did not know if God looked favorably upon any of my actions that night. I had upset the natural balance, and defied death, by bringing the Koldun back.

Dr. Badmaev finally arrived sometime after Alix and the tsarevitch had left. I might have fallen asleep briefly, because Petya shook me gently to get out of the doctor's way. I stood up and moved away from the sleeping Koldun.

The Tibetan doctor smiled at me. "You have done a very brave thing, Duchess. Why don't you return to Smolny and get a good night's rest?"

I shook my head, stifling a yawn. "I want to stay. Please."

A pair of arms wrapped gently around me, steering me toward the hallway. "You need rest, or you will make yourself ill." George led me to a leather settee in an empty sitting room a little way from the noise of the Great Hall.

I got a good look at him under the gaslight lamps. "George, you need rest more than I! You're pale as a ghost!" It filled me with alarm. "Were you injured?" Without thinking, I grabbed his coat and went to open it. "Did Danilo hurt you?"

He gently grabbed my hands with his and pulled me off of him. "Duchess, please refrain from undressing me. And no, *Danilo* did not injure me."

I ignored the sarcasm in his voice. "But you are hurt. What is wrong? Can Dr. Badmaev help you?"

"I will be fine. Do not worry about me, Katiya. I will have your brother take you back to Smolny."

My heart sank. I knew I had to return to the institute, but I had hoped that the grand duke would take me in his own carriage. I should have realized he had more important things to tend to.

"Katiya, I want nothing more than to accompany you. But I'm afraid if I had you in my carriage I would take you far away from all of this and never let you go again."

I almost laughed as I realized he was reading my thoughts again. I threw my arms around him, laying my head on his chest. "George, you've come back to me."

"I never left you."

"But you were in Paris, and I was behind the empress's spell at Smolny, and you couldn't hear me. And I was hearing such terrible things about you." My fingers curled around one of his golden buttons.

"From Crown Prince Danilo?" He pulled back from me, an eyebrow raised.

"The devil! Is there no way I can nullify the blood bond with him?"

George gathered me in his arms again and pulled me close. "We'll find a way, love," he murmured against my ear.

"Ahem." My brother sheepishly cleared his throat, just outside the door. "Katerina? Dr. Badmaev said the Koldun is being taken back to Vladimir Palace. He should recover with no difficulty. Are you ready to return to school? It's almost morning."

"*Mon Dieu!*" I said, leaping up. "Elena. She came with me tonight. I haven't seen her in hours."

George stood as well. "No one has mentioned seeing her. Perhaps she has already returned."

"You shouldn't worry about that Montenegrin witch, Katiya," Petya said. "Most likely she was part of the crown prince's plot to make sure you were here."

I shook my head, frowning at the scorn in his voice. "I don't think so." I had to believe that Elena had been ignorant of her brother's treachery.

"You must hurry." George took my hand and kissed my fingers. In front of my brother. I couldn't help blushing. "I will see you soon, Duchess."

I curtsied. "Your Imperial Highness."

Petya bowed his head as well, with a military click of his heels. "Your Imperial Highness."

In the carriage, Petya seemed embarrassed as he escorted me back to Smolny. He was silent for a long time before asking, "Does Papa know?"

"Know what?" The sky was already beginning to lighten. An enormous gray bird swooped over the roof of our carriage as we crossed over the Fontanka Canal, and it landed on the elaborate iron railing that lined the bridge. An owl, apparently resting its belly after a successful night of hunting. Its enormous green eyes seemed to follow us as we rolled past. The sun would be coming up soon. I would be expelled for certain.

"About you and the grand duke. Maman will be pleased."

I groaned. "Please do not say a word to Maman. Or Papa. There is no way the tsar would approve of a marriage between his son and me. Do not get Maman's hopes up for nothing."

"What do you mean, for nothing? The grand duke has no business behaving in such a manner if he does not intend to marry you."

"Calm down, Petya," I said with a sigh. We were pulling in through the open gates at the school. I grabbed my brother's arm. "The grand duke still has hopes for his parents' blessing. But until he receives it, I don't dare to even dream. Please promise me you'll say nothing of this to anyone."

He looked as if he would object, but finally nodded his head. "All right, Katiya. But I don't see why you should worry about their approval. Why wouldn't they want you as a daughter-in-law? You're an Oldenburg. With imperial blood."

"And aligned with the Dark Court. You know the empress is jealous of anyone who is friends with Grand Duchess Miechen." The footman opened the door of the carriage. "Please, Petya. Not a word to anyone."

He looked troubled, but he nodded at last. "I promise."

My brother stepped out of the carriage after me, intending to escort me inside, despite my hope to sneak in silently before the school was awake. "You were tending to a family crisis," he said. "I will vouch for you."

"A family crisis?" I smiled as I took his arm.

"Imperial blood, Katiya," my brother said, his chin jutting up in the air. "We are family."

CHAPTER FORTY-NINE

I was not expelled, much to my disappointment. I had hoped
that I would create a horrible scandal and my parents would
pack me off to medical school in Zurich in disgrace. But Madame Tomilov accepted my brother's apologies, and even ex-
cused me from classes for the day. "You will need to rest after
such a stressful night, Katerina Alexandrovna. Sister Anna
will look in on you later."

Elena, however, was in far more trouble than I. She had
frightened the new kitchen girl when she tried to sneak back
inside, and the poor girl had screamed, waking the entire
school. Madame Tomilov sent a letter to the king and queen
of Montenegro requesting that Elena return home immediately, as she had disgraced herself and the Smolny Institute for
Young Noble Maidens. Grand Duchess Militza, who was already aware of her brother's imprisonment at the Fortress, had
arrived early that morning to pick up Elena and her belongings.

Elena was tearful as she watched her sister's maid pack her trunk. "Katerina, I have behaved so badly to you. And to Alix and Aurora. I never believed Danilo could be so cruel. Please forgive me."

"Of course," I said, relieved that she was indeed innocent of her brother's plot, and too surprised to say anything else.

She sniffled. "It's not because of what I did, but because of Danilo. He has disgraced our entire family. I would already be on a train home if it weren't for Militza."

I couldn't help feeling sorry for her. She embraced Alix and Aurora and begged them not to forget her. Aurora promised to write and entreated Elena to do the same.

Elena asked me to tell the Bavarian princesses goodbye for her. "I cannot bear to face anyone else right now."

"Of course," I said, giving her a hug before she and her sister left.

Alix had been much luckier when she sneaked back inside the school that night, and had even managed to get a few hours of sleep. "How nice it must be to spend the entire day in bed," she grumbled, fixing her pinafore for breakfast as I finally crawled into my cot. She grinned shyly at me from the mirror, though, before she and Aurora left. "Tonight, I will tell you all about my ride home with Nicholas Alexandrovich."

I smiled back at her as I snuggled under my quilt. *Perhaps, I thought, if the empress could approve of a werewolf as a daughter-in-law, she might approve of a necromancer as well.*

∽⊘∾

I awoke that afternoon still feeling bruised and sore but decided I needed some fresh air. I took a walk in the Smolny gardens with the Bavarian princesses after tea. Augusta and Erzsebet were distressed to hear of Elena's departure. "But what about the Spring Ball?" Erzsebet wailed. "Elena wanted to go so badly with her sister!"

I did not think Grand Duchess Militza would be attending any balls for the next few weeks. I would not have been surprised if she accompanied her sister home to Montenegro until the scandal died down.

Augusta picked a lonely snowdrop that had bloomed earlier than all the others. "Still, Elena frightened me sometimes," she said. "Even more than the ghost in the library."

"How could you say such a thing?" Erzsebet fussed. "Elena never hurt anyone."

Not that anyone would remember. I grabbed Augusta's hand and squeezed it. She smiled back.

"Look! An imperial carriage!" Erzsebet squealed. A handsome black carriage pulled into the circular drive in front of the Smolny gates. "Do you think it's the empress? And her daughters?"

A footman approached us with a curt bow. "Duchess Katerina Alexandrovna, Her Imperial Highness Grand Duchess Miechen invites you to take a ride with her through the gardens."

The Bavarian princesses gasped. "Katerina! What have you done to catch the grand duchess's attention?"

"I do not know," I said, even though I knew it could not be good. "Will you tell Madame Orbellani?"

"Of course!" Augusta said excitedly. "Imagine! All the handsome young men on the street will see you riding with the grand duchess!"

"Don't be silly. No one can see inside the carriage

unless they press their face to the windows," Erzsebet said. She tugged on her sister's arm. "Come along, let's go and find Madame."

I followed the footman back to the grand duchess's carriage, and he assisted me as I entered the vehicle. Grand Duchess Miechen sat like a queen, dressed in a deep-navy-blue walking dress, her gloved hands folded serenely in her lap. She nodded to me but did not smile as I sat across from her.

"Katerina Alexandrovna."

"Your Imperial Highness. Is the grand duke in better health?"

She said nothing for a moment but merely stared at me. I tried very hard not to fidget. "Yes. My husband is feeling much better, thanks to you and Dr. Badmaev. I owe his life to you, Duchess. I suppose you will consider this your debt to me repaid."

"If it pleases Your Imperial Highness."

She did not deign to answer. The grand duchess actually looked quite displeased, her lips twisted in a thin frown. "The grand duke was extremely foolish to attempt the werewolf spell, even if he did believe he was protecting the tsar. I hope the young princess of Hesse will not look unfavorably upon the Dark Court because of his ill judgment."

"I'm sure that is not the case, Your Imperial Highness," I hurried to assure her. The grand duchess Miechen had never seemed more lethal to me than she did now, when she seemed most in danger of losing her tenuous hold on the Dark Court. I knew Miechen's weaknesses, and I was a liability to her. "Princess Alix would not say or do anything that would upset the balance between the Light and Dark Courts."

The grand duchess's eyebrow rose sharply. "Wouldn't she? Does she not hunt the darkness one night a month?"

"The evil men she pursues are not under your protection, Your Imperial Highness. No one except Monsieur Sucre. He never belonged to the Light Court, did he?"

Instead of answering my question directly, she countered, "And neither do you, Katerina Alexandrovna. You must remember that, no matter whom you love."

It was the cold, hard truth. Regardless of the fact that I tried to use my dark powers only to help people, the empress would never look upon me as a daughter-in-law. She would always see me as a tainted, Dark Court creature. And she and the tsar would never allow me to even dream of a future with George Alexandrovich. I looked away through the window, at the gray and barren gardens passing by. "I shall never forget, Your Imperial Highness. May I return to my friends, please?"

The grand duchess smiled at me, her tiny fangs showing. "There is hope for you yet, my dear. Your young man is in line for the position of Koldun one day, once my Vladimir is gone. A Koldun is almost as powerful as the tsar. It is much easier for a Light Court member to fall into the shadow of the Dark Court."

Was that what had happened to her husband? I felt nauseous at the thought. "I would never let that happen to George Alexandrovich."

The grand duchess's smile was malicious. "It's too late, Katerina. His descent has already begun."

"*Mon Dieu*, no!" I could not listen to her anymore. The carriage had just pulled into the circular drive, but had not come to a complete stop. I opened the carriage door anyway, not bothering to wait for a footman, and flung myself out.

"Duchess!" the dark faerie called to me. "You'll break your neck doing such foolish things. Remember, our accounts are now balanced. But I am sure we will see each other again soon."

I did not look back, but instead ran until I reached the front door of the institute. I kept running up the stairs. I was out of breath and almost collided into Madame Orbellani.

"Katerina Alexandrovna! We have been looking all over for you! Madame Tomilov has a visitor in her parlor who wishes to speak with you. You must hurry!"

It was the tsar's eldest daughter, Grand Duchess Xenia Alexandrovna, with her lady-in-waiting. I stopped as I entered the parlor, making a hasty and clumsy curtsy. She smiled, her gloved hands clutching a small purse anxiously. "Katerina Alexandrovich, I am so happy to see you. I come with a message from my mother and father. The imperial family is indebted to you for your recent bravery. I told Mama that I wanted to come and thank you personally, Duchess. I only wish I could be as brave and strong as you."

I blushed. But I also heard what she was not saying, that even though the grand duchess had wanted to come to Smolny, the empress did not wish to see me. I smiled tightly. "You are too kind, Your Imperial Highness. My life is to serve the tsar and the empress."

She took a step forward, and shyly grabbed my hand. "I am not supposed to tell you this, but George is feverish from his injuries. He . . . has been asking for you, although my parents forbid him to have any visitors. I thought that perhaps if I could bring him some encouraging message from you, it would allow him to rest more comfortably?"

I turned pale. "Injuries? He did seem unwell. . . ." I felt weak and the grand duchess's lady-in-waiting was kind enough to help me to a chair before I slid to the floor. "He assured me he was fine when I last spoke with him."

The grand duchess frowned. "It seems that the duel between him and Crown Prince Danilo was not the usual sort of duel," she said, glancing at her lady-in-waiting. "Anna, could you please find a glass of water or some tea for the duchess? She still looks unwell."

"Of course, Your Imperial Highness." Anna curtsied and smiled at me before hurrying out of the parlor.

Xenia Alexandrovna sat down in the chair next to mine. "It is some sort of magical wound, Katerina. The court doctors do not know what to do. It's as if the very life is draining slowly out of my brother."

"*Mon Dieu,*" I whispered. "Has Dr. Badmaev seen him?"

"I do not recognize that name."

"He is a Tibetan, and attends the grand duke and grand duchess Vladimir. He has great skill in illnesses that are . . . not usual. Your brother knows who he is."

Xenia Alexandrovna nodded. "I will mention his name to my parents, but if he attends the Dark Court . . ."

"He tends to all, I believe," I said, knowing her mother would be extremely suspicious of the Tibetan doctor. "Please give your brother my warmest wishes for his health."

"And your affection?" she asked hopefully.

I blushed. "Yes. Please tell him that . . . that I hope to see him soon."

Anna returned just then, with a servant carrying a tea tray. The grand duchess stood up. "Thank you, but we must be leaving. Goodbye, Katerina Alexandrovna. I hope we see each other again before too long."

"As do I, Your Imperial Highness." I stood and curtsied to her again.

She smiled warmly, and impulsively embraced me. "I have great hopes for you and Georgi," she whispered. "And for Alix and Nicky as well. Give her my best wishes, won't you?"

"Of course, Your Imperial Highness."

As soon as the grand duchess left with her lady-in-waiting, I sank back into the chair, taking the cup of tea from the kitchen servant gratefully. How had George hid his injuries from me? How could I have been so stupid?

The empress's spell had been recast after Elena's and my escape. There was no way I could reach George, now that I was back at the institute. I did not know what plans the tsar had for me, but I had made my own decision. I would be graduating from Smolny in a few months and there was nothing the imperial family could do to keep me here after that. I had fought off Konstantin in the Graylands, and there was no way the tsar could say I still needed protection. I would ask Dr. Badmaev to forgive my rudeness at Christmas and beg him to accept me as his pupil. My mother would probably not approve, but then again, she did not have to know of it. I would do everything in my power to take care of my grand duke. He needed me now.

CHAPTER FIFTY

～∾～

Our graduation ceremony at the Smolny Institute for Young Noble Maidens was as beautiful and boring as it had been any other year. Medals were presented to the students with the highest marks, talented students entertained our imperial guests with music and dancing. The empress and Grand Duchess Xenia attended, along with several of the ladies of the Light Court. I won no medals, nor displayed any musical talent. Of course, if I had been pressed, I could have resurrected a dead butterfly or a toad for their amusement, but I did not believe it would have provided much entertainment.

I stood up and walked across the front of the dining hall to receive my certificate of completion from Madame Tomilov and dutifully kissed her cheek. She handed me a teaching diploma as well, as the girls in my Blue Form class applauded. My family sat with the other students' families, behind the imperial party. My mother clapped politely, and, curiously, I saw my father dab at the corner of his eye. Petya and Dariya clapped the loudest.

I felt a little sad packing my things up for the last time. Aurora promised to keep in touch with us all, as she was going to stay at her grandmother's summer estate in the country. Alix was going to her sister Ella's palace in Moscow. "Do you think the tsarevitch will forget about me?" she whispered as we gathered up the last of our things. "He is going to be on maneuvers with his regiment this summer."

"How can you think so little of him?" I teased. "He worried so much about you when the Koldun kidnapped you. He cares a great deal for you, Alix." I knew this to be true, since she'd told me about the kiss they'd shared in the carriage ride home from Vorontsov Palace.

She smiled, blushing. "You will keep in touch also, will you not? My sister and I will visit St. Petersburg again before I return to Wolfsgarten in a few months."

I gave her fingers a friendly squeeze. "Depend upon it."

It seemed strange not having Elena with us. I almost felt bad for her, wondering what her life would be like, banished to the tiny court of her father in the Black Mountains. A well-placed marriage seemed almost impossible now for her, but I suspected her mother would make sure that everything ended up happily. Surely they could find one eligible prince of Europe to cast a spell upon. But I would never let her interfere with Alix and the tsarevitch again.

❦

Dinner that night at Betskoi House was wonderful. Dariya came with her stepmother, and Petya teased Aunt Zina by insisting she hold Sasha. The dark faerie did not realize what was wrong with the poor creature, but she could still sense something unnatural about it. Sasha shed clumps of fur on her lap and hissed when she tried to pet him. Aunt Zina looked horrified. "*Zut alors!*" she whispered.

"For goodness' sake, Petya," Maman scolded. "Leave Sasha alone and get ready for dinner." Dariya and I grinned as her stepmother tried to get the odor of undead cat out of her clothes.

Maman had made certain our cook prepared all of my favorite foods and surprised me with a raspberry and vanilla bombe glacée for dessert. It was wonderful to be home, and I decided that for just that one night, I would not worry about my future.

But when we were finished eating, and Papa and Petya had joined us in the drawing room for a game of cards that did not involve fortune-telling, the footman delivered a letter to Maman.

"So late at night?" Aunt Zina exclaimed. "It cannot be good news."

Papa frowned. "What is it, my dear?"

Maman opened the letter and a gray feather fell out of the folds, tumbling gently to the floor. My mother's face grew pale. "*Mon Dieu,*" she whispered.

I was reminded of the owl we'd seen on the Anichkov Bridge the night I saved the Koldun. The hair on the back of my neck stood up as I bent down to retrieve the feather. It had grown uncomfortably warm in the already cozy room. "Maman?" I asked as I held the feather out to her.

"*Merci,*" she said faintly. "This message carries the seal of Madame Elektra. She has come to St. Petersburg and is staying at the Hotel Europa. She is asking for me."

"But does it say why?" Aunt Zina seemed perplexed as she started to get up and reach for the letter. Just then, Sasha poked his nose inside the drawing room and twitched his tail menacingly at her. My aunt sank back onto the love seat with Dariya.

Maman hastily stuffed the letter back in its envelope. "She is ill, the poor dear. I must go to her immediately." She glanced around at all of us as I stood up to accompany her. "No, Katiya. You must stay here."

"Should we send for Dr. Ostrev?" I asked. "He should go with you if she has no doctor attending her."

"That will not be necessary." My mother swept out of the room without another word. Papa followed her.

Dariya looked at me. "Will she be all right?"

"Papa won't let her go alone," Petya said. "Nor would I." He stood up as we heard our parents arguing in the hall.

Maman rushed in again, with her coat in her arms. She looked at my aunt. "Zenaida Dmitrievna, I'm afraid I must ask you to go with me."

"But Maman," Petya and I both started to protest. Aunt Zina gathered her things and told Dariya to stay where she was.

Dariya looked as bewildered as me. Maman and Aunt Zina were gone before anyone could say another word.

"Papa?" I asked as he returned to the drawing room holding the letter. "What is happening?"

The news had apparently shaken him as well. His hand seemed to tremble slightly as he laid the letter on the card table. "It appears your mother is Madame Elektra's heir."

"Is she very rich?" Dariya asked.

Papa's laugh was hollow. "Rich? No doubt." He went to the sideboard and poured himself a glass of vodka. He finished his drink before looking at me and Petya. "Madame Elektra is . . . or was . . . the last living striga in Russia. Your mother must now carry that title."

No wonder my father was trembling. "How could this happen? Why Maman?"

He looked at all of us, sitting nervously. "I suppose you should all hear this," he muttered, making himself another drink. "When Katiya was born, your mother bled heavily. Madame Elektra was there and was able to save her from death by giving her a glass of striga blood."

I thought back to the day in Yalta, the day that Dariya and I performed the play for everyone. Now Grand Duchess Miechen's words made sense. Maman owed the striga her life. "And Maman's been a blood drinker since I was born?" I asked.

Papa shook his head. "No, but she agreed to take the striga's place when she died. A striga lives a long time, but is not immune to old age. I wish I'd been there, but your mother was delirious from the birth and from the loss of so much blood. I doubt she knew what she was agreeing to at the time."

Petya looked angry. "So Maman willingly accepts this legacy from Madame Elektra and becomes a blood drinker? Are we in danger?"

"A striga only drinks the blood of other blood drinkers," I said, remembering the rest of what Miechen had told me.

"How frightening for the St. Petersburg vampires," Dariya said, laying a hand on my arm. "The Montenegrin veshtiza will not be happy."

301

And neither would the empress, I thought unhappily. There was no way we'd be able to keep this a secret. What would the imperial family think? There was no hope now of Maman ever returning to the Light Court.

Dariya and I played cards until we thought we'd die of boredom. It was after midnight when Maman and Aunt Zina returned. I stood up to greet my mother but was met with a surge of intense, suffocating heat. She was causing everyone's cold light to bend. Already, her new powers were frighteningly strong.

After saying their goodbyes, Aunt Zina and Dariya left. Petya and I kissed our mother goodnight on her cheek. But she stopped me. "Stay for a moment, Katiya. I must speak with you alone."

"Yes?"

Maman took my hands in hers and squeezed them. The room was not quite so warm anymore, now that everyone else had left. There was only my own cold light for her to affect. "I wanted to apologize for not taking you with me tonight. I had no idea how violent the ceremony was going to be, and I did not want you to see it."

There were tears in my mother's eyes.

"Did you know this was going to happen?" I asked. "How could you have told me that blood drinkers did not exist anymore?"

"For all I knew, they had all been banished from Russia. And Elektra was not the same as the others." She tucked one of my curls behind my ear, like she'd done a thousand times before. It seemed like such a normal action. Not something that a striga would do. "And she traveled to St. Petersburg so seldom."

"What was the ceremony tonight like?" I asked.

Maman pursed her lips. "Dreadful. She was on her death-bed and gave me a glass of her own blood, mixed with that of an upyri. It didn't taste bad, but it had a hint of rosemary. And after that delightful fennel salad at dinner . . . well, you just can't have two strong herbs competing for your palate."

"Where on earth did she find upyri blood?" I wanted to believe that the striga had found the primitive blood drinker somewhere far from St. Petersburg. But what if that was what she'd been hunting here in the city? Petya and the rest of the imperial guard would have to be warned.

"Who knows," Maman said. "Now off to bed with you, dear. We've been invited to the ballet tomorrow and I think I shall let you attend with your aunt Alexandra. I have an atrocious headache, and I don't see how it could possibly be gone by tomorrow afternoon."

I was happy to hear that my father's sister had returned to St. Petersburg from Kiev. She was much nicer than Aunt Zina. And much less ambitious. "Good night, then, Maman. Do you want me to send Anya in with some tea?" I stopped. "Or are you able to drink tea anymore?"

"Hmm? Oh, I'm sure it will be fine. Of course, Elektra preferred cocoa." She kissed both my cheeks. "Just have her bring it to me in my room, dear."

She no longer seemed as upset as she had when she'd first received Madame Elektra's letter. I could have sworn I heard her humming a gypsy love song as I left the drawing room. It was as if turning into a striga had been no more traumatizing than changing one's hairstyle. I sighed as I went upstairs to find Anya.

CHAPTER FIFTY-ONE

The next afternoon, my elderly but kind aunt Alexandra took me to the graduation ceremony of the Imperial Ballet School. Here, the dances were much more impressive than the ones Aurora and my other classmates had performed at the Smolny graduation. The imperial family was present, including the tsar and his eldest son. And Grand Duke George Alexandrovich. I marveled at my good fortune. He sat down next to his mother and brother in the row of chairs in front of me. I had a glorious view of the back of his neck.

Whispering to his brother after the first dance, he quietly stood up and changed seats so he could sit next to me. The empress never said a word to him, but I'm sure she noticed. "Katiya," he whispered in a low voice. "We have much to discuss."

"Do we?" I whispered back. Fortunately, Aunt Alexandra was too deaf to hear our conversation.

"Maman is rather displeased that you ruined her spell at the institute."

I glanced nervously at the back of the empress's head. She had even more reason to dislike me now that my mother had become a striga. What if Mother Dear chose me to be her heir? A blood drinker could not marry a Romanov. That was a conversation I was not willing to have with the grand duke just yet. "The empress's spell set the ghost loose within the school. Still, I must apologize to her. I never meant to go against her will."

"Somehow, I think that might make it worse. The night at Vorontsov, you brought the Koldun back from the dead. How is that possible? He is not a ghoul like the others."

I sighed. I knew all along that eventually he would want to know everything about that night. There was only so much Danilo and Sucre had told the imperial investigators. They knew nothing about what had happened in the Graylands. "The Koldun was close to death when I found him, but he did not die. I think that is why he did not turn into a ghoul."

George frowned at me. "Katiya, the Koldun's body never vanished. He stopped breathing and his body grew cold. And then you were there, and he was breathing again."

I looked at him in shock. "How could that be? I found him in the Graylands!" What had I done to the Koldun?

"No," George whispered. "I know everything was chaotic that night, but the Koldun died. You brought him back to life."

My head was swimming with a million questions. But who would have the answers? "Please forgive me. I could not leave

305

him there. I know it was horribly wrong, but it would have been worse to leave him there with Konstantin and Sophia."

The grand duke's whole body stiffened. "The lich tsar? You saw him?"

"He cannot return without the throne. It must be destroyed. Along with the Talisman of Isis. Danilo took the talisman from the Koldun when he thought he was dead. He believed he could bring the lich tsar back and control him with the talisman."

"The blood-drinking crown prince will die."

I could feel the anger in the grand duke's voice. It frightened me. "He will be punished by his own father for destroying the tsar's trust. Won't that be enough?"

"It is treason, Katiya. There is still much to sort out in the mess of the Order. That was one of the reasons I spent so much time in Paris, learning the secrets of Papus and Sucre. I am not sure the tsar will allow Uncle Vladimir to remain as the Koldun. I am not even certain the grand duke is well enough to resume those duties."

It did not surprise me that a man who had returned from the dead was not up to fulfilling his previous obligations.

George laughed, hearing my thoughts. "Still, Katiya, you will be summoned to speak with the tsar about that night. You will be required to explain exactly what you did. And to tell him everything you learned about Konstantin Pavlovich." He paused as the dancers onstage finished their pas de deux, and everyone clapped politely. "Katiya, who is this Sophia you mentioned?"

"Konstantin's daughter. She was the ghost who was terrorizing everyone at Smolny. She was responsible for the kitchen girl's death."

"Good God, Katiya. The daughter of the lich tsar? Why didn't you tell me?"

"How could I? It does not matter now. I banished her to the Graylands, and that is why she came after me there. She cannot hurt anyone anymore."

George grew silent. I glanced up at the stage, where the entire graduating class of the Imperial Ballet School stood. Suddenly, he slumped back in his seat. "George, what is wrong?" I whispered. His brother twisted around in his seat and looked at him with concern.

"Nothing," he answered finally. "I am only a little overheated. Is it not warm in here to you?"

The tsarevitch turned his attention back to the stage.

I had actually been chilly since sitting down in the drafty theater. "Are you feverish?"

"Don't be ridiculous. I am going to get some fresh air. Excuse me," he whispered as he stood up to make his way to the exit. His mother turned around and looked up at him questioningly, but, seeing his pale face, nodded. She caught my eye briefly before turning her attention back to the stage. If she knew about my mother already, she was not going to say anything. I wanted to get up and leave right then and there.

"Do not follow me, Katiya," George whispered, loud enough for only me to hear. "It would only cause a scene. I will be fine."

"As you wish." It annoyed me that he assumed I would leap to his rescue, but that had been my first impulse. Even though I knew it would not be proper at all.

He smiled weakly. "Do not be vexed with me," he murmured. "We will see each before long."

But I noticed he held his hand to his chest as he walked

down the aisle toward the exit. He looked paler by the second. At a nod from his father, a member of the imperial guard followed him out.

I could not concentrate on the rest of the graduation dances. George's health was still in danger and I felt helpless. I promised myself that I would speak with Dr. Badmaev the very next morning. Becoming the Tibetan's pupil would at least give me something to take my mind off my worries. And I hoped that Eastern medicine would provide a way for me to help George. Perhaps a way to help my mother as well.

Having a plan made me feel somewhat better. I tried to enjoy the final dance of the ceremony, performed by the best student of the ballet school's graduating class.

She was the most accomplished dancer that day, a beautiful young girl of seventeen named Mathilde Kchessinska. She bewitched everyone in the audience with her grace and beauty. Including the tsarevitch. His eyes never left her as she twirled and spun across the stage. *Mon Dieu.*

ACKNOWLEDGMENTS

Thanks to my agent, Ethan Ellenburg, and his minion, Evan Gregory, for all the hard work they do for Katerina here and abroad. And to my Random House family: especially Françoise Bui, who makes the words sing; Elizabeth Zajac, my PR guru; and Trish Parcell, who designs the most beautiful covers. Thanks to my hospital family, who have been so supportive over the past few years of this nurse who wanted to write books. Especially the ghouls who work with me at night. I love you ladies! *Spasibo* to my online groups: the Class of 2K12, the Apocalypsies, and the Elevensies. I would never have made it through pre-publication (and post-publication!) without the support of such good friends. Julia Karr, Maurissa Guibord, Randy Russell, Amanda Morgan, and Jill Myles— you all saw Volume II through its ugly early stages and helped it grow into a real story. Vodka and chocolates for all of you. And finally, a Russian-sized thank you to all the readers for your enthusiasm and support for Katerina. You guys make every word worth it. *Spasibo!*